RED MOSCOW

R.C. REID

Jumpmaster Press
Birmingham, AL

Copyright

Artwork Generated by Midjourney
Library Cataloging Data
Names: Reid, R.C., (R.C. Reid)
Title: *Red Moscow* / R.C. Reid
5.5 in. × 8.5 in. (13.97 cm × 21.59 cm)
Description: Jumpmaster Press™ digital eBook & paperback edition |
Alabama: Jumpmaster Press™, 2018 - 2025. Alabaster, AL 35007
info@jumpmasterpress.com

Summary: In the summer of 1991, KGB Major General Anastasia Zolotova, nearly assassinated and marked for death, seeks to escape from Moscow. With the help of her long-ago lover, CIA assassin Jonathan Cole, the two of them fight to bring down the abusive KGB Chairman whose mistress she once was, thereby shaping what history will one day call the August Coup.

ISBN 978-1-964526-19-5 (eBook) | 978-1-964526-07-2 (print edition)

1. Thriller 2. Espionage 3. KGB 4. Soviet Union 5. CIA
6. Assassination 7. Romance

Printed in the United States of America

MOTHER RUSSIA SERIES BOOK 1

RED MOSCOW

R.C. REID

To my dear wife Susan, who always believed, and my daughter Carolyne, who gave me the inspiration.

CHAPTER 1

10:15 PM, Moscow Time, Wednesday, August 7, 1991

Major General Anastasia Zolotova, head of the Special Investigations Directorate, hurried down the deserted hallway of KGB headquarters at Dzerzhinsky Square. The clack of her polished heels echoed about the narrow space as she glanced over her shoulder, her knuckles white around the handle of her briefcase. Gorbachev would not return for another two weeks, and she needed to safeguard her evidence.

Tasia breezed into her small, darkened office and ignored the light switch. The door to the secure file room was in the back. One of the pins popped loose from the bun at the nape of her neck and a lock of red hair dropped down over one eye. She reached up to drag it behind her ear.

A rough length of rope blurred past her eyes, bit into her neck, and pinned her left wrist to her face. She dropped her briefcase, jerked her right arm backward and connected with something soft. She hard-elbowed repeatedly into the attacker's gut and forced him into the heavy oak bookcase along the wall. Picture frames and other mementoes crashed to the floor.

She shoved backward to keep her attacker off balance. Her heels barely found purchase on the polished hardwood floor. She burrowed her free hand underneath the rope and stretched the fibers enough to rotate her trapped hand.

Tasia heaved with her arms and pushed backward with her legs. Onion-laced breath puffed with exertion along the back of her neck. The rope inched forward, and she sucked in sweet oxygen. A feral grunt escaped from her attacker's throat as the cord snapped onto her chin.

Little by little, she edged it past her nose, then shoved it the rest of the way off.

Tasia's now-loosened hair flowed free as she spun to face her attacker. Even in the dark, she could tell he was small, almost emaciated. Piggy-black eyes shone underneath his protruding forehead. A curved scar marred his left cheek. Tasia raised her fists and prepared to lunge.

The man tossed the rope to the floor and jerked a double-edged knife from his black raincoat. Tasia stopped herself barely in time. She tried to yell, but only a squeak came from her mouth. The knife slashed toward her eyes, and she thrust both arms up to block it. The blade sliced through both her shirtsleeves and across the soft flesh below her wrists.

She backpedaled and her heel bumped into one of the chairs in front of her desk. She snatched the wooden piece of furniture and, despite the raw sting from the knife wounds, swung it toward the man's midsection. The killer gasped at the impact and grabbed hold of the obstruction to yank it aside. Tasia turned and ran behind her desk.

The man rushed around the side as Tasia tugged open the top drawer. Her fingers grasped the PSM pistol as the killer loomed over her, knife raised. She stumbled backward, aimed by reflex, and pulled the trigger three times. Multiple booms accompanied the muzzle flashes in the darkness.

The man fell backward and hit the floor with a muted thump.

Tasia kept the PSM pointed at the man's head as she stepped into the open area of the room. Her labored breathing echoed in the silence. The metallic smell of blood mixed with the acrid stink of gunpowder. She nudged the man with her shoe, but he did not move. She attempted to spit on him but could only muster a small amount of saliva.

The hallway door slammed, and Tasia spun her PSM toward it. The outside lights silhouetted three men. The two in security uniforms, looks of disbelief on their faces, pointed Kalashnikovs at her head. The third was Andrei.

"Code Forty-Seven," Tasia rasped as she lowered her pistol. "Lock down the building!"

The taller security man, a sergeant, dropped his weapon into safe-hang position. "Did you say—a Code Forty-Seven, Comrade General?"

"Yes!" Tasia croaked, slightly louder than before. "Code Forty-Seven! We have been breached!"

"You heard the general!" Andrei said. "Intruders have entered this facility. Get to an intercom and activate the protocol!"

"Yes sir!" The sergeant ran out the door and down the hallway.

Andrei turned to the second guard. Tasia thought he looked scarcely more than a teenager. "Private, the general has been seriously wounded. Run to the infirmary and send help. I'll stay with her." The boy ran from the room like the building was on fire.

KGB Major Andrei Bolskov flipped on the overhead lights, stared at his director, and whispered, "Comrade General, you're bleeding to death."

Tasia looked down. Blotches of bright scarlet covered the front of her white shirt. Dark blood saturated her torn shirtsleeves and fell to the floor in a thin, continuous stream.

Perhaps the killer had succeeded after all.

The Lubyanka building at Dzerzhinsky Square in Moscow served as the central headquarters of the *Komitet Gosudarstvennoy Bezopasnosti*—the KGB. This granite symbol of Soviet dominance was considered the most impregnable intelligence facility in the world. That had changed.

Tasia stepped over to the nearest chair and extended her arm. The blond major took the PSM from her hand, flipped on the safety and sat it atop her desk. She slid into the chair as Andrei crossed to a credenza along the far wall, picked up a handful of napkins, wet them from a nearby pitcher of water, and returned. Tasia jerked as Andrei laid the dripping cloths across her abraded throat and over the cuts along her arms. She did her best to hold them all in place while he filled one of the glasses on the credenza. The lukewarm water soothed her burning throat as she gulped it down.

Footsteps echoed in the hallway. Doctor Greorgi Chernyshevsky charged into the room with two stout-looking nurses. Tasia groaned inside. The tall, gangly man with the bald head and stained white coat reminded her of an awkward praying mantis. Widely believed to be an alcoholic, he somehow managed to retain his position, despite Tasia's and other directors' urgings.

"Get her on the gurney," he said.

Tasia's stomach gurgled as the two expressionless women in tan medical smocks helped her stand. They removed the sticky, blood-soaked napkins, gingerly ripped away the tatters of her sleeves, walked her to the gurney, and helped her onto it.

The doctor peered over his half-frame eyeglasses at the bleeding slices on Tasia's arms. He stepped in close, pinched the wounds open and closed with his ungloved fingers and nodded. He wiped his liver-spotted hands across the front of his coat and turned to the closest nurse.

"No damage to the radial arteries," he said. "Staunch the bleeding, please. We'll suture when we reach the infirmary."

"No one is to leave this room, Doctor," Tasia said in a raspy voice. She motioned Andrei for the glass of water and took several more sips. Her next words sounded stronger. "You need to make do with whatever you have here."

"Comrade General, I strongly suggest—"

"We are under a Code Forty-Seven, Doctor. No one is allowed in the hallways except the search and destroy teams."

The old man peered at the puddle of blood near his shoes. "Very well then." He nodded to each nurse in turn. "Prepare the areas along her arms. I need to examine her neck."

The two women applied cold compresses to the cuts as Chernyshevsky bent close to Tasia's throat. The stench of alcohol on his breath nearly made her gag. It took a moment for him to speak.

"Comrade General, it appears your carotids and jugular are intact. You are indeed fortunate. At best, maybe one person in a million ever survives a strangulation attempt."

"She is Mother Russia, Doctor," Andrei said. "What else would you expect?"

"Of course," Chernyshevsky replied. He took a suture kit from one of the nurses and Tasia jerked as the other applied cold, brown iodine to the wounds on her arms. The old doctor met her gaze for the first time. "Comrade General, you're still bleeding significantly. We could treat you far more effectively in the infirmary."

"Not until I issue the all-clear, Doctor," Tasia said. "You may proceed with the stitches."

"I will have to work without anesthetic."

"Understood," Tasia said. She moved her head to look past the old man. "Andrei, come here please."

Chernyshevsky, needle in hand, bent toward Tasia's right arm. Andrei maneuvered to stand behind her on the left.

"Call the main switchboard," Tasia said. She winced as the needle pricked her skin. "Get me a connection to the head of the search and destroy teams. Pull my phone to the back of the office where no one can—"

She glanced up. The door to the secure file room was open.

"Andrei, are you armed?"

"No, Comrade General."

"Belay my previous order." She jumped again as the needle pierced her arm. "Pick up my PSM. Stay on this side of the desk and keep your eye on the file room door as you call the switchboard. I want a strike squad sent up immediately. We may still have an intruder."

"Yes, Comrade General."

The doctor took what felt like an eternity to apply the sutures. Four uniformed men rushed into the room as he snipped the last thread. Tasia recognized the squad leader and pointed to the file room.

"Sergeant Petrov, secure that room. Anyone found in there is to be brought to me alive."

The tall, square-jawed sergeant with the blond buzz cut nodded. "Right away, Comrade General."

Chernyshevsky and the two nurses scurried to the walls as the four-man squad spread into a diamond-shape formation. Each man held his assault rifle to his eye, primed to fire. The sergeant motioned with two fingers and one of his comrades slid up behind him while the other two circled around. Two men flanked each side of the open door as they approached. The sergeant slipped into the room first, followed quickly by the other three men in turn.

An eerie silence filled the air, punctuated with the occasional creak or scrape from the other room. The huge sergeant finally stepped back into Tasia's office and adjusted his *pilotka* cap.

"The room is secure, Comrade General. No one is there."

"Has anything been disturbed?"

"Not that we can tell, Comrade General."

"Very well then," Tasia said. "Thank you, Sergeant. You and your men may return to your previous duties."

The phone on her desk rang. Andrei set her PSM on the desk and picked up the receiver.

"General Zolotova's office."

The color immediately drained from his face, and he put a hand over the receiver.

"Comrade General! It's Chairman Kryuchkov! He demands to speak with you!"

CHAPTER 2

KGB Chairman Vladimir Kryuchkov's voice assaulted Tasia as soon as the receiver touched her ear.

"You stupid bitch! A Code Forty-Seven? Do you realize what you've done?"

"Chairman, our central headquarters has been breached." Tasia's voice cracked. "I was attacked and nearly killed in my own office. We have no way of knowing the number of enemy forces nor the extent of their penetration. I thought the proper course—"

"You thought nothing, you idiotic cow!" Kryuchkov yelled. "Half a dozen other protocols could have been issued, yet for some reason, you select the one that shuts down everything and notifies the Central Committee! I've had to field nearly a half-dozen panicked phone calls asking me if a nuclear attack is imminent! Are you really that stupid?"

"Vladimir, I—"

"Don't *Vladimir* me! How dare you presume upon our prior relationship, General! I have rescinded the Code Forty-Seven so operations can return to normal. Furthermore, your astonishing lack of judgement tempts me to relieve you of your position here and now."

"You will do no such thing," Tasia said with a tone of equal menace. "Only President Gorbachev can dismiss the head of the Special Investigations Directorate."

"*Yerunda*! I sponsored your appointment to that position. I can still break you into tiny pieces should I choose. Never forget that, Tasia."

The KGB chairman paused as if he had suddenly run out of steam. "What is your status?" he asked in a softer, more conciliatory tone.

"An unidentified assailant nearly strangled me in my office," Tasia reported. "I escaped and shot him dead." She paused for effect. "The medical team is treating my wounds."

"Very well," Kryuchkov said with a sigh. "An investigation into this incident will need to be conducted and evidence collected. I presume you have no objection if I assign Yuri to oversee this?"

"Yuri? Well, no but—"

"But what, General? Surely, he is someone you would trust?"

"Why yes, of course. I did not realize he was qualified for such a task."

"You should really take the time to get to know him better. Yuri has worked as my adjutant ever since he graduated from the Institute last year. I will send him to your office with an investigative team presently."

"Ahem," Chernyshevsky interrupted. "Given your amount of blood loss, Comrade General, I recommend a transfusion as soon as possible. Now that the, uh, emergency has subsided?"

Tasia muttered something under her breath and turned back to the phone.

"Comrade Chairman, I must get to the infirmary. Can Yuri see me there?"

"I will inform him," the KGB chairman replied.

The line went dead, and Tasia slammed the receiver onto its cradle.

"You just wait," she whispered. She bolted upright. "Where's my briefcase?"

"Here, Comrade General." The burlier of the two nurses plucked the sticky case from one of the puddles of blood.

"Wipe it off and give it to me, please."

"We can have it cleaned and disinfected in the infirmary, Comrade General," Chernyshevsky said.

"That briefcase must not leave my sight, Doctor," Tasia said. "Andrei, please give me my pistol plus the two extra magazines from the top drawer."

The major handed her the PSM butt-first then laid the extra magazines in her lap. A few moments later, the nurse wedged the wiped-down briefcase inside the gurney's rail.

"Please get me to the infirmary now, Doctor," Tasia said with a disarming smile.

KGB agent Yuri Vladimirovich Zolotov opened the door to Tasia's office and glanced around the room. The round-faced clock on the wall showed a few minutes before midnight and the young man yawned.

A corpse in a black raincoat lay on the other side of the large wooden desk. A gooey-looking lake of coagulated blood surrounded the body, and a long double-edged knife lay inches from its hand. A short piece of what looked like industrial rope, tied around two pieces of wood, sat a foot or so away, amidst a haphazard pile of books, picture frames and broken glass.

Yuri turned and raised his hand to the three-man investigative team in the hallway before they could enter the room.

"Not yet," he said as he closed the door in their faces.

The overhead lights were bright florescent tubes. As Yuri walked over to the corpse he caught a glimpse of his reflection in the desk's glass top.

His dangerously premature birth twenty-two years earlier had rendered him both small-in-stature and abnormally thin. He adjusted his thin black tie to better fit his slightly-too-large shirt collar. The nearly unlimited power that came from his position as adjutant to the KGB chairman demanded he maintain proper standards of dress at all times.

The young man knew he was resented and had heard the nickname he had been given—*mudak* or turd. His age, height and high-pitched voice caused nearly all his KGB comrades to ridicule him. They were simply envious of his quick rise and feared his authority. Despite their opinions, he would make certain they obeyed him. One way or another.

Yuri pulled a pair of rubber gloves from his pocket, carefully skirted the blood on the floor, and squatted beside the corpse. He took a closer look at the pieces of wood and rope.

Homemade and amateur, he thought. *A professional would have used piano wire to slice the victim's carotids at the outset. No wonder she was able to escape him.*

He leaned over, careful to avoid the blood, and systematically patted down the corpse. It took him no time to find the silver key in its coat pocket. He stood up, put the key into the pocket of his own mustard-yellow trenchcoat, then walked back to admit the investigative team still waiting in the hall.

The others set about their duties as Yuri weaved around the blood and walked to the back of the room. He stepped through the open, vault-like door into the Special Investigative Directorate's file room and looked around. Row after row of metal cabinets of varying size, age, and color filled the space. He checked them all, one by one. The aroma of decaying paper hung in the air, and he coughed periodically.

He turned off the lights, exited the room, and locked the heavy door with the key taken from the assassin's pocket. He brushed some unseen dirt from his coat, straightened his tie again, and walked into the main office area.

"Are you finished?" he asked.

"Yes Comrade," one of the men replied.

"Good. You are to take all this down to Sub-basement Room Six and incinerate it."

The three men looked at each other. "Did you say incinerate, Comrade?" the same man asked.

"I did. Is something the matter with your hearing?"

"No, sir. We will incinerate it all right away."

"Good. Report to me when you've finished. I will be in the infirmary."

The investigative team left the room, their metal carts loaded with black bags and the rest of their equipment. The floor, furniture and walls were clean once again and Yuri ran a hand over his reddish-brown buzz cut. He stepped into the hallway, looked both ways, then closed and locked the door.

He started with the desk. Three of the drawers opened when he pulled on them but contained nothing of interest. He pulled a thin pocketknife from his pants and pried open the locks on the other three. There were plenty of file folders and loose reports to go through and it took him some time to check each one. He moved over to check the credenza, then the shelves along the wall and anywhere else papers might be kept.

The young man sat on the edge of the desk, picked up the phone and entered a complex string of numbers. All phone lines in or out of KGB headquarters were monitored and recorded twenty-four hours a day, except for certain private lines known only to a select few. He took pride in being one of those few. A man's voice answered on the first ring.

"Well?"

"The general somehow overpowered her assailant, sir. I have disposed of the body and all the evidence."

"What about the files?"

"I made a thorough search. They must be elsewhere."

"What do you mean she overpowered the man? He was a known killer, right?" A brusque edge tinged the voice, and Yuri knew he grew impatient.

"Yes, sir, but I recruited him quickly from the local drug trade. We could not use KGB personnel for obvious reasons. He was supposedly one of the best."

"Apparently not good enough."

Yuri switched the receiver to his other ear.

"I have an idea how we can work this to our advantage, sir."

"Go ahead."

"General Zolotova will soon deduce this attack could only have happened as it did with support from inside Dzerzhinsky. It will therefore be easy to confirm her suspicions that powerful forces seek her death."

"So? Powerful forces really do seek her death. Get to the point."

"With this groundwork laid, sir, it will be a small matter for me to persuade the general to make an escape attempt to the West."

The voice snorted. "Ridiculous."

"Not at all, sir. Contrary to the facade she's no doubt displaying, she's frightened now. If I frame this properly, as an escape instead of a defection, it will make sense to her."

"I find that hard to believe."

"I can easily build the narrative that this is her only choice. We can then catch her in the act and kill her on the spot without any questions. Her reputation would be forever destroyed, so any uncomfortable investigations she might have undertaken would be quickly forgotten."

Silence.

"It could be an elegant solution," the voice finally said, "but only if you can convince her to run. I have a hard time believing one of the most famous faces in the Soviet Union—a KGB major general who heads one of its most powerful directorates—could ever be convinced to do such a thing. What power do you possess with her?"

Yuri smiled. "The obvious one, sir. How could she not trust her own son?"

CHAPTER 3

Tasia was seriously queasy when the gurney rolled into the infirmary.

Chernyshevsky walked away without a word and an enormous charge nurse suddenly appeared. She reminded Tasia of a lumberjack, with huge arms, legs the size of small tree trunks, and a face locked into a perpetual scowl. Tasia felt as if she were being sized-up as the other nurses wheeled her into one of the empty rooms.

"You will take off all your clothes, Comrade General," the charge nurse said.

"I'm afraid I'm rather nauseated. If I could have some assistance?"

The big woman snapped her fingers, and the other nurses helped Tasia up. They stayed beside her while she slipped out of her shoes, then unbuttoned and removed her bloody shirt. The room began to spin as she unzipped her skirt, and unfastened her grey nylons from the garter belt she wore. The two nurses helped her out of the stockings, but when she reached for the patterned hospital gown, the charge nurse grunted, "Everything, please."

Tasia detested Soviet women's underwear. Although sturdy and serviceable, they were universally plain and ugly. Some time ago she had ordered a large collection of expensive silk and lace undergarments from Paris. Tasia could see the jealous avarice in the eyes of the charge nurse. Without a doubt, and purely out of spite, her beautiful intimates would promptly disappear if she took them off.

"That's *Comrade General* to you, nurse," Tasia said with all the authority she could muster. "I will decide what I remove, not you. Now step aside before I decide to make your life most unpleasant."

The big nurse hesitated but complied. The other nurses moved to help Tasia into her gown and then into the hospital bed. The smaller of them handed over her briefcase, leaned in close and whispered into her ear.

"Thank you, Mother Russia. We appreciate you putting that loudmouth *suka* in her place."

Tasia smiled and remembered.

When she began her rise within the KGB, she had been persuaded to pose for a series of governmental propaganda posters. Designed to glorify the ideal Soviet woman, the beautiful high gloss productions showed her in various poses and settings.

In one, she wore a red-and-white print dress and headscarf and portrayed a smiling Soviet mother with her then-five-year-old son. In a set of heavy-duty blue coveralls and holding a huge hammer, she depicted a sweaty and hard-working female Soviet factory worker. Finally in her full-dress KGB uniform, complete with medals and officer braids, she saluted the hammer and sickle as the ideal female Soviet patriot.

Tasia's radiant smile, authentic charm, and natural beauty, along with her busty physique and flame-red hair, transformed her overnight into a cultural icon. The Soviet press had dubbed her "*Mother Russia*" and many of her posters still hung in prominent places all over the Soviet Union. She could not walk the streets, even these many years later, without being recognized.

The sharp stick of the transfusion needle brought her back. She sighed and settled into the proper position as a knock sounded at the door.

"Prince Andrei," Tasia whispered as the major, still in his sweat-stained tan duty uniform, entered the room. His name always reminded her of the dashing Prince Andrei Bolkonsky in her favorite novel, Tolstoy's *War and Peace*.

"How do you feel, Comrade General?"

"Better I suppose. Deathly cold inside. The nausea is the worst part. I cannot even adjust myself without nearly vomiting."

"A common symptom of blood loss, I'm afraid."

She motioned for him to come closer.

"We need to keep our voices down," she whispered when he knelt beside her bed. "I'm taking a serious chance by saying certain things within Dzerzhinsky's walls."

"I understand."

"Only three keys will open the doors to our file room. Mine—the one used by you and the other SID staff—plus the one in the Secretariat's secure archive. I have my key for certain. Do you know if the departmental key is secure?"

Andrei paused. "I used it myself to come in via the staff-side door earlier this evening. Everyone else had already left. I can see the safe from my office window. No one could have approached it unnoticed."

"Then it all fits. The only way my attacker could have gained access to that room would have been with the Secretariat's master key."

"How is that possible?" Andrei whispered.

"I'm not certain how, but I definitely know why. I've conducted a top-level investigation these past many months into an enormous amount of Party funds diverted outside the country. Two days ago, I finally identified the specific source accounts being drained and ordered them frozen by SID edict."

"You did what?" He pursed his lips into a sour-looking circle. "But by using our edict, whoever stole those funds knows it was you who locked them out!"

Tasia frowned. "Andrei, I need you to take care of a few things for me. First, go down to the gymnasium and get access to my locker. I have some extra clothes and a pair of shoes in there. Bring them to me right away."

"Then what?"

"Contact Yulia first thing in the morning. Have her go to my apartment and gather enough clothes and personal items for at least a week." Her fingertips slid across the long white bandage along her neck. "I'll need some scarves too. Make certain she gets the leather-bound book from my nightstand. Tell her to be careful, it's irreplaceable."

"I will. What is she to do with these things?"

"Have her take them to the Savoy and leave them with the concierge. Andrei, this is important. I have to go into hiding until President Gorbachev returns. Other than you and Yulia, absolutely no one can know where I am. My life could depend on it, do you understand?"

"Yes, of course. But you should get some security."

"I will take care of that, no need to worry. I'll be alright tonight."

It took Tasia three phone calls to locate Pyotr Gusarov. The loud, raucous noise in the background nearly drowned out his deep baritone.

"Anastasia! I heard what happened. Are you alright?"

Tasia had always enjoyed her conversations with Gusarov. Second-in-command of the *Devyatka*, the KGB Directorate responsible for providing bodyguards to Communist Party leaders and their families, the handsome rogue with the flowing black hair and dazzling smile had relentlessly tried to convince her to become his mistress for well over fifteen years. She had come close on several occasions, but it was only her aversion to drinking too much that had stopped her. She often wondered if he really was as amazing a lover as he had always claimed.

"I have definitely had better days, Pyotr," Tasia said. "I very much need your help, I'm afraid."

"Mother Russia, I am yours to command!" Gusarov slurred. "Perhaps you might join me in drinking some of this excellent vodka before I make love to you tonight? I could have a car pick you up in just a few minutes?"

"Pyotr, you know straight vodka makes me sick to my stomach. And yes, I would love nothing better than to have you kiss me all over like you've always promised. Right now, I need you to be serious. I require some personal security right away, and this needs to be kept secret, especially from you-know-who."

"Kryuchkov? I wouldn't piss on that scumbag if he were on fire," Gusarov roared. "I will have two of my best security men report to you within the hour. You can arrange for around-the-clock protection with whoever's most senior."

Tasia heard him speak to someone nearby.

"Are you sure I cannot convince you to stay with me tonight, my beautiful goddess? I can promise you not only safety, but a night of love like you've never experienced."

"Oh, Pyotr," Tasia said as several images flew unbidden through her mind. "I so look forward to it one day. I might even promise not to tell your wife."

Gusarov hung up the phone with a grunt.

Yuri was surprised when he entered the infirmary and found an armed guard.

"This room is off-limits," the beefy young man said with polite firmness. "Only those authorized by the General."

Yuri stood up straight. The guard was only a few years older than him, his Kalashnikov and full uniform set and shined to parade levels. His eyes appeared neutral, but Yuri could tell he was not one of the common simpletons the KGB often used for such duties.

"I am General Zolotova's son," he said in a clear voice. "She can verify my identity if you insist."

The guard did not move, and Yuri decided maybe this one was not as smart as he had given him credit for. He was about to escalate the discussion when the guard stepped aside, opened the door, and clicked his heels. Yuri did not bother to thank him.

Only the nurses' light behind the bed was on. His mother appeared sound asleep, so he closed the door with a deliberate clack. Her eyes flew open, and she grabbed for the PSM in her lap.

"No need to shoot me, Mother."

"Hello, Yuri," Tasia replied with a yawn.

Yuri leaned against the wooden doorframe. "I have some information for you about the attack."

"I'm feeling much better now, Son. Thank you for coming to see me."

Yuri did not make eye contact, but instead directed his gaze toward the white plaster wall beyond her. "We have not yet identified the assassin who attacked you, but it appears he belonged to some local criminal element. He undoubtedly accessed the SID file room, as that door was open when the investigative team arrived."

"I sent a strike squad inside when we discovered that. They found nothing."

"Neither did the investigative team. How the assassin gained access to KGB Headquarters is still uncertain. We think he used one of the side entrances on the ground floor below your office. The surveillance cameras in that area have malfunctioned."

"That is next to impossible," Tasia scoffed. "It sounds like this assassin had assistance from inside Dzerzhinsky."

"I'm afraid that is exactly the case." Yuri reached into his pocket. "I found this on the assassin's person." He showed her the key. "It opens the door to your file room. I take it you know where it had to have come from?"

"Yes," Tasia said. "The other two keys are accounted for. Whoever took that key could only have done so with the Chairman's knowledge. It requires his personal security code to access that room."

Yuri struggled to keep from smiling. "Then you understand, Mother. It seems my father is trying to kill you."

CHAPTER 4

Bile burbled into Tasia's mouth. She fought the urge to vomit, swallowed it down, and blanched. "Until you showed me that," she said. "I did not actually believe this could be true. Now, it's undeniable."

"Mother, I do not wish to upset you, but the situation is far more dangerous than you realize. My father can mobilize the forces of the entire KGB, including our blood-wet killers from the *Mokryye Dela*. When that happens, the outcome is inevitable."

"Yes, I know."

She took a deep breath and swallowed again.

"Father would not resort to such drastic measures unless something threatened him. Based on the things I've seen and heard these past many weeks, I think I know what that might be."

Tasia arched an eyebrow. "What are you talking about?"

"Father has hosted many secret meetings of late with a multitude of high-ranking officials. This afternoon, I'm being sent to Washington with a sealed packet of information for Ambassador Komplektov. Enormous plans are being set in motion on an international scale, like nothing we've ever seen before. I do not know any details, but if something you know or have done was perceived as an impediment to those plans? Well, that would explain what just happened."

"It certainly would," Tasia said. She laid her head in her hands. "Yuri, what am I to do? If what you say is true, there's no one I can trust and nowhere to hide."

"Mother, you can trust me. I may not have the power to stop my father, but I can still help you."

"How?"

"You need to leave the country. Go somewhere Father and the KGB cannot reach you." He lowered his voice. "I can reach out to the Americans for you."

Tasia's face blanched. "That is insane. Mother Russia defect?"

"Not defect, Mother, escape." Yuri stepped to the edge of the bed. "Think about it. This is a means to save your life. The Americans are greedy to a fault. I'm certain your conscience can be assuaged with the right amount of negotiation once you're over there."

"Yuri, there must be some other way. I have to figure this out."

"You haven't time, Mother. The forces arrayed against you are both enormous and without pity. The only way to checkmate them is to leave the game entirely."

Tasia considered her son's words.

If what he says is true, even approaching President Gorbachev might give Vladimir reason to have me shot. I can go into hiding, but that merely buys a little time. Could the Americans send someone quickly? If only there was someone in the United States I could trust—

Her head shot up. She looked at her son and turned slightly in the bed to better face him.

"Yuri, I think you're absolutely right."

"Well, of course."

"If you're willing to help me like you say, I need you to carry a message from me to the United States government. To one particular person in fact."

"A particular person?"

"Yes. Tell the Americans what just happened. Say I want to defect and require extraction from Moscow as quickly as possible." She nervously adjusted the blanket on her lap. "This next part is critical, Yuri. Make certain the Americans understand it is non-negotiable."

Yuri sighed. "Yes, Mother."

"My defection is conditional on them sending one man in particular. His name is Jonathan Cole. He is likely still with the CIA in some capacity."

Yuri cocked his head. "You know an American? A CIA officer?"

Tasia kept her gaze even. "Yuri, there are many things about me you do not know. I met Jon many years ago during my time with the KGB Foreign Office. We were each on assignments when we became—entangled, I suppose you could say."

Yuri's reddish eyebrows shot up like little flames. "You and an American? You were—lovers?" He spat the word as if it were poison.

"Yes, Yuri. This was several weeks before I met your father. Jon and I were very young and what we had was beautiful. We made promises to each other before I decided not to go with him to America. He will remember them, I'm certain."

Tasia reached behind her pillow for her briefcase. She laid it on her lap and took out paper and pen. "I'm going to write a note. I want you to deliver it to Jon personally."

Tasia wrote her message, folded the paper into quarters, and handed it to her son.

"You can read it if you like. It should only make sense to Jon. Bring me his reply when you return. I'll be at the Savoy, but no one must know that." Tasia stared at her son and sighed. "Thank you, Baby Boy. Considering how rarely I've seen you these past many years, I'm grateful you love me at least a little to do this for me. I have so many regrets regarding us."

"Don't worry, Mother," Yuri said without expression. "I will deliver your message."

He pocketed the note and left the room.

The morning sun streamed in through the tall, squared windows as Andrei entered the common work area at Dzerzhinsky assigned to the Special Investigations Directorate. The staff appeared diligently at work as the sound of clacking typewriters filled the high-ceilinged space.

Miss Yulia Gradenko, Tasia's personal secretary, sat at her customary desk near the front of the room. The young woman with the shiny-blond hair stayed perpetually cheerful, which grated on Andrei's nerves. Unfortunately, the general liked her sunny disposition, so he endured it.

"I have completed the assignment you gave me, Major," Miss Gradenko said in a voice significantly louder than Andrei thought proper.

"Did you retrieve all the items?" he whispered.

"Oh, yes, sir," the young woman replied, still at the same ridiculously loud level. "I took every uniform, dress, scarf, and pair of shoes from the general's closet, along with all the makeup on her dresser. I gathered all the underwear and stockings from her drawers but could not find any slacks."

Andrei wondered if perhaps the girl had been dropped on her head as a child. "General Zolotova prefers skirts and dresses," he said. "I doubt she has many pairs of pants. Did you retrieve the book she wanted?"

"Oh, yes, sir. Everything is at the Savoy just like you asked."

"I did not ask for anything, Miss Gradenko," Andrei said in a menacing tone. "I gave you an order."

The smile fell from the young woman's face. "Yes, sir."

"Furthermore, you are not to answer any questions about General Zolotova's whereabouts. She is away on a classified matter, that is all. Any inquiries are to be directed to me and none of this may be shared or discussed with the staff. Am I clear as to the seriousness of this matter?"

"Y—you are, sir," the young woman whispered. Her lower lip trembled, and Andrei feared she might burst into tears. He headed down the hallway as fast as possible.

He opened the door to his office and found Yuri asleep in one of the chairs, feet crossed on top of the large oaken desk.

"What are you doing here?" Andrei asked as he hung his uniform jacket on the coat tree.

Yuri dropped his feet to the floor, sat up straight, and yawned. "I've been here for several hours." He pulled a loose key from his trenchcoat pocket and held it up. "I needed to return this."

"Give me that!" Andrei reached across the desk and jerked the key from the young man's fingers. "It needs to go back into our safe."

"You are the one who is late, Major. Did it not occur to you someone might need that key this morning?"

"Obviously, no one did," Andrei said as he sat down.

"The only thing obvious here is that you are fortunate. Still, the Secretariat thanks you for your cooperation."

"I thought you needed access to the files! I had no idea you planned on killing her! Murder? Here? Do you not think there will be an investigation?"

"Of course. I completed it myself, hours after the incident occurred."

"You did?"

"It wasn't difficult to arrange."

Andre mumbled something under his breath, placed his palms on the desk, and wheeled his chair closer. "Do you require anything else?"

"Only this, Comrade Major. Everything we have discussed is classified far above your level. You have never seen nor spoken with me. That key has been in your department's safe this entire time. To mention anything contrary to that to anyone will result in the gravest personal consequences for you. Am I clear?"

"I've been a KGB officer for well over a decade. I know how the game is played."

"Good. You can let me out through the back exit." Yuri stood, smoothed the front of his trenchcoat and checked his watch. "I have a plane to catch."

CHAPTER 5

10:00 PM, Washington Time, Sunday, August 11, 1991

Jessica Bolton rose with the rest of the audience at the Kennedy Center and applauded.

The National Symphony Orchestra had performed nearly two hours of Russian classical favorites, including Shostakovich, Rimsky-Korsakov and Mussorgsky. The biggest treat had been the finale from Tchaikovsky's 1812 Overture, complete with firing cannons.

The performers stood for their accolades and Jessi watched the Soviet delegation clap in unison. Russians often applauded in what they called rounds for an exceptional performance. The practice dated from the days of Stalin when the dictator would often single out for special punishment whoever stopped clapping first at State events. Soviet diplomats in particular, like the embassy members present tonight, Jessi thought, had long memories.

The houselights came up and she turned to the man in the seat beside her. "Jon, it's time."

Jonathan Cole nodded. His thick brown hair was precisely trimmed, and his evening-black tuxedo displayed his athletic physique in an understated yet flattering style. His square jaw retained the same frown it had held all afternoon, and the brows over his pale grey eyes scrunched in an angry manner. Jessi did not understand his agitation, but knew it started when they learned about the KGB general who wanted Jon to personally negotiate her defection.

Jessi and Jon rose from their seats along the second level balcony. Jessi led the way up the steps to the exit, careful in her high heels. When they reached the top, Jon touched her shoulder.

"You look great tonight, by the way."

"Thanks," she said with a wink. "Was hoping you'd notice." The long slit up the leg was far more daring than she had ever attempted, and she felt a little self-conscious at the profound neckline that plunged way too low.

The two of them worked their way to the stairway that led to the main lobby. The crowd was tightly packed, and when someone jostled her, Jessi wobbled for a second and reached to steady the elaborate pile of brown hair atop her head.

"Careful," Jon said as he moved in closer. "Just because we're in friendly territory does not mean we shouldn't be vigilant."

Jessi looked around as they reached the bottom of the stairs. It was unlike her to forget her training, especially in a large crowd.

"You're right. I'm sorry."

The two of them strode across the huge, carpeted lobby. Most of the crowd headed for the stairwells that led to the parking garage, but Jessi put her arm around Jon's waist and steered them toward one of the smaller theaters along the side.

The security personnel raised eyebrows at their special passes for the invite-only diplomatic event but asked no questions. The bulge under Jon's left arm told anyone who cared to look he was armed. Jessi kept her Agency-issued Smith & Wesson in her handbag.

Tall tables and chairs haphazardly surrounded the open reception area. A small set of musical instruments and chairs lined the back of the stage area where the Soviet and American flags hung side by side. Smiling servers in formal attire swarmed everywhere with trays of finger foods and the dozen or so drink stations along the periphery were already busy.

Jessi spotted their contact against the far wall. The CIA man with the straw-colored hair could not have been much over thirty. Jessi thought he blended in well, not too tall or intense like so many Company personnel, and he did not appear to be nervous. She nodded at Jon, and they rapidly crossed the crowded room.

"Mr. Moore, nice to meet you in person," Jessi said without extending her hand. She had to speak up to be heard over the noise of the growing crowd.

"Likewise," the man replied. "I presume this is Mr. Cole?"

"Yes," Jon answered in his mild Boston accent. "Nice to meet you."

"Same to you, sir. Have you put on your wire? If so, can we test the audio?"

"Sure." Jon reached into his pants pocket for the wireless microphone's transmitter and asked in a normal voice if everyone could hear him. Moore and Jessi both nodded as they reached up to touch their barely noticeable earpieces.

"I'll turn it off for now," Jon said. "No sense draining the batteries."

"I see you're wearing the purple pocket square our Soviet friend requested," Moore said.

"Yeah, I feel like a damn target." Glasses clinked nearby and Jessi waved away an approaching waiter. "How many of us are in the room?"

"Six, counting myself and Officer Bolton. We're all connected via audio and will converge at discrete distances once you make contact. Officer Bolton will accompany you, of course."

"How many KGB?" Jon's head moved in a slow circle as he scanned the room. Jessi copied his movements. Russians were generally unmistakable by their dress and demeanor. They appeared to be everywhere.

"It's difficult to say, but we've identified ten strong potentials. Given this meeting is supposed to be about a runner, we assume they're unaware."

"Unless something else is going on," Jessi said.

"I hate assumptions," Jon said, "but sounds like we're as ready as we're going to be. I'm going to get a drink. That should put me on display easily enough."

Jessi and Jon walked side by side over to the nearest drink station. The line was long but appeared to be moving well.

"I presume young master Moore doesn't know who we really are?" Jon asked.

"Definitely not," Jessi said. The chatter around them seemed louder than before so she raised her voice again to compensate. "Neither of us needs the grief nor the condescension. Moore and his friends believe we're run-of-the-mill CIA, just like them. They have no idea we're Eagle Group."

Saying the name out loud felt wrong to Jessi. Eagle Group was the covert assassination arm of US intelligence, and while technically part of the CIA, it was generally viewed as an embarrassing remnant of a more brutal time.

Jessi and Jon were what Eagle called a unified pair, a euphemism for an attack dog and its handler. Eagle's enforcement officers were called wolves, and Jon was their most experienced. Codenamed Archangel, his kill record was unmatched by anyone in its near-thirty-year history.

It was Jessi's job to coordinate assignments, provide support and most especially arrange for cleanup services after a removal—Eagle's term for an assassination or killing—took place. Unlike other handlers, however, Jessi had allowed her personal connection with Jon to become complicated.

Jon touched her arm. One of the bartenders pointed at them.

"I'd like a cranberry juice over ice," Jessi said.

Jon studied the selections behind the bar before he pointed to one of the bottles. "I'll take an Old Forester on the rocks. Make it a double."

The bartender prepared and handed over their drinks. Jon dropped a tip in the jar, and they moved into the crowd.

"Jonathan Cole?" A high, squeaky voice came from Jessi's right.

A short young man, in a too large, powder-grey suit, stood a few feet away. His reddish-brown hair was cut down to the nub in the common Russian fashion, and his babyface cheeks displayed an odd, off-center smile. Jessi wondered if he could grow facial hair.

"Yes, I am Jonathan Cole. Are you the person I am to meet this evening?"

Jessi noticed Jon sneak his left hand into his pants pocket. The noise of the activated microphone popped in her earpiece.

The young man stepped closer but did not offer Jon his hand. A huge bear of a man with shaggy black hair, bushy beard, and impatient eyes appeared at the young Russian's shoulder.

"My name is Yuri Vladimirovich Zolotov." The signal from Jon's microphone was crisp and the young man's English impeccable, if a little deliberate. "I presume you have somewhere we can talk privately?"

"Yes," Jon said. "If you would walk with me?"

Jon led the young man toward the far wall. The big Russian fell in step behind them at the same moment Jessi did.

"Be careful, little girl," the bear said as the two of them walked side-by-side. "I would hate to snap that soft and pretty neck of yours."

"You'll need to threaten better than that if you want to get my attention," Jessi replied with a curt smile.

The big Russian showed his husky yellow teeth. "I have not begun to threaten you, little girl. You'll know when I do."

Jon pulled out a chair at a tall table next to one of the velvet draperies that lined the walls. He gestured to the chair on the other side and the young Russian sat down. Jessi drained her glass and set it on an empty table, then took up station a few feet behind Jon. The huge Russian did the same directly opposite her. Yuri spoke first.

"Since you are likely recording this conversation, I will be direct. I am here on behalf of Major General Anastasia Zolotova of the Special Investigations Directorate of the KGB. She asks for extraction from the Soviet Union immediately, and for protection in the United States as a defector. I believe you know her personal history?"

"I am aware." Jon said as he set his glass on the table. "We are happy to assist with her defection. I do have some questions, though."

"By all means, ask whatever you like."

"Let's start with the obvious. What has happened to bring this about? Given General Zolotova's rank and position, not to mention her fame, why would she do this?"

"To put it simply, Officer Cole, she wants to live."

A young server with a blonde ponytail and a large tray of bacon-wrapped shrimp came out of the crowd. Both Jon and the young Russian politely declined her offer, and Jessi promptly shooed her away.

"Are you saying she has enemies?" Jon said when the girl had gone. "I would think that would be part of her everyday concerns. Considering the anti-corruption aims of that directorate?"

Yuri sighed as if annoyed. "General Zolotova was nearly killed in her office four nights ago. All evidence points to an assassination attempt from within the KGB. She is currently in hiding and asks for asylum in the United States where she believes they cannot reach her."

Jon took a drink of his bourbon. "Why does the KGB want her dead?"

"She is not certain, but believes it has to do with a recent investigation. I was not given any details, I'm afraid."

"Of course not," Jon said. The musicians on the stage at the other end of the room began to tune their instruments. "My next question is for you personally. Why are you effectively committing treason to help her? That seems an enormous risk."

Yuri's smile broadened. "Perhaps my answer will alleviate your doubts, Officer Cole. General Zolotova, you see, is my mother. She told me of yours and hers—previous relationship, shall we say?—and how she would trust you alone to come to Moscow and help her escape."

Jessi's mouth dropped open, and she felt her face go flush. She glanced at the Big Russian and saw his teeth were bared. He appeared to be salivating, hard eyes focused squarely on Jon. She could not tell from where she was standing if Jon noticed or not.

The young Russian reached into his jacket pocket, pulled out a piece of paper and handed it over. "My mother wrote you a note that should prove I am telling the truth." Jessi tried to peer over Jon's shoulder but was too far back to see clearly. Jon appeared to read the note several times.

"I presume you have read it?" he asked as he refolded the paper and slipped it into the pocket of his tuxedo jacket.

"Of course," Yuri said, "although the names she mentions make no sense to me."

"Then you are not as well read as you should be," Jon said. "If your mother did not explain, then neither will I. Please give her this message from me, word for word."

"Very well."

"You tell her I'm coming," Jon said. "And that I love her, too."

Jessi erupted into a sudden coughing fit. She saw Jon crook his head toward her, as did both Yuri and the big Russian. It took her several seconds to regain her breath. Jon and the Russians turned back around.

"Uh, all right," the young man said. "Is that everything you want to tell her? Surely you have more questions for me?"

"No, that's all," Jon said. "Good evening and enjoy the reception."

Jon abruptly rose. He moved toward Jessi, his face a cold and impassive mask, and she felt his strong grip on her bare arm as he gently tugged her into the crowd.

The big Russian—Anatoly Turgenev—stepped forward as Yuri pushed back his chair. "What's the matter, Turgenev?" he asked in Russian. "Our mission is complete. You are free to enjoy the evening."

"What I am going to do, boy, is kill that sonofabitch you were just sitting with. I intend to carry his head all the way back to Moscow in triumph."

"What are you talking about?"

"That man is the American assassin, Archangel."

"No, that man is a CIA officer named Jonathan Cole. He just confirmed it."

"I don't care if he told you he was Josef Stalin. He's the one who nearly killed me in West Berlin. It took me a few minutes to put everything together, but I tell you it's him!" Turgenev nearly shouted.

"Guard your mouth," Yuri whispered through clenched teeth. "We are in a public place on foreign soil. Are you an idiot?"

"Watch your own mouth," Turgenev said. "I'd already slit a dozen American throats by the time you stopped crapping your diapers." He raised his arm and pointed into the crowd. "That man has been at the top of our kill list for nearly a decade. Until this moment we have never been able to discover his true identity. I will not allow him to walk this earth a second longer!"

Yuri stepped in closer. "You do realize there are at least four armed American agents watching us? Do you really think you could kill this man in here and survive?"

Turgenev dropped his arm and stared at where Jon and Jessi had disappeared.

"Comrade Turgenev," Yuri said. "This Archangel, as you call him, is being used to flush out a traitor at the highest level of the Soviet government. That mission takes priority over everything else. I presume you know who my father is?"

"Yes, comrade," Turgenev said with a tone of annoyance.

"You know I speak with his authority. This American has just agreed to come to Moscow on what he thinks is a defection mission. You want justice for your fallen comrades? So does the Chairman."

Yuri stood on his tiptoes and pointed his finger at the bigger man's face.

"In his name, I order you to leave this man alone. In Moscow we will arrange a proper, public revenge against both him and the evil capitalist government that spawned him."

Turgenev glared at him, turned on his heel and headed into the crowd.

CHAPTER 6

Jessi jerked her arm away and followed behind Jon as he elbowed through the crowded hall. He did not look back and neither did she. He hit the crash bar on the huge wooden exit doors and the two of them rushed into the main lobby.

People still milled about, although not near as many as before. Jessi, unsteady in her high heels, caught a wrinkle in the ornate floor rug and nearly fell. Jon did not seem to notice.

"Will you please tell me what's going on?"

Jon did not answer and kept moving. Jessi struggled to keep up, her frustration growing with every step. Finally, they reached the other side. Jon turned around, placed his back against the wall and motioned for Jessi to stand beside him. The door to the parking garage was a few feet away.

"Will you answer me!" she said, slightly out of breath.

"Did you see that big-bearded Russian?" Jon said as he fumbled in his pants pocket. His eyes scanned the room.

"Of course."

Jon pulled out the wireless microphone transmitter, disconnected it, and tossed it into the garbage can beside them.

"That was Anatoly Turgenev."

A chill went down Jessi's spine. "Turgenev? But—you said he died in that warehouse fire."

"Apparently, he escaped like I did." Jon brushed the front of his jacket and raised his chin. "He knows who I am, Jessi."

"How do you know that? Did he see your face in West Berlin?"

"No, I was masked, but he heard my voice and saw my body movements. Apparently, that was enough for him to piece things together. We locked eyes when I was talking with Zolotov. There's no doubt, trust me."

"Damn." Jessi's pulse throbbed in her ears. "What do we do?"

"Get him out of the city. Someplace remote where we can remove both him and whoever he brings along."

Jessi mulled over what he was saying. "Wait a minute. You mean to lure them to your place?"

"Exactly. I've got almost a hundred acres of woodland surrounding me, and my closest neighbors are literally miles away."

"Holy hell," Jessi whispered, then took a deep breath. "Okay, what's the plan? You do have one, right?"

"We wait. It won't be long."

A distant elevator dinged, and Jessi saw Turgenev push his way into the bustling lobby with three men in tow. Jon took Jessi's hand and whispered for her to stay still as they watched the men scan the space. Turgenev's eyes finally locked on them, and Jon quickly opened the heavy fire-door and drug them both inside.

The door slammed shut and Jessi let go of Jon's hand so she could remove her high heels. The two of them ran down the steps, burst onto the first level of the garage, and sprinted across the concrete to her silver Mustang. Jessi threw her shoes into the back seat and plopped into the driver's seat. The engine caught with a throaty growl, and she jammed the car into gear. She pulled out of their parking space and headed toward the exit line.

Jon turned to look behind them.

"Do you see them?" Jessi asked as she edged into the line of cars.

"Yeah, they're on this level, too. We're getting lucky so far. Black Crown Victoria, do you see them?"

Jessi glanced at the rearview mirror. "Yeah, I got 'em. You want me to take I-66 to the Georgetown Pike?"

"Yes, but do not speed. I want them to think we don't see them."

Jessi pulled out of the garage, drove up the ramp to the interstate and crossed the Theodore Roosevelt Bridge into Virginia. Traffic thinned out as they moved north and away from the city. The black Crown Victoria kept its distance but stayed in sight. Thirty miles later, she left the interstate and watched her pursuers follow. The narrow two-lane highway was pitch black and virtually deserted, penned in from all sides by thick tall trees.

"Turgenev is predictable to a fault," Jon said. "He'll want me to know it's him. I suspect his preference would be to tail us to wherever we're going, sneak into the house and kill us in bed."

"That's a comforting thought," Jessi whispered.

"Turn up ahead onto Towelston Road as usual, okay?" Jon said. "Slow down when we get close, so they see us make the turn."

"Not a problem."

"When you reach the stop sign at Old Dominion, we'll make our move. Turgenev's ready to spit fire about now because of these narrow, unfamiliar roads. When I give the word, turn right and floor it. We need to get to the driveway ahead of them."

"Then what?"

"You know the open field along the side of the driveway? The one that runs beside the river?"

"Yeah?"

"Run off into it when I tell you and go all the way to the tree line. You'll need to spin the car around, so it faces the road more or less."

"Spin the car around?"

"Don't worry, you can do this."

Jessi gripped the wheel tight with both hands. Her palms were sweaty. Her eyes flittered from side to side in the darkness, wary of encountering the many deer that were no doubt all around them. She tried to visualize the field Jon mentioned, even though she had seen it many times. She trusted him and had been well trained by both the CIA and Eagle, but this was the first time she had ever been directly involved in an actual operation.

The sign for Towelston Road appeared ahead, so Jessi flipped on her blinker. The Russians had kept back, but she knew they could still see her. It took her no time on the curvy side-road to reach the stop sign at Old Dominion Highway. A few seconds later, headlights appeared behind them.

"Go!" Jon whispered.

Jessi turned right and punched the gas pedal to the floor. She held the Mustang steady as it picked up speed, and peeked into the rearview mirror to see the Crown Victoria pull out after them. The entrance to the long driveway appeared in the glare of her headlights. She threw the wheel hard to the right and felt the tires spin gravel. The Russians sped past them, and Jessi heard their tires screech.

"Cut left! Now!"

The little Mustang jumped the edge of the drive and hit the open field so hard Jessi almost lost control. In August, the weeds were still high. The tree line along the riverbank jumped into view as Jon's finger shot in front of her face.

"Hard left!"

Jessi yanked the wheel, and the Mustang spun around. She mouthed a silent prayer they would not flip over. All four wheels stayed on the ground, and they ended up parallel to the river; the tree line a few feet from her bumper. Her headlights pointed back at the road like a beacon.

"Bullseye," Jon said. "Looks like you lost control and spun out. Grab your weapon and follow me. Leave the lights on and the engine running."

Jon grabbed Jessi's hand as they ran into trees. Thorns, undergrowth, and composted leaves assaulted her bare feet. Jon pulled her into the stinking grey mud below the slope of the riverbank. Jessi heard rushing water below them. The underside of the narrow concrete bridge loomed above their heads, several dozen yards to the right.

"Wait," Jon whispered.

Jessi raised her 10mm and willed herself to focus. Through the underbrush, the glow from the Crown Victoria's approaching lights flooded the tops of the weeds. The big car pulled nose-to-nose with the tiny Mustang, doors slammed, and Anatoly Turgenev stepped into the circle of light between the cars. The bearded giant pointed at the Mustang and two of his companions, armed with submachine guns, stepped forward and opened fire. Bullets shattered the windshield and riddled the passenger compartment. Another man with a handgun appeared and added his fire into the car.

"When they stop," Jon whispered in her ear, "shoot the machine gunner closest to you, then the one with the pistol behind him. I'll get the other two."

Both submachine guns clicked on empty chambers. Jessi and Jon simultaneously fired. The Russians, illuminated by the Crown Victoria's headlights, were sitting ducks. Jessi nailed her first target in the center of the chest. She tracked her pistol toward the second man, who scanned the trees in search of the source of the shots. She fired again and a burst of blood erupted from the man's neck before he fell backward into the matted grass. Her ears rang as she turned to look at Jon. He was gone.

She scanned the tree line and saw him, moving with the speed of a leopard, heading toward Turgenev. The Russian still stood, despite being hit, and blood soaked the left side of his suit. Jessi saw his eyes widen and he turned in time for Jon to plow into him like a locomotive. Both men went down. Jessi glanced over and saw Jon's 10mm in the mud beside her.

Jessi clambered up the slick riverbank, careful not to slip because of her pantyhose. Jon's back rose and a wet smacking sound filled the air as his right hand flew up and down. Jessi picked her way through the dense undergrowth and saw a long blade in Jon's hand, red with dripping blood.

Jessi watched with mute fascination as Jon walked over to the wounded men. Without a word, he turned the first KGB man over with the toe of his shoe and in two swift motions, slit his throat on both sides. Crimson immediately doused both the man's shirt and Jon's hands. The other two KGB men died the same way.

Jessi limped into the light; her pistol held in front of her with both hands. Somewhere along the way she had stepped on something sharp. Her hair had come loose and a portion of it hung in front of her face. She looked over at Jon and stopped.

The glow from the Crown Victoria's headlights reflected off his face. His tuxedo was drenched in blood. Hair askew, eyes wide and wild, he looked like a werewolf sprung from the darkness. Jessi half-expected to see him throw back his head and howl.

Jon walked back to Turgenev and Jessi stepped in behind him. Thick blood bubbled out of the dying Russian's lips and stained his black beard.

"Thought you had me, didn't you, Anatoly?" Jon said in English. "The wolf beats the bear every time. You should know that by now."

"Go to hell, Archangel," Turgenev spat. "We finally know who you are—you are as dead as me." The big Russian choked one final time and stopped breathing. Jon spit on the corpse, said something Jessi could not make out, then turned to look at her.

"We need to get up to the house."

"What?"

"You need to call in a cleaning crew."

Jessi did not understand. Everything happened so fast. Jon tossed his knife to the ground and grabbed her by the shoulders.

"What's the matter? Are you hurt?"

Jessi searched his face for a moment before she found her tongue.

"No, I'm fine. Sorry."

"It's okay," Jon said in comforting tone. "No amount of training can prepare you for something like this the first time. We can't drag evidence up to the house. We need to strip naked right here and toss everything into your car."

"Okay."

The stench of blood and ozone in the air almost made her gag as she drew her mud-encrusted dress over her head. Sweat glued the pantyhose to her skin; she peeled them off like an orange. Jon tossed his own clothes near the Mustang and motioned for Jessi to place her handbag on the grass where he laid his keys, wallet, and the note from the young Russian.

They gathered the weapons, theirs and the Russians', then threw both them and their clothes into the front seats of the bullet-riddled Mustang. The spent brass and dead bodies, now covered in flies, stayed where they fell. Jon turned off the Crown Vic's engine and a multitude of stars shone down through the clear sky.

"Let's go," he said.

Completely nude, Jessi scooped up her handbag then hobbled off through the high grass. Jon picked up his items, caught up with her and reached for her hand, but she smacked it away. The two of them reached the gravel driveway and Jessi took one last look through the darkness at the spot where she had witnessed death up close for the first time.

She shook her head and began the long walk to the house.

CHAPTER 7

10:15 AM, Moscow Time, Wednesday, August 14, 1991

The morning light streamed through the high windows into Vladimir Kryuchkov's office at Dzerzhinsky Square. A dust-filled aura formed on the polished hardwood floor as the KGB Chairman sat patiently on one side of the rectangular conference table. His guest sat across from him and threw up his arms in frustration.

"What the hell are we waiting for?" Soviet Interior Minister Boris Pugo yelled. "Gorbachev is scheduled to come back on Tuesday. If he signs that damn New Union Treaty, both of us are out on our asses and everything we've done will be thrown open to the light of day. We need to move now."

Kryuchkov picked up the crystal tumbler in front of him and took a slow drink. He had decided on one of his favorites, Chivas Regal. He had not offered Pugo any.

"Not everyone is onboard," he said. "There are still a few arms we need to twist."

"Whose?"

"Only minor players, but it's essential everyone is informed before we move. We'll stick to the original timetable."

He set the tumbler back on the table, folded his hands and met Pugo's gaze with what he hoped was serene confidence.

"I will send three officers to Gorbachev's dacha in Crimea Sunday afternoon. Their orders will be to cut communications to the outside world. Gorbachev and his family will be placed under house arrest and the briefcase with the nuclear codes will be confiscated and returned to Moscow. We will announce the state of emergency at six Monday morning. Yazov's troops will move into the city soon afterward. Are your forces prepared to handle the press outlets and television programming?"

The circle of complete baldness in the center of Boris Pugo's head was surrounded by a swatch of thick, grey hair which stood nearly upright. Kryuchkov always thought it made the man look like a portion of his head was missing. With his reading glasses on, he looked almost grandfatherly. When outraged, like he was now, he reminded Kryuchkov of a ferret which had gone too long without eating.

"We will preempt normal programming at precisely six with a replay of Swan Lake over all state channels," Pugo said. "The documents declaring the state of emergency will be read over the air soon after that. All press outlets, except for our own state-controlled newspapers, will be shut down by noon. Yanayev will need to host a press conference, preferably Monday evening, but I can arrange that quickly enough. Are you sure he's ready for this?"

Gennady Yanayev was vice president of the Soviet Union. Kryuchkov had always been ambivalent toward the lackluster-looking man who was widely rumored to be an alcoholic. If their new regime was to be recognized by the rest of the world, some appearance of legality had to be maintained, so Yanayev would assume the office of acting president and serve as the public face of the Committee on the State of Emergency—the *GKChP*.

"Pavlov and I can control him," Kryuchkov said with a confidence he did not quite feel. "We will tell him Sunday evening after everything's in motion. Don't worry, he'll do as he's told."

"He'd better." The Interior Minister leaned back in his chair. "What about internationally?"

"The key is, of course, the United States. I will get the details when my son arrives back in Moscow, but he reports Komplektov is fully prepared and will present our information to their State Department Monday morning. Due to the time difference, it will be afternoon here before we can gauge their reaction."

"What about internally? Those who will not support us?"

"No one who matters would dare," Kryuchkov said as he took another drink. "But if you're worried about Yeltsin, one of my Alpha Group commando units will be at his home early Monday morning. They can arrest him whenever we wish."

"Yeltsin is a pragmatist and fond of making deals. I'm not particularly worried about him. Your bitch, on the other hand, is another matter."

Kryuchkov sighed, set his glass on the table, and folded his arms. "What about her?"

"She has frozen our funding sources! The accounts we've bled away are traceable. Even though we will sideline Gorbachev before he finds out, we're still vulnerable."

"General Zolotova has gone into hiding after an attack on her in this very building several nights ago." Kryuchkov gave the Interior Minister a hard stare. "You wouldn't happen to know anything about that, would you Boris?"

Pugo paused. "No, I would not, but whoever was responsible very nearly did us a favor."

Kryuchkov pushed the papers in front of him aside. "Boris, I know you are concerned. After what happened, General Zolotova has hidden herself at the Savoy. Her supposedly trustworthy security all report to me. She has not set foot out of there since the attack. I say let her be. We have more important things to worry about."

"What is it with you and this woman, Vladimir? You vacillate every time she enters the picture. She's a blazing whore of incredible beauty, I grant you, but you have to see what she knows can upend everything! No woman, no matter how spectacular, is worth all that!"

"General Zolotova and I parted company years ago," Kryuchkov said with an icy tone. "Anything else is none of your business. I agree she's a potential liability, but she has gone to ground. That's enough as far as I'm concerned."

"Not for me," Pugo said. "Do you remember how she deposed Rudestenklov to gain her current position? She practically knifed the old man in the back to get him to retire. He's lucky he did not go to prison."

"Rudestenklov was an incompetent ass."

"Precisely my point. She saw the weak player and went for his jugular. Do you think she's changed since then?"

Kryuchkov did not reply.

"She is rabidly loyal to Gorbachev," Pugo said. "He and Raisa have hosted her at the presidential residence on several occasions. She's also been the darling of the press for well over a decade now."

"Your point?"

"Let me put it this way. What do you think Mother Russia will do the moment we announce Gorbachev is unwell and the *GKChP* is assuming control? She will find the closest press outlet, that's what, and they will listen to her. We are going to be screwed from the very outset unless we deal with her now!"

"Dammit Boris!" Kryuchkov pounded his fist on the table. "What do you want?"

Pugo's chipmunk cheeks spread into a wicked smile. "She must have written documentation of some kind about our financial activities for her to have frozen our funding sources. Take that away and she has no proof. If you want her to continue living, you need to secure those papers. That is the bare minimum I will accept, Vladimir."

Kryuchkov studied Pugo's face. "Very well," he finally said. "I will retrieve those papers."

Pugo frowned. "We do not have a lot of time."

"Leave it to me. I only need remind her who's boss."

"Very well," Pugo said, "but be warned. I will personally blow the brains out of that beautiful red head of hers if you do not handle this quickly."

Yuri yanked his suitcase from the baggage claim carousel at Moscow's Sheremetyevo Airport. He walked quickly toward the exit, stepped outside, and inhaled the familiar air of his city. He was glad to be home.

Twelve hours inside multiple commercial airliners had made him feel soiled. The people were rude, the food was awful, and the smell of so many closely packed human bodies reminded him of sour garbage.

A black Zil limousine pulled to the curb a few feet from him. The driver got out, opened the back door, and motioned for Yuri to get in. Boris Pugo sat on the other side of the brown leather seat with a scowl on his face.

"Well?"

"I met my mother's long-ago lover as expected, sir. He has agreed to come to Moscow to help her escape."

"Good. What's he like?"

"About my mother's age, mid-forties, with a ridiculous flair for the dramatic. Seriously handsome, overly tall, and built much like an American football player. I can see why she spread her legs for him. The best part, however, is he is much more than we knew."

"How so?"

"Apparently he is one of their Eagle assassins, codenamed Archangel."

"The name means nothing to me."

"I was told he has killed a great many of our operatives over the last ten years and stymied several of our operations. Until now, we have never been able to discover his true identity."

"This could have possibilities."

"Very much so, sir," Yuri said. "If we capture him alive on Soviet soil in the act of facilitating my mother's defection, you and my father would secure an enormous propaganda victory. His public trial would cement your new regime as a force to be reckoned with, while at the same time prevent the Americans from taking the moral high ground against us."

"When will he arrive in Moscow?"

"No later than Saturday, I should think. The CIA will want to create a plan for him and there is the travel time."

Pugo's mouth drew up into a tight circle. "Your mother needs to run before Monday. Her presence is causing your father to waffle again."

Yuri raised an eyebrow. "What?"

"He says he can convince her to cooperate with us."

"No!" He kicked the seat in front of him. "He needs to stay away from her. She will just manipulate him again! She always ruins everything!"

"Listen," Pugo said as he turned around. "I had to boldface lie to your father a little while ago about the attack on your mother. I can only get away with that so many times." He took a deep breath and turned to face the front again. "What is the American going to do when he arrives?"

"Meet her in the restaurant at the Savoy. I expect he will try to smuggle her into the American Embassy soon afterward."

"I'll see to it she's shot in her room before that happens," Pugo said.

"What about the proof you need? It's guaranteed my mother has hidden it somewhere by now. She knows how important it is. No doubt she's made contingency plans in case something happens to her, and you can be sure they all involve the press."

"We would not have to worry about any of this if your assassin had succeeded."

"This is a chess match, sir, not a street brawl. My mother has always been a wizard at the game, but she's not infallible. She blunted our first attack by removing a pawn, that's all. The next move is ours. We need to be clever."

"Where would she hide it? The hotel safe?"

"Too obvious and out of her control. No, she's got it offsite somewhere, but not far. We just need to follow her when she runs. Capture her, the evidence, and the American all at the same time."

"This American sounds dangerous. What are your plans regarding him?"

"He's only one man and past his prime. I have three *Mokryye Dela* men at the hotel, plus one of our finest technicians on standby."

"This sounds better than your father's insane idea. Make sure it happens. We need first the proof, then your mother dead, in that order." Pugo looked out the window as the car moved through the crowded streets. "Where do you need me to take you? Dzerzhinsky Square?"

"Thank you, sir, but please take me to the Savoy. I need to further my mother's romantic notions about this American savior of hers. It also sounds like she will need to be inoculated against my father's forthcoming intimidations. We do not want her to lose her resolve."

Tasia flinched at the harsh jangle of the phone across the room.

The front desk or her bodyguards could call her, of course, but in the seven days she had been at the Savoy, it had yet to happen. She took a deep breath, pulled her bare feet from underneath her on the red-and-gold velvet couch and laid the large leatherbound book on the marble coffee table. The phone rang again, so she fast-walked to the credenza along the far wall and grabbed the heavy receiver. "Yes?"

"General, we received a call from the front desk," one of her bodyguards reported, his voice bored. "I'm down here now. Someone who claims to be your son is asking for you."

"What does he look like?"

"Slight young man with short reddish-brown hair and a yellow coat."

"That's him. Make certain he is alone. If so, you can bring him up to me."

"Yes, General."

Tasia padded across the golden marble floor and glanced around the room. She grabbed the small leather thong which held together something like a horse's tail and marked her page in her book. She fluffed the pillows on the couch, smoothed her pink-patterned sundress, and adjusted the plastic band on her wrist. She toyed with the device, but did not push the button on the side. She did not want the men across the hall to burst into the room, guns drawn. *Not unless needed,* she thought.

A resounding triple knock broke the silence and Tasia opened the door, PSM in hand. One of her bodyguards, a burly KGB man with a flattop haircut, stood there with Yuri at his elbow. The young man, with hands in the pockets of his grey slacks and eyes directed at the tops of his shoes, looked like he had been sent home from school for bad behavior. Tasia might have thought the idea funny if it did not hurt so.

"Thank you, Corporal," she said. The KGB man nodded and stepped to the door across the hall.

Tasia noticed Yuri frown as they entered the sitting area of her grand suite. His eyes darted over the red-and-gold-patterned velvet curtains, the enormous Baroque and Renaissance paintings on the walls and the elegant furniture which Catherine the Great would have found familiar. Tasia set her PSM on the marble coffee table and picked up the leatherbound book next to it. She sat and motioned for Yuri to take the chair across from her.

"This was your grandfather's," she said as her fingers rubbed the cracked, black-leather binding. "It's been in our family for four generations. I've read it countless times. Papa would set me in his lap nearly every night when I was little and read to me from it."

"You've told me," Yuri said. "You do realize Tolstoy was a tool of the tsarist elites?"

"Why Yuri, what an ugly thing to say. Your grandfather would be hurt to hear you talk like that. *War and Peace* is our national epic."

"Our greatness began with the Communist Revolution," he stated. "It is there we owe our loyalty, not to the foolish imperial garbage Tolstoy preached."

Tasia smirked and changed the subject. "So, were you able to contact our, uh, friends?"

"Yes, Mother, I met them Sunday evening. They are happy to assist with your needs."

"Did you meet, uh, Jon?"

"Yes, Mother, I met your old lover."

Tasia's face flushed. "What did he say?"

"He said to tell you he was coming for you." Tasia saw him swallow. "And that he loved you, too."

Tasia's mouth dropped open. "He said that? He told you that?"

"Yes, Mother, I saw the determination in his eyes. I'm certain he was telling the truth."

"My God," Tasia whispered. "What happens now?"

"He read your note about meeting him for breakfast. I presume he will arrive in a few days and make contact like you asked."

Tasia pulled the book to her chest and encircled it with her arms. "This is really happening," she whispered. "Yuri, I—I didn't realize how hard this would be. Only now that you've completed your studies am I able to see you—" she slipped her fingers inside the folds of the book, "—but if everything goes as planned, I may never see you again!"

Yuri snorted and dismissed her with a wave. "Mother, please do not forget what happened a few days ago. The power of the forces out to destroy you is beyond imagination. Promise me you will stay the course and keep focused on escape."

Tasia tried to read her son's face and failed. "Alright," she said. "I promise."

"Good." Yuri stood and brushed his hands down the front of his trenchcoat. "I have to go."

"So soon? I hoped we could talk some more. There are so many reasons why I couldn't be there for you growing up. You need to hear them now that you're on your own and able to understand."

"Father expects me at Dzerzhinsky, and you know he does not like to be kept waiting," Yuri said. "Contacting you again could cause suspicion, so I should say farewell now."

Tasia set the book on the couch and stood up. She searched her son's face for some sign of emotion, anything. Anger, hurt, even disdain. All she saw was a frozen impenetrable wall. Her heart ached. The young man extended his hand which only confirmed her anguish at how she had so obviously failed him.

"Goodbye, Mother. I will see you again soon."

Tasia moved in before the boy could react and caught his slim body in her arms. She hugged him tight and felt him go rigid with discomfort, his arms held low against his stick-like waist. She kissed him forcefully on the cheek several times. His skin tasted cold.

"Goodbye, Baby Boy. Your mommy loves you so much. I will find a way to thank you properly one day."

Tasia let go and Yuri took two quick steps backward. Still no expression showed on his face, yet his skin had grown horribly pale and drawn. Without another word, he turned as if on parade maneuvers, walked to the door, and left.

CHAPTER 8

Approximately 5:10 AM, Washington Time
Wednesday, August 14, 1991

Jon could not see a horizon. There was no ground, no sky, no reference point of any kind. Everything was white, empty, blank.

He spun in a circle. The void was everywhere. No smells, no light source he could detect. He stood on something but did not feel it. Only he existed.

He looked down and saw he was naked, yet he was not cold. A pistol was in his right hand. A Browning automatic, like he kept in the drawer beside the bed. The familiar weight gave him comfort. His pulse raced, his head throbbed, and his stomach tightened. He was in danger, but did not know how he knew.

"Please don't kill me!"

A face appeared in front of him, disembodied, oversized. The pistol in his hand moved by reflex. It pointed at the face and Jon sighted down the barrel, finger on the trigger.

"I'll give you what you want!" the face said.

Pierre, that was the face's name. Pierre Bogrov, KGB killer.

Jon fired.

Bogrov's face exploded. Blood flew in all directions. Another face replaced it in the same spot. He had seen this man before too but could not remember his name.

"For God's sake, don't!" it screamed.

Jon fired again. The same thing happened again. Jon's confusion was replaced by rage. These men had to die, but he could not remember why.

Over and over, Jon banished each face with a bullet, only for another to appear. Sometimes he knew their names, most of the time he did not. The void around him gradually changed color, becoming redder with each shot as if he were staining reality with the blood he shed. His anger grew with each bullet fired until Anatoly Turgenev's face appeared.

"We have you now, Archangel! We know who you are!"

Jon pulled the trigger again, but Turgenev only laughed. Jon ran toward him, pistol firing over and over as he approached. Turgenev's face moved away at the same speed. Always the same distance, constantly laughing.

"Jon!"

A new voice called out to him. He could not tell where it came from. Turgenev's face vanished and so did his pistol. He was weaponless. His anger still burned, desperate to be quenched. His senses were in overdrive, searching for the unseen enemy but there was no input to direct him. The now-red void had consumed everything. It wanted him too. He would not let it.

"Jon!"

The other voice again. He stood still. It was in front of him.

"Jon, for God's sake!"

He leapt toward the voice, hands extended. He saw nothing, but somehow grasped hold of something. It was soft and warm but also real. It had to be whoever was responsible. The real enemy at last.

He swung his fist. A scream erupted in his ears. The dream vanished. His bedroom leapt into existence. He was sitting upright in bed.

It was still dark outside. The shades were open; he could see the woods at the back of his property through the windows. He felt something squirm beneath him and looked down.

"Jessi! Oh my God! Jessi!" he cried.

"You maniac!" Blood streamed out of Jessi's nose and her voice sounded like she was underwater. "Get off me!"

Jon rolled to one side and Jessi slid out from underneath him. She bounded to the floor, ran into the bathroom, and slammed the door behind her.

Jon scooted to the edge of the bed and let his legs dangle off. Silence reigned and he shivered slightly. He stared at the bathroom door for several seconds, then looked around the darkened room. Shadows played on the wall from the interacting clouds and moonlight outside. The bedcovers were a mess. There was blood on them. He put his head into his hands. Reality flooded back into his brain, and he slowly remembered what had happened.

Jessi had made arrangements for a cleaning crew as soon as they got to Jon's house after their encounter with the Russians. She had cut her foot, but it was not serious. Jon tended to it at the kitchen table while she was on the phone. Eagle Group's director, General Gerald Stone, had been furious about the incident and ordered them to stand by for further instructions.

Once certain the cleaners were on the way, Jon and Jessi scrubbed the filth and grime from each other in the master bath's oversized shower. Normally, this would have led to them making love under the spraying jets, but they were both bone weary. They quietly collapsed into bed after drying off.

Jon walked down to the river in the morning and saw nothing but flattened weeds and tire tracks. Eagle Group had remained unnoticed for so many years due to their nearly foolproof evidence removal techniques. They had arrangements in every major city around the globe, usually with local criminal organizations that loved to moonlight for cash funneled through untraceable accounts. Bodies, murder weapons, and physical evidence disappeared from the face of the earth with a simple phone call.

Jessi declined Jon's invitation on Tuesday to help him scout for some suitable firewood trees. He found her asleep later that afternoon, wearing only one of his t-shirts, as she shivered on one of the upstairs beds. He covered her with a quilt, gently kissed her forehead, and went downstairs.

Jon had fetched two large ribeyes from the freezer and grilled them in Irish butter and fine-ground black pepper. The smell of cooking steaks eventually brought Jessi downstairs with the big quilt haphazardly wrapped around her thin frame. She livened up a little at dinner, and afterward they sat under the quilt on the couch. They drank nearly two bottles of red California wine and watched TV. They made love soon after.

Jessi had always preferred for Jon to take the lead in bed, but this time her behavior bordered on frantic. She insisted Jon stay on top, but all his movements seemed to startle her. He tried to kiss her several times, but she turned her head away. Eventually she grasped his shoulders and let out a long, deep moan like always, but instead of staying together, she pushed him off, reached for their discarded covers and curled up in a ball near the edge of the bed.

Later, in the depths of the darkness, his nightmares returned.

The bathroom door slammed and brought Jon back to the present. Jessi wore a way-too-short silk robe and held a wet bath towel to her nose. She plopped onto the bed, stretched out on her back, pulled her long hair in front of her shoulders, and stuffed two pillows under her head. Both her eyes were black and had swollen, nearly shut.

"Jessi, we need to get you to the hospital. It looks like your nose is broken."

"It is," she replied as if speaking to a small child. "I'm going to lay here for a minute first. We need to talk."

"Alright."

"I know you don't want to hear this, Jon, but the time has come. You have to stop. Resign, retire, whatever you want to call it."

Jon's eyes traced the mortar lines between the stones of the fireplace on the other side of the room. Jessi had pestered him for many months to seek professional help. He detested her constant pecking, mostly because she was right.

"Jon, do you realize how close you came to killing me just now? If you'd hit my nose a little differently, I'd be a corpse."

Silence.

"I don't know if it's medication, therapy, or even hospitalization you need. The Company can provide plenty of good and reputable doctors to help you work through the unimaginable traumas that have built this messed-up version of you." She took a loud, phlegm-filled inhale through her mouth then turned her head. "Jon, you either can't sleep or have nightmares. Do you know how many times I've had to wake you from whatever kind of hell is going on in your brain?"

Jon jumped off the bed, walked to the window, clicked open the latches and heaved up. The pre-dawn air flooded the room, along with the sounds of nightbirds and numerous insects. He felt the coldness on his naked skin, and it invigorated him. He took a slow, deep breath and turned around.

"Jessi, I am so sorry for hitting you. It was an accident, please believe me. I would never dream of hurting you."

"You literally just did," she snapped. "While this may be the only time you've ever physically harmed me, you hurt me in other ways all the time."

"What are you talking about?" he said as he walked back to the bed. He stayed standing and tried to focus on her face in the dim light.

"Don't play stupid with me. It's insulting, okay? This Russian woman who wants you to come get her. I want to know if you meant what you said the other night."

"What?"

"God, you are a master at dragging stuff out. You said you loved her! Words I would kill to hear you say to me!"

"Jessi now is not the time. We need to get you to the hospital."

"Don't change the subject! I can't get you to take me out to a restaurant except maybe two or three times a year, but this Russian bitch writes you a note and suddenly you love her?" Jessi sniffled. "Do you realize how that makes me feel? Do you even care?" She choked on the last word.

Jon moved toward her, but she held up her hand. She raised her head, coughed several times, then spit a clot of dark blood onto the sheet next to her. Jon looked down at the blood, then at her swollen face.

"I swear, I've about had it with all this, Jon. I have no desire to just be your sex partner, and you should know that. Maybe it's time for me to reconsider my life and our relationship."

"What?"

"You heard me. I'm seriously thinking of going back to CIA proper. My friend Sara's been trying to get me to come over to the marshal's service for years. Maybe that would be the right move."

She raised herself onto one elbow.

"I love you so much, Jon. I worry about you constantly and would do absolutely anything for you, but I can't bear being with you if you don't feel the same. You need to decide if you want us to be together. If you do, we both have changes to make." She paused. "But if you don't, I deserve to know."

Jessi's pager buzzed on the nightstand. The unexpected noise shocked them both into silence. A moment later the device buzzed again, and Jessi rolled to the edge of the bed and picked it up.

"It's Stone. We're to be at the State Department at two this afternoon. Fifth floor."

"State Department? Why there?"

"Don't know," Jessi said. "But you can bet it can't be good."

Jessi sat in the passenger seat of Jon's Explorer while he drove her to the closest emergency room, about five miles away on Leesburg Pike. They had thrown on whatever clothes were laying around—t-shirts, sweats, and sneakers—and even though Jessi had pulled her seat prone and tried to remain calm, her bath towel was soaked with blood by the time they arrived.

She made up the excuse of a minor car accident to counteract the suspicious looks of the hospital personnel. Their questions and attitudes all indicated they believed her a victim of domestic violence. It truly was an accident, she told them, although she fibbed about the details. The whole affair only strengthened her resolve to get Jon professional help, although she fretted over how to best convince him.

When they got back to Jon's place, she screwed up the courage to look in the mirror. A large white bandage, held in place by surgical tape, covered her nose. Her swollen eyes had turned a deep, mottled purple, which in combination with her now-chalky white skin made her face resemble a cadaver's. She wanted to crawl back in bed, cover herself with a blanket and never set foot outside again. Unfortunately, they had orders.

They arrived at the State Department Building early. Jon wore a cordovan-brown, two-piece suit with a plain knit tie and penny-loafers. Jessi decided on a canary-yellow jacket with a white open-collared blouse, black polyester slacks, and heels. She did not have time to wash her hair, so she pulled it back into a messy ponytail and grudgingly called it good enough.

They sat alone in the Fifth-Floor conference room at the State Department Building as the afternoon sun streamed through the large windows that looked out over downtown Washington. General Gerald Stone, a small man with bug-like eyes and a military haircut, entered the room without saying anything. He wore his customary nondescript black suit, plain white shirt, and thin coal-colored tie that looked like a relic from 1962.

"Give me an update on the removals in Virginia," Stone said as he sat down at the head of the table. His gaze zeroed in on Jon.

"Cleanup was one hundred percent, sir," Jessi said in her muffled voice. "No traces remain and there's been no activity on the local law enforcement front. The Russians have been silent on the matter, which would tend to confirm our suspicion that Turgenev had indeed gone rogue."

"You were sloppy, Archangel," Stone said, ignoring Jessi completely. "I don't have much patience for that, no matter how long you've served."

"Sir, there's no way we could have anticipated this," Jessi said. "It was just an unfortunate coincidence."

"I don't believe in them," Stone said. "If the damn Russians get wind of what really happened, reprisals are guaranteed. Also, we can't be sure Turgenev didn't tell anyone else your true identity."

The door opened and Secretary of State James Baker, National Security Advisor Brent Scowcroft, and Acting CIA Director Richard Kerr entered the room. A handful of aides followed and stood before chairs stationed along the walls.

"General, you are in my chair," Baker stated in his soft Texas drawl.

"Come again?" Stone said.

"That's my chair, General. Please remove yourself over there." Baker motioned to an empty chair on the other side of Jessi. She noted that it was as far from the head of the table as could be, and still be *at* the table. Stone did not move, but neither did Baker's outstretched hand. Scowcroft, Kerr, and the aides all stood in silence.

"General?" Baker said again.

Stone said nothing. A sour look scrunched his face as he rose and moved to the indicated seat. Baker sat down at the head of the table. Jon, Jessi, and Stone sat to his right, Scowcroft and Kerr on his left.

"Thank you for coming over to our house, as it were," Baker began. "I'm flying out to Wyoming shortly for a late start to my vacation, so this makes things easier for me. I realize State's involvement here is outside standard protocols. I ask for your forbearance on this as the president has asked for us to be looped in." He turned to look at Kerr. "Dick, the floor is yours."

"Thank you for your hospitality, Mr. Secretary," Kerr said as he opened the folder in front of him. "We will try to make this brief. CIA has the ball on this one and that trumps any other involved agencies, including Eagle. I want to be clear on this up front, General Stone, since this involves one of your people."

Stone looked around the table as the air conditioning clicked on. "This is insane."

Baker's eyes widened. "I beg your pardon, General? Do I need to remind you where you are and to whom you're speaking?"

Jessi suddenly felt very small as she looked back and forth at the two men.

"I know exactly who I'm talking to," Stone said. "This Russian general headed the KGB Personnel Directorate for well over a decade. Her knowledge regarding moles and sleeper agents here in the United States will undoubtedly be the most detailed we've ever been able to acquire. Eagle needs to be in charge of this woman's exfiltration so we can forcibly obtain those names and details."

Every other head in the room turned toward Baker.

"We are not medieval torturers, General," the Secretary of State said. "Nor do we see acquired intelligence assets as property or disposable pieces of meat. Major General Zolotova wishes to defect, and we will honor that." He turned to Scowcroft. "Brent, do you have anything to add?"

Brent Scowcroft was famous for his abilities as a peacemaker in Washington. A disciple of Henry Kissinger, and staunch Bush ally like Baker, the former Air Force Lieutenant General's strength was in fostering conciliation.

"General Stone, I am certain the issues you raise can be given a fair hearing at a later date," Scowcroft said. "At the moment, interdepartmental coordination under CIA's oversight makes the most sense to ensure General Zolotova is brought over safely. Based on her message, we do not have the luxury of time."

Scowcroft paused and glanced at Stone, but the old general stayed silent. Jessi felt she could hear the breath of everyone else in the room.

"Can we count on your cooperation, General?" Scowcroft asked.

Stone's brow furrowed. "It seems I have no choice." The short, wiry brigadier looked at the tall man in the expensive suit at the head of the table with undisguised venom. "God help you, Baker, because sooner or later, he'll be the only one who can."

Baker appeared both unfazed and unimpressed. "Thank you, General." His gaze stayed on Stone until the old general finally looked away. "Dick, please continue."

Kerr nodded to one of the aides behind him who rose and passed out folders to everyone at the table. "This material is classified," Kerr said. "It contains a copy of CIA's file on General Zolotova as well as the transcript of Officer Cole's conversation with her go-between on Sunday night. During the course of that conversation, we learned of Officer Cole's, uh, previous encounter with the general."

Jessi sat up straighter.

"Officer Cole, this is not a witch hunt," Kerr said as he looked at Jon. "I want you to feel completely at ease. In order for us to make a fully informed decision about the general's request, and for that reason alone, please take your time and tell us what happened."

"Thank you, sir," Jon said. "Anastasia Zolotova and I had a brief but powerful romantic affair in Marseille in late August of 1968. I was part of a CIA translation team on a reacquisition mission. I'm fluent in both French and Russian."

"Your mother was French, is that right?" Baker asked.

"Belgian, sir. She was a literature professor at Ghent University who fled Europe during the Nazi occupation. That's how she met my father. He was a foreign language professor at Yale assigned to intelligence operations in London due to his multiple fluencies. Both my parents were professors at Yale after the war. I, uh, believe they both taught the president when he was a student there."

"They did indeed," Baker said. "The president said to tell you they were both very formative to him as a young man."

"Please thank him for that," Jon said. "They've both been gone a long time and that's good to hear."

"Please, continue," Kerr said.

"We were in Marseille meeting with a third-party intelligence broker attempting to sell stolen French defense plans on the open market. Heinrich Mueller was his name, although I'm fairly certain that was an alias. Anastasia was on the translation team for the Russians.

She's also fluent in French, which was the language of the negotiations. She and I sat across the table from each other and, uh, caught each other's eye."

"I see," Kerr said.

Jessi could not identify what she was feeling. Confusion, curiosity, and dread all washed over her at once. In the end, curiosity won out, although just barely.

"In the end, Mueller drove over a cliff into the ocean with the plans. Anastasia and I were able to be together for a week in a hotel room there in Marseille; the Beauvau Vieux Port along the waterfront."

"Yes, I believe Hemingway used to frequent that place," Scowcroft commented. "So why do you think she's reached out to you now?"

"It may be as stated, sir," Jon said. "If she was the target of an internal assassination attempt, it makes sense she'd want to get out of there fast. I guess she thinks if I can verify her request as genuine, things will happen quickly from our end."

"So, you believe this request is really from her?" Kerr asked.

"Oh, I'm certain of that, sir," Jon said. "The details in her note could only have come from her."

"We have not seen the note," Scowcroft said.

"I have it here, sir."

"Go ahead and read it for us, Officer Cole," Baker said.

Jon pulled the note from his jacket pocket, unfolded it, and read aloud.

"*Edmund, it really is me. Please meet me at the Savoy for breakfast. You are the only person I can trust. Remember our promises in Marseille. I certainly do. Love always, Mercedes.*"

He handed the note to Kerr, then looked around the table. "Edmund and Mercedes are the two lovers from *The Count of Monte Cristo*. My mother used to read to me from that book, and much of it takes place in Marseille. I purchased a French language copy there in 1968 and since both Anastasia and I were afraid of being seen, we stayed in our hotel room that entire week, ordering room service and, uh, reading aloud to each other from it. No one else could know of this connection, I'm certain."

"I'm quite sure you were doing more than just reading," Scowcroft said with a slight smirk. "I understand your desire to keep this encounter a secret, Officer Cole, but thankfully this is a different time.

No matter how it came about, it seems your relationship with the general back then has brought us a unique opportunity today."

"Based on your remark to her go-between," Kerr said. "I presume you want to go to Moscow like she asks?"

"Yes, sir."

"I won't lie to you, Officer Cole," Kerr said. "The potential advantages this woman could provide us are enormous. Normally a prior relationship such as the one you've just laid out would disqualify you from taking on this assignment. General Zolotova, however, seems to have made you a requirement."

"I speak Russian without an accent, sir, and have conducted operations within the Soviet Union on several occasions," Jon said. "I promise you; no one can accomplish this mission better than me."

"I don't like feeling pinched," Kerr said. "But time and circumstance have given us very few options." He adjusted his glasses. "I will hold you to your promise, Officer Cole."

"Thank you, sir."

"We should fly you into St. Petersburg via Paris," Kerr said as he closed the folder in front of him. "It's safer than Moscow, although it will eat up some extra time. You can use one of your Eagle covers. We'll have our Moscow Station Chief, Tripper McKenzie, pick you up at Pulkovo airport and from there deliver you to the Savoy. I believe you two know each other?"

"Yes sir. Tripper's an old friend."

"Perfect." Kerr turned to Jessi, and she sat up straighter. "Officer Bolton, I know you and Officer Cole usually work in tandem. The nature of this mission makes that somewhat impractical."

"I'm happy to accompany Officer Cole, sir," Jessi said. "Tripper McKenzie has been my mentor since I first joined the Company. He arranged for me to come over to Eagle when he went to Moscow, in fact. I would love the opportunity to work with him again."

"Tripper has spoken highly of you on several occasions," Kerr said. "I see you have an injury?"

"A small accident, sir. My nose is broken, but I'm fit for duty."

"Do you speak Russian, Officer Bolton?" Kerr asked.

"No, sir."

"Then I'm afraid you will need to stay behind." Jessi's heart sank. "We'll use on-site CIA support folks on this one." Kerr turned to look at Jon again. "Officer Cole, you are to create a plan with McKenzie's help to get the general to our embassy as quickly and quietly as possible."

"What about getting her out of the country?" Baker asked.

"McKenzie created a system for such things when he arrived in Moscow several years ago," Kerr said. "We've used it successfully on several occasions." He glanced around the table. "It utilizes a series of locals who, via their homes and autos, help us smuggle defectors to an isolated extraction point along the northern coast. We use local watercraft to rendezvous with our people in international waters under the cover of darkness. Due to its compartmentalization, it's a near-bulletproof exfiltration system, or as close as anything ever could be."

"How long does such a thing take?" Baker asked.

"A matter of weeks," Kerr said.

The Secretary of State leaned back in his chair. "Makes sense if we can get the general into the embassy quietly," he said. "Should she come in hot, though, we'll need something quicker. Something to provide us deniability on the diplomatic side."

"The Soviets watch the air channels extremely close, Mr. Secretary," Kerr said, his hands folded on the table in front of him. "No way is that an option."

"What do you suggest?" Baker asked.

Kerr paused for a moment. "Well, the new *USS Kentucky* is on her shakedown cruise in the North Atlantic. They're testing a new prototype that could help us. Using that option, we could exfiltrate via sea in, I'd say, less than 48 hours."

"You want to divert a US ballistic missile submarine into the Russians' backyard?" Baker said. "That seems an enormous risk, no matter how important this defector is."

"The Finns keep a sharp eye on the Soviets for us, sir," Kerr said. "They've supplied us with multiple safe spots in international waters where we won't be detected. We've used them before without difficulty."

"Alright then," Baker said.

"We'll get our folks to work on the details right away." Kerr turned once again to look at Jon. "I expect, Officer Cole, we'll need you at Langley tomorrow morning for a final briefing prior to departure. Let's say 9:00 AM?"

"I'll be there, sir."

Kerr rose and everyone in the room followed. Stone was the last to stand. One of the aides collected the folders, then Baker, Scowcroft, Kerr, and their people all filed out of the room in orderly fashion. Jon was about to push in his chair when Stone spoke.

"Sit back down, Archangel."

Both Jon and Jessi did so. Stone walked back around to the head of the table and took the seat Baker had vacated.

"You do realize you've just confessed to fraternization with the enemy?" Stone said. "I don't care what Kerr says, this makes you a security risk, if not downright treasonous."

Jon leaned forward and brought his face to within inches of Stone's.

"Your security clearances should all be forfeited since you've obviously lied for every single one of them," the old general said without blinking. "Not to mention there's the question of how you've managed to fool your regular polygraph certifications all these years."

Jon's gaze stayed locked onto the old man's face. Jessi held her breath and heard Jon's breathing increase.

"If I had my way," Stone continued, "I'd have you prosecuted—if not shot—for what you just admitted."

Jessi reached for Jon's leg under the table. She gently squeezed and heard his breathing slow. She kept hold, knowing if Stone noticed, her career might very well end right there.

"I don't respond well to threats, General," Jon said.

His tone was even, but Jessi had heard the cold menace underneath many times. She shivered at the thought of what might happen if they did not get out of there quickly. She squeezed Jon's leg again.

"If you come after me, you'd better send an army," he said. "Anything less and there won't be enough to bury."

"We'll see, Archangel. We'll see."

Jessi shoved back her chair and stood. Both men looked up at her. She nodded at each one, first the general, then Jon. It was apparently enough. Both men rose and Jessi hustled Jon to the door and out of the room as fast as she could.

She did not breathe again until they were in the hallway and on their way to the elevators.

CHAPTER 9

Shortly after 1:00 PM, Moscow Time, Saturday, August 17, 1991

Jon looked down the long line of yellow taxis, hand above his eyes in the bright sunlight. The afternoon breeze contained a heady blast of rural autumn. Dried leaves and decayed compost overpowered the more industrial smells from the city only a few miles away. Pulkovo International Airport lay just south of St. Petersburg, newly renamed back from Leningrad, and since Jon's flight had been on time, his pickup should be close by.

The temperature felt significantly cooler than either Washington or Paris. He wore generic brown work pants and a collarless Brunswick-green wool pullover—with no tags and made to look homespun—plus a slightly oversized slouched woolen cap. These were paired with a plain but heavy wool jacket and Russian-made brown work boots.

Someone emerged from a taxi down the line and waved. Jon waved back and the man got back in, pulled out of line, and practically slammed the faded yellow car into the concrete curb. The driver, slightly slouched with a grizzle of gray stubble, stepped out of the car and took Jon's suitcase. A near-toothless smile peeked out from underneath his short-brimmed cap.

"Welcome to Russia," he said in thickly accented English.

"Thank you," Jon said, also in English. "Are you taking me to my, uh, friend?"

The man looked up at him, and much slower this time, said the same thing again and motioned to the back seat. Jon moved to get in and saw he was not alone.

"Dude!" The medium-sized black man with the tight afro and greying temples grinned with all his teeth. "Get your old fart ass in here. Don't you know how long a drive we've got?" Dressed in a navy windbreaker, sky blue oxford shirt and khaki trousers, he patted the seat next to him.

"Tripper!" Jon said with a smile. "Old fart, yourself."

"Yeah, yeah, yeah," Tripper McKenzie said as he adjusted himself in his seat. "Cathy tells me that all the time. I told her there's none better, at least not that she could ever find. She rolls her eyes."

"Yeah, putting up with you is a full-time job. How is she?"

"Back home, actually. Her mom fell about a month ago, so she's been staying with her. Gives her a chance to catch up with the kids."

"How are the girls?" Jon said as the car pulled away from the curb.

"Lizzie's shacking up with a nice boy there off campus. He'll probably pop the question before too long. Grace is figuring herself out. What about you? Still hiking those trails at Great Falls?"

"Every chance I get," Jon said as the car made its way southwest towards the M-11 Highway. "Best decision I ever made buying and building out there. I owe you for introducing me to it."

"You know, if you finally gave General Asshat the drop kick, you'd have more time for stuff like that. It's not like you need the money."

"You sound like Jessi." Jon nodded toward the driver in the front seat. "How freely can we talk?"

"Don't worry. I haven't introduced you to Maxim yet. Hey, Maxim!"

The old driver looked into the rearview mirror and smiled. "Welcome to Russia."

"The only English he knows," Tripper said. "Practiced the damn thing all morning. He's one of mine here in St. Petersburg. He'll drive us south for a bit to where some of my other friends are waiting for us."

"Sounds good. So, what're you hearing?"

"Change is in the air over here. Yeltsin is a damn fireball. Gorbachev looks like he's sitting still compared to him."

"Mikhail's still popular, isn't he?"

"Not so much. The regular people like him mostly, but they're tired of this halfway crap. They actually have choices now about what clothes to wear, what milk to buy, or whatever. Hell, Moscow even got a McDonalds not long ago."

"Yeah, I heard about that. Lines around the block they said." Jon stared out the window as traffic built around them. Any one of them could be KGB.

"It's amazing the things we take for granted back home that folks over here have never seen. They're willing to change everything to keep getting it."

"That's a good thing, right?"

"Not for those in power. I hear the old guard is fed up with all this change. Gorbachev's up-and-coming New Union treaty is a huge threat to the establishment. Rumors are some sort of reaction is in the offing."

"You think what happened to Tasia might be connected to that?"

"Maybe. If what you say is true, she sure pissed somebody off."

"Her son implied that. He was less than forthcoming with the details."

"Yeah, Yuri. Daddy's little prodigy. You know Kryuchkov is allegedly his father, right?"

"I'd heard that."

"Supposedly your girl became Kryuchkov's mistress sometime in late 1968, shortly after he took over the KGB Foreign Office."

"Yeah, that's where she was when we were in Marseille."

"Her son was born sometime in early 1969, but we're not exactly sure when. She stayed Kryuchkov's mistress for quite a few years after that, even though the guy was married with two older kids. He's still married to that same woman even now, believe it or not. Ekaterina is her name."

"Yeah, a lot of things are hard to believe."

"Well, Russians are all about family, a lot more so than we Americans, even when there's illegitimacy involved. Apparently Kryuchkov's other kids weren't interested in following in daddy's footsteps, but this little guy sure was. Speaking of daddies, I get the impression most folks haven't noticed the timing here. You think the kid's yours, don't you?"

Jon wondered if anyone else had done the math. "It's on my mind. I don't have exact numbers any more than you do. I plan on asking her eventually."

"So, this is more than a routine exfiltration?"

Jon sighed and pulled his cap down to block the sun reflected from passing windshields. “I don’t know. It’s been twenty-three years, Trip. I have no idea what I’ll find when I see her again.”

“She’s bound to be a different person now, but then again so are you. You worried she’s using you to get out of Russia?”

“No, any qualified operative could get her out of here. It’s rather bold of her to request me personally, especially how desperately she appears to need our help.”

“So, what is it then? You think the Russians know who you are?”

“If they did, you would’ve found me dead in a public bathroom stall somewhere. No, her note was way too personal. Almost as if she regretted her decision in Marseille not to come with me to the States like I begged her to.”

“Sounds like wish fulfillment on your part, dude. Be honest with me. You still carrying a torch for this Russian princess?”

Jon turned and looked out the window. Trees flew by now that they had cleared the worst of the traffic. Large trucks zoomed past, their cargos bound to feed the city or take ship to foreign ports. The life of this country was not something he had ever considered before. He had buried everything about it with his feelings long ago. Tripper had a habit of asking uncomfortable questions.

“God, I hate it when I’m right like that,” Tripper said. “A whole lot of things are starting to make sense now.”

“Like what?”

“Like how you can never make a romantic relationship work without things eventually falling to pieces. This woman’s been in the back of your mind all this time. I guess only Mira ever came close to breaking that cycle.”

“Let’s not go there, Trip.”

“Okay, but that doesn’t invalidate my point. Kerr was right to be worried about you taking on this assignment. By all rights I should call him, and we should come up with another plan.”

“But you won’t.”

Tripper shuffled in his seat. “No, I won’t. Your feelings for her are a powerful motivator and the goal is to get her out of here safely.”

“I appreciate that.”

“There’s still a big issue in your way on the personal side. What do you think the general is going to say when she finds out you’re the guy who's killed—what?—over thirty of her KGB comrades? If her memory and connections are like they say, she's bound to have known some of them. Maybe even well."

"One more example of how all the blood I've spilt keeps haunting me. Can't sleep worth a damn and I'm long past sick of it."

Tripper turned in his seat. "What about Jessi? Thought you two had something pretty good? Do you really want to kick her to the curb like this?"

"No, of course not."

"Dude, don't hurt her. She's been so good for you. She's an amazing lady and one of a kind. She deserves better than this and you know it."

"I don't want to hurt her, Trip."

"But you'll dump her?" Tripper sighed. "This is not cool, Jon. You don't get to avoid this one and you can't have it both ways. If you plan to pursue things with Mother Russia, Jessi needs to hear it from you right away."

Jon again stared out the window. Grey clouds passed by overhead, obscuring the sun. He and Jessi had fought again before he left. The last thing he wanted to do was hurt her.

"I don't know what I want, Trip," he finally said. "Let's talk about something else, okay?"

"Alright," Tripper said. "You think your Red Sox got a chance this year? Or are my Phillies finally due for their comeback?"

The conversation continued into familiar, safe territory until the driver put on his blinker.

"Looks like we're ready for our change over," Tripper said. "Grab your bag so Maxim can get on home. I'll introduce you to *Babushka* Sophia."

"Grandmother?"

Tripper smiled. "Who do you think's really in charge around here? Russia's more of a matriarchy than you realize, dude. Women run the show over here and the men fall in line. You have to take care of the *babushkas* if you want to get anything done."

The rendezvous took place down a farm road several miles off the main highway. *Babushka* Sophia appeared to be in her early eighties. The stooped old woman, dressed in a cranberry-colored headscarf and ankle-length skirt, walked speedily without a cane. Two huge male attendants she called her grandsons accompanied her.

"I hear she's still a sex maniac, even at her age," Tripper told Jon. "She's gonna love your hunky white ass, so get prepared to be felt up."

The old woman grabbed Jon's crotch as soon as Tripper introduced them. She grinned with glee as she fondled him through his pants. Jon simply smiled. Sophia giggled all the time, although the frowns on the faces of her grandsons seemed set in concrete. They perked up a little when Tripper handed over a large envelope stuffed full of rubles.

"We've got to get moving if we want to reach Moscow at a decent hour," Tripper said. "Let me show you the goodies." He took Jon over to the ivory-colored Mosckvich sedan, opened the door on the passenger side, and fiddled with the dashboard. The entire right-hand section flipped down.

"They call this the hidey-hole. It has a special hidden release switch here on the side. Russian drug trade uses them all the time and the Interior Ministry boys have yet to find any of them, or so the story goes anyway. Here's your stuff, courtesy of *babushka*."

Tripper pulled out a small cloth duffel bag. Inside was a Makarov pistol with three extra magazines, a shoulder holster, and a black dress-leather belt.

"The Makarov's the easy thing, but check out the belt," Tripper said. "I know you prefer to work with blades, so you should love this. It's local workmanship, actually."

Jon fiddled with the buckle until it came loose. The square piece of shiny metal formed the handle of a double-edged knife, several inches long.

"That's the big daddy," Tripper said. "Razor sharp on both sides, so be careful. The belt hooks together on the inside, so your pants don't fall down when you pull out the knife."

"Yeah, that would be a fatal design flaw."

"The best part is in the back, see? Looks like two adjustable clips, like on a cummerbund for a tuxedo. Twist with your fingers and pull."

Jon did so, and two smaller versions of the razor knife slid out. Both were long and thin, almost like double-bladed needles.

"These are the little brothers, made of stainless surgical steel, like scalpels. Unless they strip you naked, these should give you a hell of an edge."

"Pun entirely intended, I'm sure," Jon said.

"Hell yes! You do know the pun is the highest form of humor, right?"

Jon put on the new belt, stowed his old one and everything else into the duffle bag and put it all back into the secret compartment. The two of them walked back to *Babushka* Sophia who was still smiling with grandsons on either side of her. Tripper said their goodbyes, Jon got felt up again, and the two of them pulled back onto the highway with Tripper behind the wheel.

"Okay, let's walk through this," Tripper said. "We need to get the general over to the embassy. We can work out what comes next once she's there. She's at the Savoy, which should make things easier, although it's highly likely she's being watched."

"She told me to meet her for breakfast, which I presume means the restaurant. I'll go down there in the morning and find a way to give her my room number."

"Big surprise," Tripper said. "You know the Savoy is where all the foreign big money stays in Moscow. Supposedly the whole damn place is bugged, and we've been told it's not that garden variety stuff you can find and remove."

"I've got something to mess with whatever they're using."

"Alright, let's keep this simple. Assuming you can make initial contact tomorrow morning, and then something more meaningful later on, we can meet in the alley near the kitchen receiving door at, say, five on Monday afternoon? We can quietly get into the evening business rush and make the embassy in maybe thirty minutes, even with traffic."

"Sounds doable," Jon said. "I presume I'm going to have to do this solo?"

"Unfortunately, yes. I'll have some folks watching, but they're locals and won't interfere. You've got to be careful as hell, Jon. If the KGB boys get even a sniff of what's going on, they'll have a wall around you fast. This is some dangerous stuff you're attempting in the very heart of their domain."

7:00 AM, Moscow Time, Sunday, August 18, 1991

KGB technician Stanislav Alekhin exited the elevator on the second floor of the Savoy and adjusted the sleeves of his maroon wool jacket. His long delicate fingers seemed appropriate to an artist, something he had always considered himself.

His dexterous precision, in addition to his lack of conscience, had cemented his reputation inside the *Mokryye Dela* as the technician who could provide the longest-lasting torment for a captured enemy. His current record topped thirty-six continuous hours of torture on a single living subject, a feat unmatched by any of his peers.

Anyone could pull a trigger, or wield a butcher's cleaver, but Alekhin's weapon of choice was the scalpel, and his target the largest organ in the human body, the skin. He viewed his flaying process as a sacred attempt to reveal the innermost secrets of his victims, a reduction of the human person to its truest, most basic self. He saw himself as the anti-priest, the final confessor no one could deceive. Rivers of blood were the result of his efforts and continuous screams, the music of his symphony.

They had promised him a beautiful victim this time. His whole body trembled with anticipation. He would retain a large lock of her beautiful red hair as another trophy for his collection.

Alekhin reached into his pocket for the key he had been given. At this hour, he did not want to disturb the occupants of the room if they were still asleep, although he doubted that was the case. He silently slid the key into the lock and opened the door.

The smell of old cigarettes nearly knocked him over as he entered the room. The elegance astounded him, red velvet furniture, huge paintings on the walls. A man in a threadbare tank top sat at the round table reading a newspaper as the morning sun invaded the room through the tall square window.

"You by yourself?" Alekhin asked.

"Kostin's in the shower," the man said without taking his eyes from the paper. "I have morning watch. The lieutenant's sacked out in the adjoining room."

"I presume we're close?"

"Trigger gets pulled this afternoon. Boldin, Baklanov, and Verennikov are going down to Crimea to place Gorbachev under house arrest. Looks like by tomorrow morning, the *mudak*'s daddy is going to be in charge of everything."

"What about our beautiful redhead?"

"Her *Amerikanski* boyfriend checked in late last night." He set down his paper and reached for the pack of cigarettes on the table. "The *mudak* says she will sneak up there once she knows."

"Sounds like it will be hours or even days before my services are needed. Why did I have to be here so early?"

"If you have issues with the *mudak*'s timing, take it up with him. We've all been ordered to wait. Daddy is supposed to call the bitch to Dzerzhinsky before long."

"What for?"

"He wants to talk to her for some crazy reason. *Mudak's* pissed as hell about it." The man put his lighter to a fresh cigarette.

"How long is this supposed to take?"

"The *mudak* expects her to bolt as soon as she gets back here." He blew a long stream of smoke out through his nose. "The guys across the hall from her have doctored her door so they know whenever it opens. We're one floor below, so we should have plenty of notice to tail her."

"Only if she runs from there," Alekhin said. "What if she's somewhere else?"

"The *mudak* brought in the Personnel Tracking System people. He says we can always use that to locate her if we need to."

"How's that?"

"He won't give us any details. Big state secret of some kind." The man shook his hands in the air. "Apparently she has no clue about it either."

"When is daddy supposed to call?"

"Who knows? The guys upstairs will escort her to Dzerzhinsky whenever he does. When she runs, you will come with us to recover the documents she's hidden somewhere around here. The lieutenant will take you and her, along with the *Amerikanski* boyfriend, to one of our safehouses after that."

"They only told me about her."

"The *mudak* has something special planned for the boyfriend. The lieutenant will fill you in." The smoking man smiled. "Kid's a vicious little bastard."

CHAPTER 10

8:00 AM, Moscow Time, Sunday, August 18, 1991

Blue-white water trickled down the marble fountain in the restaurant of the Savoy Hotel. The fresh scent of clean linen, and a hint of rosemary, filled the air. Floor length, white tablecloths and patterned fine China covered the dozen tables nearby.

Tasia loved the ornate grandeur of the place. The gold latticework, the muted eggplant-colored walls, and the shiny brass chandeliers all came from another time; before the Revolution and the blood of the First World War. She imagined herself a Nineteenth Century Russian aristocrat every time she entered the rooms, even though she had been taught disdain for such things her entire life. She had always felt herself a poor communist.

The Fountain Room appeared the same as it did the previous morning. Tasia had decided to wear her champagne-colored business dress and shiny black heels, with matching lace gloves and stockings. An opaque scarf covered the marks on her throat and her PSM rested in her clutch-purse. She noted several patrons glanced at her—some twice—as she walked past. One of the tables near the fountain was empty, so she set her purse atop it and looked around. Her heart skipped a beat.

Jon sat barely ten feet away, long legs crossed in front of him, the most recent copy of *Pravda* in his hands. A China cup of what looked like steaming Russian tea sat on the table. His dark blue two-piece suit looked ordinary enough, but fit him splendidly, pressed and cuffed, and his black lace-up dress shoes looked suspiciously like KGB issue. The crisp white shirt and silver silk tie completed the portrait of a man at ease with himself and his environment. No gray whatsoever showed in his thick brown hair, although she had expected to see at least a little.

He had not yet looked up from his newspaper, and she needed to see his eyes, so she pulled out her chair and made certain to scrape the feet along the marble floor.

He looked up. Their eyes locked. He smiled.

God, he was still so beautiful, she thought. No other word about him ever came to mind as easily as that one. His eyes still mesmerized her like they did in Marseille. Soft pale grey, gentle and tender like the fingers that had caressed her delicate, innermost places those many years ago. His eyes were unmistakably the same, yet somehow different. She needed to see him up close to discern what it was.

Her bodyguard settled in behind her, a few tables away, no doubt where he could watch the entrance. He could see Jon's face but not hers. Any communication of meaning would have to come from her.

She sat down and ordered fried eggs with dill, kielbasa sausage, a side of cottage cheese dumplings, and hot black tea with sweet cream. Trusting her bodyguard could not see her face, she silently mouthed in exaggerated English. "Where are you?"

He nodded with the barest level of motion, pulled a pen out of his jacket and wrote something on the inside fold of his newspaper. He set the paper on the table and kept his eyes away from her as he reached for his tea.

The waiter appeared with Tasia's food, and she saw Jon stand up. He put his hand on the paper and nodded at her. She tipped her chin ever so slightly and saw in his eyes he understood. He drained his teacup, reached into his pants pocket for some rubles, and placed them next to the empty cup. He strolled past her toward the hotel lobby.

Tasia glanced around the room. A few patrons stared at her, but quickly looked away when she caught their gaze. Satisfied, she stood up, eyed her bodyguard, walked over, and snagged the discarded newspaper. One of the uniformed busboys came for Jon's cup as she opened the paper and laid it beside her plate. In blue ink, on the top of the inside page, were three handwritten numerals—414.

His room number, one floor above hers.

The battleship-grey door to Sub-basement Room Six at Dzerzhinsky Square opened with a hardened creak. The stink of wet mold permeated the concrete rooms, a persistent reminder of the rarely circulated air that inhabited the underground spaces.

A metal folding table and chair sat in front of a long wall of red industrial iron that featured four heavy cast doors with elaborate opening mechanisms. In the days of Stalin and Khrushchev, these were the coal furnaces which heated the building above. The metal monstrosities had been retrofitted in the late Seventies to operate on natural gas, and now produced temperatures close to two thousand degrees Fahrenheit. Enough to dispose of nearly anything deemed necessary.

Yuri entered the room, accompanied by a tall, dark-haired man in a dull-brown KGB enlisted uniform. The young man dropped a red file folder onto the table as he laid his briefcase on the floor beside the chair. The other man took up position several feet to his left.

"How far behind do you think they are?" Yuri said as he sat down and crossed his legs.

"Yushin said to expect them within five minutes."

Major Andrei Bolskov entered the room right on time. The man called Yushin was three steps behind him.

"Alright, here I am." Andrei brushed some unseen cobwebs from his olive-green shirt as he approached the table. Yuri nodded at Yushin who locked the door. "Why do we need to meet down here?"

"Less likely for us to be overheard," Yuri said.

"So, what do you need?"

Yuri sat up straighter. "We can now confirm the August seventh attack on Major General Zolotova did indeed have assistance from inside Dzerzhinsky."

"Well, of course."

Could this man be any denser? Yuri thought. "I'm pleased to say we have finally discovered the culprit."

"Well, who is it?"

"You."

"What?" Andrei sputtered. "Why, that is complete and utter bollocks! You know exactly who's responsible—"

Yuri cut him off. "I have the proof right here." He tapped the red file folder in front of him. "Multiple signed affidavits from witnesses who say they saw you escort the assassin through the hallways on the evening in question. Furthermore, you were the last person to access the safe which contained the only unaccounted for key to the SID file room, which we know the assassin penetrated. The case against you is complete. I have a full confession for you right here. Would you care to sign it?" Yuri held up a pen.

"I will not sign anything! These are lies!" Andrei shrieked. "You know who let that man into the building. You also know how he got the key. I have a mind to tell everyone—"

Yuri lowered his hand. "Golovkin," he said.

The side of Andrei's skull exploded. The shot sounded like a cannon blast in the enclosed space. Blood and brain matter splattered across the forward edge of the table and along the concrete floor. Warm gore sprayed Yuri's face and shirtfront, but the young man did not move a muscle except to close his eyes. The *Mokryye Dela* man named Golovkin holstered his Makarov nearly as fast as he had deployed it.

Yuri pulled out a handkerchief and wiped the sticky mess from his face and neck as the corpse collapsed to the floor. "Looks like I'll need to sign his name after all," he said to no one in particular. "I suppose after all the others, one more won't matter."

He threw his bloody handkerchief onto the table, pulled the papers out of the stained folder and scribbled on the signature line of the top paper in the stack. He then pulled a clean folder from his briefcase and tossed the bloodstained one over the front of the table.

"I will take these files to the Chairman after I've cleaned up," Yuri said as he placed the new folder in his case. "Dispose of the major's body in one of the incinerators."

"Won't his disappearance be noticed?" Yushin asked.

"It seems the major lost his life in a classified operation," Yuri said. "Unfortunately, his remains could not be recovered. I will arrange for a letter to go to the widow which expresses the Chairman's condolences. The other members of the SID will be informed of his heroic death within the week."

Yuri loosened his bloodstained tie on his way to the stairs. He needed to stop by the gymnasium for a quick shower and a change of clothes. His tie and dress shirt were certainly ruined, but a thorough dry-cleaning should salvage his coat. The KGB provided such services in-house and knew better than to ask questions.

Everything was now in position with all the loose ends tied off. He only needed his mother to behave as expected.

CHAPTER 11

9:15 PM, Moscow Time, Sunday, August 18, 1991

Tasia had circled the length and breadth of her grand suite's sitting area all day like a caged lioness. She did not dare sneak out until the lights in the hallway dimmed for the night.

The time finally grew close, and she drew herself a bath. The steaming hot water soothed both her angst and skin, although the stitched wounds on her arms were still tender. She thoroughly washed her hair with Amber Imperial shampoo, left the bath, and spritzed perfume over her entire body.

It took nearly twenty minutes with a brush and blow dryer provided by the Savoy to craft her long hair into a loose, full-bodied, free-flowing chic that satisfied. Then came the makeup, lipstick, and eyeliner. She stood and made a frank appraisal of herself in the mirror.

The raw, red abrasions on her neck were horrific to her eyes, as were the wounds on her arms, but since she could do nothing about them, she decided to focus on everything else. Her lashes were full, her eyes clear and bright, her mouth sensuous when formed for a kiss. Her bare skin was supple and pleasantly pale, her arms strong but slightly heavy. She had always been worried about her height and bone structure, thinking it overly large. The words *trim* or *dainty* would never apply to her.

She turned from side to side and agonized about the weight she had put on in the intervening years. She was certainly curvaceous. Broad, round and Rubenesque, she filled out her form with lush bounty and healthy strength. Her hands slid down her waist and hips. She was older too, but her body was still solid, yet also soft. She turned and looked at her behind and thighs. Slightly pronounced, certainly not flat, but beautiful enough.

She put her hands on her hips and tried to look wanton, sultry, desirous. She laughed out loud at how ridiculous she appeared. She was never one to show off, even when the cameras and spotlights were on her.

Her reflection stared back at her. It had been twenty-three years yet seemed only a brief time. Her insides trembled like a schoolgirl on her first date. His eyes in the restaurant seemed to reforge their connection instantaneously, but what if she was wrong?

She thought back to the handful of lovers she had entertained after freeing herself from Vladimir. The memories were pleasant enough, and they had assuaged her loneliness for at least a time, but none had ever come close to Jon. Perhaps that was why she had always pushed them away. In her mind, the bond somehow created during that week in Marseille had been unbreakable. She had given her entire self, body and soul, and still did not understand how it happened. Nor did she know why she told him no when he had asked her to come to America and marry him. She whispered a prayer to a God she did not know and shook her finger at her reflection.

"Second chances rarely happen. Don't screw this up. Just be yourself."

She padded into the bedroom, bare skin chilled by the air conditioning, and slid on her favorite black lace bra, a pair of barely-there French-cut panties, and a charcoal silk slip. A light raincoat came next, with the PSM in its pocket. The final piece was a black sheer scarf, woven loosely around the marks on her throat, with the excess stuffed inside the raincoat to conceal her seriously exposed cleavage. It would have to do.

The door to the hallway soundlessly opened and a quick glance both ways confirmed no one was about. She slipped out of her room and casually walked to the fire door. Her pounding heart echoed in her ears.

Her satin slippers made no noise in the concrete stairwell, but the heavy door to the fourth floor creaked when it opened. She walked with a normal gait onto the brown-patterned carpet and noticed Jon's room was at the other end.

The elevator dinged as she came close, and the doors swished open. An older couple dressed in a black tuxedo and floor-length evening gown got off and Tasia had no alternative but to smile and hope they did not recognize her. Perhaps they thought her a prostitute meeting a client. She nearly laughed out loud at the thought of Mother Russia moonlighting as a hooker. The older couple stopped at their room, and she stepped around them. At 414 she took a quick breath and rapped three times.

The door opened and he stood there tall, brown hair perfectly ordered. His shoes were off, and he still wore the same pants and shirt from that morning, minus the jacket and tie. Her eyes drank in the moment she had not known she had wanted until a few days earlier.

"Hello, Edmund," she whispered in English.

"Hello, Mercedes," he whispered back with a warm grin.

She leapt into his arms.

Their tongues found each other and danced wet caresses as Jon quietly shut the door. His fingers washed through the red waterfall of hair that cascaded down her back. Their kiss went on for several heated moments and Tasia tasted wintergreen in his mouth. She reluctantly pulled back to look at him.

He put his finger to his lips, and she nodded. He took her hand and led them around the corner to the bed area. A plastic cylinder, like a small caramel-colored cake, sat on the round wooden nightstand. Jon flicked a switch on its side and the device began to whirr.

"White noise machine," he whispered in Russian. "Supposed to help me sleep. The Customs folks tested it, of course. Guaranteed to garble everything we say as long as we don't get too far away."

Tasia glanced at the green-brocaded queen-sized bed and smiled. "We're staying right here, darling, I promise."

Jon took her hand and stroked the ends of her fingers. "You smell wonderful."

"It's *Red Moscow,*" Tasia replied, and she heard the husky desire in her voice. "Most popular women's perfume in all of Russia. I'd hoped you'd like it."

"I like anything you decide to wear."

"Really?" She took a step back, reached for her scarf, pulled it free and tossed it onto the dressing bench at the foot of the bed. She unbelted and unbuttoned her raincoat. The blended rayon slid down and landed on the rug behind her.

"What do you think of this?" she swung her hips gently from side to side. The black silk clung to her body like a second skin.

"You are so beautiful," he whispered.

Tasia smiled. "My favorite word." She slid her fingers under the slip's shoulder straps, swished it over her head and let it fall to the floor.

"Come here, my beautiful darling," she whispered. "Let me touch you."

Jon stepped closer and Tasia placed both hands on his chest. She fingered the placket of his shirt, and they kissed again. He reached around her back and unfastened the catches of her bra while she worked on his buttons. The white Oxford cloth plus his cotton undershirt came away quickly, as did her black lace.

"You are so much more developed, darling," Tasia said in Russian as her hands roamed over his pectoral muscles with shameless desire. "Your biceps and forearms are so much larger." Her fingers dipped lower and traced the curves of his abdomen. "It feels so good to touch someone so beautiful."

"You've hardly changed," Jon said as his palms slid down her bare arms.

The rest of their clothes came away quickly. The sheets were cool, but her skin felt flushed, although whether that was with angst or desire she did not know. Their mouths found each other again and so did their bodies. He felt so familiar, so actual and alive, like he did those many years ago. Her breath inhaled his presence, and her entire person slipped under the waves and drowned in a moment she almost did not believe was real. It ended far too quickly.

"Thank you for that darling," she said in Russian as she slid down beside him. "I didn't realize how much I missed you."

"I can say the same," Jon whispered. "Your note brought back feelings I'd buried long ago."

"So much has happened since we parted on that dock in Marseille—so many agonies and mistakes. I want to change that now, with your help."

"I told you back then I would come if you ever called. I'll get you out of here, that's a promise."

"I trust Yuri told you what happened?"

"He said you were attacked, but didn't give me any details."

"I was strangled." She dragged his fingers along the abraded tissue of her throat.

"It still hurts?"

"A bit. Bathing helps."

"Yeah, I remember you loved taking baths." He took her palm and kissed it. "That tub at Beauvau Vieux Port wasn't quite big enough, was it?"

"We made it work though," she said as she wrinkled her nose. "Can you really help me?"

"Definitely, I just need a clearer picture of the situation. Your son said you were in hiding. How many people know where you are?"

"My secretary Yulia; an associate, Andrei Bolskov; my dear friend Sivilla; and, of course, Yuri. The hotel staff leaves everything in the hallway. Beyond that, there are only my rotating bodyguards in the suite across the hall."

"Rotating?"

"Their commanding officer is a trusted friend. He guaranteed their secrecy."

"So, you've been here a week without ever venturing into the outside world?"

"Exactly like Marseille, darling. The only exceptions were my two trips to the restaurant, yesterday and today."

Jon nodded. "I'm worried more people know where you are than you realize. No matter how trustworthy, with different bodyguards passing through here for over a week, I cannot believe word has not leaked out."

"What are you saying?"

"We need to consider the possibility there's more going on here. Your son indicated the attack on you had something to do with an investigation?"

"Yes. Two months ago, I discovered a number of suspicious wire transfers that sent large amounts of Communist Party funds out of the country. The totals run well into the billions. About ten days ago, I confirmed the destination accounts all belong to a small group of high party officials, namely Vladimir Kryuchkov, Boris Pugo, and a few others."

"Are you serious?"

"Of course. I have proof of everything. When President Gorbachev sees it, Vladimir will be disgraced, dismissed, and sent to prison. I made one stupid mistake, though."

"What?"

"I should have kept the information to myself until the president returned. Instead, to stop more funds from being stolen, I froze the originating accounts. Two days after that, someone tried to strangle me."

"You've been in hiding ever since?"

"Yes." She planted a wet kiss on his bare chest. "Waiting for you."

Jon reached over and stroked her cheek. His touch was warm. "This whole situation worries me, Tasia. Anyone with the will to kill you could have easily tracked you down by now."

"The bodyguards?"

"Maybe, but if the stakes are as high as you say, I cannot imagine that would have deterred them for long. Someone's keeping tabs on you. When we move, it'll need to be like lightning, surprise them before they can react. Until then, we have to make whoever's watching think nothing has changed. You should get back to your room and stay there."

Tasia's hand trembled as she put her fingers to his lips. "Please. There's got to be a way for me to stay with you. I can check in with my bodyguards from your room phone."

"We'd be taking a hell of a chance. Besides, there's no way you can go out in public in what you wore up here." He nodded at the pile of clothes a few feet from the bed.

"That's certainly true," she said with an impish grin. "I also need to retrieve Papa's book. It's the one thing I can't leave behind."

"Book?"

"War and Peace, of course. Tolstoy himself presented it to my great grandfather, complete with a personal inscription."

"Sounds valuable."

"It probably is, but nothing could ever make me part with it. It's literally all I have left of dear Papa."

Jon enclosed her fingers with his. "Alright, take the day to get your things together, then meet me in the hotel lobby at five o'clock. We'll sneak out through the back entrance. A car will be waiting to take us to the US Embassy."

"I presume we can stop by my friend Sivilla's to get my proof?"

"You don't have it here?"

"She was to take it to the press if anything happened to me."

"We really don't have time for detours."

She let go of his hand and stared into his eyes. "Jon, Vladimir manipulated, controlled, and abused me for a long, long time. Please don't ask me to tell you anything more. This proof is my revenge against him. I need to find a way to get it into President Gorbachev's hands."

"How about this? We arrange for one of Tripper's people to retrieve this packet after you're safe at the embassy. We can discuss options with the Company after that. I'm sure they'd be on board with your goal."

"Please forgive me if I do not trust your Company. They only serve themselves and the greedy desires of their capitalist masters." She yawned and stretched her arms above her head.

"You're awfully cute when you talk communist like that," he said, "and I didn't know any of this about you and Kryuchkov."

Tasia brought her hands down and placed them on both sides of his neck. "How many regrets do you have, Jon?"

"More than I can count."

"Is your whole life nothing but regret, because mine certainly is. All the stupid mistakes I made in the name of ambition. Everything's about patronage over here. In order to rise, to achieve anything, you have to align yourself with someone powerful."

She rolled onto her pillow and pulled the sheet up to her chin.

"Andropov was Vladimir's mentor. No one was more powerful except Brezhnev himself. Vladimir's star was certain to rise, so I thought by giving myself to him, I could achieve a position that would allow me to shine as a leader of rare quality. The reality is, I simply played the whore."

"Don't talk like that," Jon whispered. "No matter what you did to get into the game, you only succeeded because of your brains, talent, and grit. You're a major general, for goodness' sake." He brushed the backs of his fingers over the red locks that framed her face. "That's pretty rare."

"Oh, how American," she said with a frown. "Rugged individualism, huh? The world doesn't work that way, at least not here." She sighed and took his hand in hers. "I was such a fool for leaving you. Can you ever forgive me?"

"Of course."

She rolled onto her side, drew his arm under her head and rubbed the edge of her foot along his leg. "Do we still have time before I have to go?"

"Absolutely. Now that we're together again, nothing can stand in our way."

3:15 PM, Washington Time, Sunday, August 18, 1991

The phone call was unexpected, especially on a Sunday afternoon. Andi Jenkins spoke quickly, put the receiver onto its cradle, grabbed her portfolio and hurried out of her office.

She stopped in the restroom to make sure she looked presentable. General Stone was a stickler for a pristine appearance in all his people, especially his command staff. She had seen him dress down administrative personnel far too many times for unshined shoes or anything remotely casual in appearance. Fortunately, she had dressed appropriately to drive into the office and finish a few items ahead of the Monday bustle.

The makeup on her coffee-colored skin appeared in order, her lipstick clear and unsmudged. She kept her dense afro pulled tight behind her head, for convenience more than anything else, so it was always more-or-less under control. Her charcoal-colored business suit appeared immaculate and, thank goodness, there were no coffee stains on her cream-colored blouse. She brushed her hands down her front and headed out.

Andi's office was on Underground Level Two. She stepped off the elevator two levels below that, into what was colloquially known as the Ninth Circle of Hell.

She walked down the deserted concrete hallway toward the double doors that divided the main Eagle Group operations center from General Gerald Stone's office and living quarters. Two US Marines stood guard as usual. After the third assassination attempt, Stone had moved himself and all Eagle operations underground, converting a series of abandoned bunkers into a hidden fortress beneath the streets of Washington. The entire complex had an unfinished, post-apocalyptic feel to it, with pipes, conduits, and metal beams visible everywhere. Like Satan himself, Stone occupied the lowest level.

"Come in, Delphi," Stone said as one of the marines opened the conference room door for her. It was strict Eagle protocol for all operatives, both administrative and field, to refer to each other exclusively by code names. She took her usual seat at Stone's right, underneath the fluorescent lights.

Andi knew every member of Eagle on sight, but the four men at the conference table were all strangers. Each was tall, well-built, and dressed in simple black suits and ties similar to the general's own. Their faces seemed familiar, but she was uncertain as to why.

"These four individuals are Eagle's newest asset," Stone said as he nodded around the table. "Their collective code name is Dagger, and they are the best in the world at, shall we say, lethal interactions."

Stone motioned toward Andi.

"Gentlemen, Delphi here will handle your integration into Eagle, as well as serve as your interim handler. Your orders will come exclusively from either her or myself. She will contact you with the details about your initial assignment as soon as we have them. Until then, you are dismissed." Stone pushed a button on the conference table. "One of the marines will escort you out."

Everyone stood. One of the guards entered the room and held open the doors. All four men filed out in silence and when the last one left Andi suddenly remembered where she had seen them before.

"I thought we weren't moving forward with those new applicants, sir," Andi said after she and Stone were alone. "You said it made more sense for us to wait and see how next year's election turns out."

"I expect the volume of field assignments to increase greatly in the coming months," Stone said as he motioned for Andi to sit. The old man had a gleam in his eye she had rarely seen. "This incoming Russian general is the biggest bonanza we've ever come across. Her knowledge of the inner workings of the KGB will be a master key to unlock the identities of potentially hundreds of Soviet spies hidden here in the US and elsewhere. I mean to use that knowledge to remove every single one of them."

"Are we being allowed access to her?"

Stone muttered something under his breath as he gathered the folders in front of him into one stack. "No, but we're going to take it anyway. That's why I've fast-tracked these new recruits. We're going to use them to acquire this woman as soon as she arrives here in Washington."

"A multi-person operation, sir? Breaking away from our unified pair model would run many risks. Also, our charter specifically forbids planned operations on American soil without presidential approval."

"This operation has impediments which require more intensive tactics," Stone said. "I intend for the Daggers to remove Archangel when they acquire this Russian woman."

An uneasy feeling crept into Andi's stomach as she folded her hands and set them on the table. "Archangel, sir? But he's ours. Only Nightjack's served longer and even Morrigan doesn't have as many removals."

"New information has come to light about him. He is disloyal to the United States and needs to be removed accordingly. That's all you need to know, Delphi."

"What about his handler, Mary Magdalene?"

The old general scowled. "She's an impertinent know-it-all. The more I think about it, she might even be a spy sent by Tripper McKenzie. I should have never agreed to take her on." He sighed, stood, and picked up the stack in front of him. "We'll remove her only if she interferes."

"Yes, sir," Andi said as she pushed back her chair and stood as well.

"Reach out to our informants within the Company proper," Stone said. "We'll need advance word of this Russian general's arrival, whenever it happens. I intend for us to give both her and Archangel a special Eagle Group welcome as soon as they land."

CHAPTER 12

2:30 AM, Moscow Time, Monday, August 19, 1991

Tasia breezed through the sitting area of her grand suite, slipped out of her raincoat, and tossed it onto one of the chairs. She was naked underneath; the rest of her clothes were still on the floor in Jon's room. The air in the bedroom chilled her bare skin; she hurriedly drew back the covers and shimmied underneath.

She fell asleep quickly, but the phone still jangled her nerves when it rang. She reached over to the nightstand, picked up the receiver, and a voice that should not have been there spoke from the other end.

"Good morning, General Zolotova."

Vladimir.

"I know you've just returned to your room, so there's no need to feign you were asleep," Kryuchkov said. "You should remember the men guarding you are mine, as is your friend Gusarov, no matter what he may think of me. They have kept me aware of your every move, including your little escapade upstairs."

Tasia gasped, gut-punched.

"Your bodyguards should be outside your door by now," Kryuchkov said. "They will enter your room as soon as I hang up."

"Enter my room?" She instinctively clutched at her sheet.

"Yes, they are to confiscate the pistol I've been told you possess. Then they will watch you get dressed to make certain you have no other weapons. Dress uniform, please. Your bodyguards are to escort you to Dzerzhinsky for an emergency meeting with the heads of the other directorates. Afterward, you and I will meet privately. Am I clear on this, General?"

"Y—yes, Chairman."

"Good." Kryuchkov lowered his voice. "There's nothing you can do about this, Tasia. You have my word you will not be harmed. I have some very important plans for you, in fact."

The line went dead just as Tasia heard the hallway door open outside her bedroom.

Vladimir Kryuchkov, sitting in his office at Dzerzhinsky, poured the final remnants of his white-label Jim Beam and set the empty bottle on the edge of the desk.

The fact that Gorbachev refused to sign the documents transferring power had not been a surprise, although everyone besides Pugo expected him to have done so.

With communication lines to the outside world cut, and Plekhanov's bodyguards on the side of the GKChP, Gorbachev is effectively contained, he mused.

Kryuchkov had a one-sentence document for Yanayev to sign when he and the other Emergency Committee members met earlier at the Kremlin. Yanayev had shown up drunk, as expected. Kryuchkov had to bully the man into signing, but once that was done, everything became official. Yanayev retired to his office after the meeting with Valentin Pavlov, no doubt to get even more drunk. Kryuchkov did not care. He could handle the details himself going forward. He drained his glass in one swallow, stood, and straightened his tie.

The walk to the auditorium was short and Kryuchkov waved away several salutes as he moved through the narrow hallways. The buzz of a dozen conversations grew louder as he approached. The door opened and the duty sergeant stepped in front of him.

"*Smer-nah*!"

All conversation immediately ceased. Close to three dozen KGB directors, all in full-dress uniforms with decorations on display, rose. They snapped their heads to the front, chins up, and looked straight ahead as the room's sound system began the Soviet National Anthem. Kryuchkov nodded. He had always favored this version, full of power and fury, performed by the Red Army Choir.

He stood near the door and scanned the faces in front of him. Everyone appeared to sing along with appropriate levels of enthusiasm.

His emergency summons had the desired effect, even though delivered in the middle of the night. Kryuchkov noticed Tasia at attention, her lovely mouth opened wide, singing. Mother Russia's many medals shone bright on her buxom chest and her long red hair appeared sloppily stuffed underneath her red-banded uniform cap.

Kryuchkov felt his loins stir. The thought of her under his control again excited him in ways he had not experienced for some time. The song ended and he stepped to the podium at the front of the room. An oversized metal emblem of the KGB sword and shield filled the wall behind him.

"Comrades, be seated," he said. "I begin this emergency meeting with an announcement of grave importance. President Gorbachev is ill. He is resting comfortably at his *dacha* in Crimea, but as of ten last night, the powers of the State have been transferred to Vice President Gennady Ivanovich Yanayev, who will now serve as acting president."

Kryuchkov eyed the faces around the room as he spoke. All listened attentively, and while many displayed a lack of concern, others—like Tasia—had lost their color.

"To assist the acting president, an emergency committee known as the *GKChP* has been formed. It consists of Prime Minister Pavlov, Interior Minister Pugo, Defense Minister Yazov, Oleg Baklanov, Vasily Starodubtsev, Aleksandr Tizyakov, and myself."

Kryuchkov glanced around the room. He made certain his expression stayed hard. The time was long past for questions.

"A little over two hours from now, at six Moscow time, a state of emergency will be declared throughout the Soviet Union. In anticipation of possible unrest here in Moscow, Marshal Yazov has ordered troops and tanks into the city, which will arrive later this morning. These army troops will be supplemented by forces from Comrade Pugo's Interior Ministry as well as our own."

He adjusted the large glasses on his face.

"Some of you have already been informed of much of this. Those of you hearing it for the first time will be required to provide your public support in some fashion over the next few days. I expect everyone's full compliance in this matter, is that clear?"

Silence.

"Good," Kryuchkov said. "You will each receive detailed information about what is specifically expected from you and your respective directorates later this morning. Until that time, you are dismissed."

Kryuchkov stepped away from the podium as the directors rose. He walked over and stood in front of Tasia.

"General, I will see you in my office now."

Tasia hated Kryuchkov's office.

The polished woodwork, high ceilings, hardwood floors, and milky plaster walls all reminded her of the places he took her in the before time. The places she would have to go if she wanted to see her son. The places where she was not allowed to say no. The places where she learned what it meant to be used. The places that never truly left her, even though she had physically left them long ago.

Kryuchkov told her escorts to wait outside. He walked behind his desk, took his seat, and motioned for Tasia to sit in one of the wooden chairs in front. She sat, uniform cap on her head, and her hands in her lap.

The KGB Chairman smiled. "How are you feeling?"

"Better, sir. The wounds on my arms are healing. I've been told the scars on my neck will likely never fade completely."

"Show me."

Tasia's fingers trembled as she loosened her tie and unbuttoned the top of her uniform shirt. Kryuchkov's eyes widened.

"Would you believe me if I told you I had nothing to do with that?" he said.

"I—I'm not sure."

"Well, I did not. One of your underlings was responsible, a Major Andrei Bolskov. We have testimonies from multiple witnesses who say they saw him escort the assassin through Dzerzhinsky's hallways. It would seem he coveted your position."

Tasia felt her mouth drop open. She closed it and swallowed in disbelief.

"I have his signed confession right here." Kryuchkov patted a red file folder on his desk. "I want you to know he has paid for his crime with his life."

"Oh, Andrei," Tasia whispered.

"Tasia, you and I have had a difficult relationship these past many years," Kryuchkov said. "I have not treated you well at times, that is true. I am willing to put all that behind us if you are."

Tasia sniffled and sat up straighter in her chair. "I—I—suppose so?"

"Good." Kryuchkov's voice sounded like it did in the before time. Smooth, arrogant, in control. Tasia had to choke down the panicked reaction in her stomach. She was not going to allow him to intimidate her again. "Before that happens, however, there are two things I require from you."

"Two things?"

"Yes, and they are simple. First, I want you to appear on one of our television channels this afternoon. You will make a statement in support of the *GKChP* and a repudiation of President Gorbachev. Having Mother Russia tell the country and the world our former leader has betrayed the Soviet Union will have an enormous impact. The statement will, of course, be preprepared for you."

"And the second thing?"

"I believe you are in possession of financial documents related to Party funds transferred out of the country. Those documents are to be delivered into my custody at once. You will then sign a sworn statement to authenticate the funds in question were handled within the rights of the Soviet officials responsible for the transfers."

Tasia took a deep breath and let it out slowly. He was doing what he always did. Boxing her in, leaving her with no alternative but to comply with his desires. Many times in the past—moments she struggled to banish from her memories—she had capitulated. Finally, she had told him *no* and it had cost her almost everything. She clenched her fists. He must not be allowed to win this time.

"Your words, sir, are—unexpected," she said.

"I regret so much of what has transpired between us, Tasia."

"So do I," she truthfully said. "But I must tell you, I've worked closely with Andrei Bolskov for several years. I've eaten dinner with him and his wife many times. I've played with their children. The picture you paint of him is simply not correct. I weep for the agony you've just given his beautiful family."

"Tasia, the man was a confessed conspirator. You know the penalty—"

"Your penalty, Vladimir!" her voice rose. "Torture, abuse, and death are all you understand. It's as if you're some kind of machine or device, devoid of anything but ambition and guile." She flexed her fingers then dug them into the chair's armrests. "I will not betray President Gorbachev, nor will I support this heinous thing you and your cronies have hatched. I would rather go to the gulag!"

"You realize that can be arranged?" Kryuchkov said, his voice stepping up in volume. "I can have you arrested at any time. I could have you executed and there's nothing you could do to stop me."

"You will not have that power for long. The people of this country will not stand for what you are doing. Millions will rise against you!"

"Enough!" Kryuchkov shot to his feet. He stepped out from behind his desk and leaned in close to Tasia's face.

"General Zolotova," he said. "I order you to turn over the documents we have just discussed. After that, you will be taken to a television station of my choosing and read the statement I provide over the air."

"No!" Tasia yelled.

She did not have time to blink as the KGB chairman's fist swung for her face. Pain exploded across her jaw. Her uniform cap flew from her head. She toppled from her chair and hit the floor. She rolled with the impact and leapt for Kryuchkov's legs. The older man fell backward and smacked into the front edge of his desk. The empty liquor bottle fell to the floor and shattered.

The two of them wrestled in a desperate embrace across the floor. Punching, gouging, kicking, biting. Kryuchkov finally managed to get her underneath him. Broken glass crunched under her back. Tasia reached up and plunged her nails deep into his cheek. She yanked hard and tore away a thick swath of bloody flesh. The KGB Chairman screamed. Tasia bucked him off and rolled away.

Kryuchkov staggered to his feet, one hand at his bleeding face. He turned toward his desk and pressed a button on the console there. Four guards immediately burst into the room and pointed their Kalashnikovs at Tasia as she lay on the floor. She raised her hands.

"Give me the documents, Tasia," Kryuchkov growled.

"Vladimir, I—"

"Now!"

"They're in multiple locations!" she lied as she crawled to a kneeling position and raised her hands higher. "All are nearby, but some are in places that are not yet open." Her palms bled from the broken glass. "Vladimir, please, give me some time! The men who escorted me here can accompany me. If you will give me that—" she paused with disgust, but knew she needed to say it "—I will submit myself to you again."

Tasia closed her eyes and prayed. Silence filled the room. She waited for his words.

"You are trying my patience, woman," he finally said.

"I only need until noon! Let me go back to the Savoy—to clean myself up so I can appear on camera. Once that's done, I will take my escorts, retrieve the documents, and bring them to you."

Kryuchkov stared at her. Time seemed locked in place.

"Very well," he said, his hand still at his face. "You may go back to the Savoy. You will be escorted to wherever you need to go to retrieve the documents, then bring them back to me at noon. If you have what I want—"

Tasia saw him lick his lips.

CHAPTER 13

5:10 AM, Moscow Time, August 19, 1991

The door to her grand suite slammed shut behind her. Tasia put her hand to her mouth.

All her teeth were still in place. Her jaw did not feel broken, although she constantly swallowed what felt like substantial amounts of blood. She had managed to slip the jagged bottleneck from the broken liquor bottle into the pocket of her skirt but had no other weapons. She picked up the phone and dialed the room across the hall.

"I would like to go down to breakfast one final time at eight. I will take you to retrieve the documents the Chairman wants after that. Is that acceptable?"

The man on the other end of the line grunted his assent. She thanked him, clapped the lever on the phone's cradle, and dialed Jon's room. The receiver picked up.

"This is General Zolotova in Room 303," she quickly said. "I am coming down again this morning at eight and demand my breakfast be hearty this time. Your recent offerings have been terrible disappointments, do you understand?"

Jon, please get it.

"We understand you, General," he said in clear Russian. "We will have your breakfast ready at eight and will take extra care this time."

She hung up and wondered what they were going to do next.

Jon placed the receiver back in the cradle. He considered calling Tripper and having him meet them out back at eight. The Savoy phone lines were certainly tapped. Everything could go up in flames if he was not careful. He needed to think this through.

He rolled off the bed and began a series of pushups. He transitioned to sit ups and had to force himself to finally stop. The wolf inside him had fully awakened and multiple plans of action ran through his mind. He needed information and Tasia had it. He would meet her as she expected. God help anyone who tried to hurt her. They would never see the sunset.

He made his way into the bathroom and set the shower as cold as he could stand it. He allowed the wolf inside him to howl as the stinging water poured over him. He needed a clear head.

He pulled his dark navy two-piece suit out of the closet. All the clothes he brought with him were Russian made, and the jackets had been adjusted to conceal a shoulder holster. He was still concerned. The Makarov was commonplace in government circles around the USSR, but he had no illusions about what would happen if the wrong people noticed the small but still-visible bulge under his arm. He dressed quickly, adding in his black button-down shirt, bluebell-grey tie, and polished black dress shoes.

He stashed his identification papers, rubles, and extra magazines for the Makarov in his pockets. He packed everything else into his suitcase and placed it in the closet. With one last look around, he left the room and headed downstairs. The Savoy's restaurant was not busy. He sat at the same table as the day before and ordered black coffee.

Tasia entered the room right on time, flanked by two oversized security men. Her long red hair flowed free, held back by a wide white band. She wore the same black raincoat as the night before, but with a navy linen dress underneath which came just above her knees. A red-and-navy checkered scarf encircled her throat inside a starched white collar. She wore neither earrings nor any other jewelry, except for a decidedly non-Soviet oversized white wristwatch. A large sailcloth bag hung from her right shoulder and a huge purple bruise marred one side of her jaw.

Jon wrestled the rising wolf inside him. He knew he could take down both her escorts, if necessary, but as he looked around, he saw two other hard-faced men sitting much further away with interested eyes upon her.

Tasia walked straight to Jon's table. One hand grasped the bag on her shoulder while the other held the edge of her raincoat.

"May I join you?" she asked in Russian.

"Please."

Tasia told her escorts to sit wherever they liked. They appeared to hesitate at first but moved and sat at a table a few feet away.

"Talk to me," Jon said in French as Tasia sat down and laid her bag beside the chair. It took her a second to adapt.

"It's a coup, Jon," she said. "Vladimir has seized control. Gorbachev's been removed from power. They say he's ill and resting at his *dacha* in the Crimea, but that's surely a lie. I—I fear he might be dead."

Jon's eyebrows shot up. "Damn."

"They took me to Dzerzhinsky last night as soon as I returned to my room. You were right, they've been watching this whole time."

"What did they want?"

"The proof I have." Tasia struggled a bit with French. "I was able to convince Vladimir to give me until noon today to bring it to him."

"He's the one who did this to you?" He nodded at her bruised jaw.

"Yes." She dropped her head.

"Hey," Jon said as he reached out to touch her chin and raise it back up. She winced slightly at his touch. "Nobody could have foreseen this."

"I should have."

"Like hell." Jon glanced at the two steely-eyed KGB watchers and then back again. "Okay, this is obviously a setup. They're letting you talk to me because they expect us to make a break for it. We've got to subvert that expectation."

"Agreed, but how?"

"Lightning fast, hit and git. If I can find a public phone, Tripper can come get us."

"Vladimir has the Army moving in. They'll block the streets any time now. Your friend will never be able to get to us, much less back."

"That might actually help. If we have to stay on foot, so will anyone else. How close is the nearest Metro Station? I assume the trains are still operating?"

"Nothing was said about shutting them down. That would be a nightmare anyway. Kuznetskiy Most is a little over a block from here, across the street from Sivilla's café. The Purple Line is there. We can be within a mile of the embassy in just two stops."

Jon's mouth tightened. "Alright, when we finish eating, tell your escorts you're ready to retrieve the documents. Walk out the front exit and take a roundabout way toward the Metro Station. I'll follow close behind."

"Then what?"

"Then we kill them."

"What?" Tasia said through clenched teeth. "Two KGB men in broad daylight? Are you insane?"

"Maybe," Jon smiled. "But I have a plan. You have to trust me."

"I do not have to do any such thing!" Tasia whispered with a sneer. "I am not committing suicide! This is crazy!"

"Tasia, there are things about me you don't know," Jon said. "It's been twenty-three years. Unlike your rather public career path, mine has been the opposite."

"So?"

"Killing is what I do. I'm not CIA anymore. Haven't been for years. I work for Eagle, our assassination group. My code name is Archangel."

Tasia's eyes went wide.

"Archangel?" she sputtered. "Archangel? You? But—Archangel is a murderer! He's killed—dozens of us!"

"The exact count is thirty-seven," Jon said, his voice tinged in ice, "and I'll add to that number here shortly."

"Holy hell, Jon!"

"I'm serious. I was going to tell you when we were out of here and you were safe."

Tasia scanned his face. "I detest liars," she whispered. She pushed back her chair and turned her whole body ninety degrees to face the fountain. Hands folded in her lap, she sighed and stared at the spurting water.

"I knew many of those men you killed," she said. "Some were friends." She spun back around and laid her palms flat on the table, eyes ablaze with fury. "If you really are one of these Eagle beasts—"

"They call us wolves."

"Oh, how American."

Jon reached for her hand, but she jerked it away and crossed her arms. Neither of them said anything for a few moments. Eventually she sighed again and looked down at his coffee cup.

"I knew there was something different about you. Your eyes aren't the same." She put a hand under her chin, elbow on the tablecloth. "I should have known the last twenty years would change you. It changed both of us, I suppose. Neither of us turned out the way we'd planned."

"Does anyone?"

Tasia sighed. "If I'd said yes back then, we could've had twenty years of happiness together. Instead, you've become a killer, and I've endured utter hell at Vladimir's hands."

She dropped her fist to the tabletop with a smack.

"I'm sick of Vladimir defeating me, Jon. Over and over again, for twenty years, he always has. Time and again, he took my dignity, my body, and pieces of my soul." She sat up straight and crossed her arms again. "I want to put him under the knife."

"I know how," Jon said. "I say we remove the bastard's goons, pick up your proof, and grab the next train to the embassy. We can release everything to the world from there."

He reached for her hand again and this time she gave it to him.

"The wolf inside me is very, very good at what it does," he said. "If you'll trust me, the two of us can throw a huge monkey wrench into all this. Bring it crashing to the ground and Kryuchkov along with it."

"The two of us, huh?" She shook her head, smiled slightly, and squeezed his hand. "God help me, you American killer. You'd better be as good as you say."

"Thought you communists didn't believe in God?"

"Don't believe everything you've heard," Tasia said. "Now tell me this insane plan of yours."

1:30 AM, Washington Time, Monday, August 19, 1991

The park area in front of the Lincoln Memorial appeared deserted. Jessi found a bench under a streetlight within sight of the front steps, sat down and yawned. She imagined Lincoln himself staring down at her.

She tried to scratch underneath the bandage across her nose. It felt like a colony of ants had invaded her sinuses. The more she fiddled with it, the worse it became. She finally shoved her hands underneath her legs to stop herself from making it worse. Her blue jeans helped keep them warm against the cool night air blowing in off the Potomac. She was glad she had worn her George Washington U sweatshirt.

She heard a noise in the brush not far behind her. The park appeared deserted, but downtown DC after dark was often not a safe place. She turned around and touched the 9mm pistol in the belt holster under her sweatshirt. Jon kept a seemingly endless number of them all over his home at Great Falls. Satisfied the noise was nothing to worry about, she turned back around. Andi Jenkins came into view, walking up the sidewalk toward her.

"Hey," Jessi said as Andi sat down beside her.

"Mary Magdalene, what the hell happened to you?" Andi said as she looked at Jessi's face.

"I'm fine. It was a small accident. Nothing to worry about."

"If you say so. You look like you ended up on the wrong end of a bar fight. Sorry to get you out so late."

"I've got nothing going on since Archangel's currently under Company direction," Jessi said as she leaned back. "What's up?"

"I'm taking a huge chance telling you this." Andi's eyes darted around the darkened park area. "But surely, it's safe to talk out here. I won't allow this to happen again, and I think maybe you can help me prevent it."

"Prevent what?"

"The boss has targeted Archangel for removal."

A cold knife cut through Jessi's stomach. "Jesus Christ, that evil son of a bitch was serious. You sure about this?"

"One hundred percent," Andi said. "Fortunately, he's got me handling the arrangements."

"Thank God for that."

"Maybe not. Since it's Archangel, Stone's taking no chances."

"Is he sending Morrigan? She's the only one I'd worry about."

"Much worse, I'm afraid. He's created a new four-person strike team. He calls it the wave of the future."

"How the hell is he supposed to keep something like that secret?"

"I don't think he cares anymore. He's always been unpredictable, but this business with the Russian general has driven him to the point of obsession. It's like a wet dream or something for him."

"Ick," Jessi said. A soft breeze rustled the leaves of the trees around them. "What does this mean?"

"The Russian woman is to be spirited away and interrogated," Andi said, "likely for the long term. Haven't got the location yet. The Dagger strike team is to remove Archangel at the same time."

"Does Stone really think he can get away with this?"

"Sure, we've done it dozens of times. The two of them will simply disappear and that's that. Lots of unanswered questions with no traces. You know the drill."

"Can't see that working here," Jessi said. "This Russian woman is under too much scrutiny. Her disappearing like that would raise a firestorm of questions. The Company would have to know it was Stone."

"Not at all. The KGB would be the prime suspects. It's happened several times already with their high-level defectors. Somehow, they always find them. The only way Stone gets outed here is if you say something now."

"Me? Why am I the person to do this?"

"Two reasons actually. First, I know about you and Archangel."

Jessi drew her mouth into a thin line. "You do?"

"Don't worry, you've both been more than discreet. Stone has no idea. Given that relationship, I knew you'd fight tooth and nail to save him."

"Damn right I will. What's the second reason?"

"This one's a little more delicate, but since Stone himself brought it up earlier, I think it's time to rip away the mask. Stone is concerned you may be working for Tripper McKenzie to undermine Eagle from the inside—" She turned and looked at Jessi. "—and I think he's right."

Jessi kept her tone even. "Why would you think that?"

"I added up the coincidences," Andi said. "The fact that you're McKenzie's protégé is well known, and it always seemed odd to me that you stayed here when he went to Moscow. Also, you were practically foisted on us through Company channels shortly after he left. Next, McKenzie and Bob Gates are known to be tight. Both are staunch George Bush allies from back in the Seventies, and it's common knowledge how much the president hates Stone. Mostly though, it's because my gut tells me I'm right."

Jessi sighed. "What do you want me to say, Andi?"

"I want you to tell me you have the goods on Stone," Andi said. "I want to know we can finally move against him before he kills any more of our own people."

"You're serious."

"Damn right. I've had enough."

"Alright," Jessi said. "Let's just say, for argument's sake, you're right about all this. What are you asking me to do?"

"Call Dick Kerr right away. Tell him about Stone's plans for this Russian woman and Archangel. Show him whatever you have."

"Who says I have anything?"

Andi frowned. "Do we really need to keep up the verbal fencing? Surely, me telling you about Archangel earns me some straight talk for at least a few minutes?"

"Think about this from my perspective," Jessi said. "I hardly know you, really, on anything but a professional level. We both work for a government subagency whose sole reason for existing is assassination. You are Gerald Stone's number two and known to be both efficient and loyal. If I were what you say, how could I know this is not a plan to confirm something you've already prepared a response to? If Stone believed I was an inside spy for the Company, you might very well ask me out here in the middle of the night to remove me. Morrigan could have an infrared scope zeroed in on my skull as we speak."

"If that were the case, Mary Magdalene, you'd already be dead. Stone doesn't need confirmation of anything once he makes up his mind." Andi yawned and stretched her legs. "Would you rather us move somewhere else?"

"No, what you say makes sense. Lord knows, I know the General's tactics as well as anyone."

"How about this then?" Andi said. "You need a reason to trust me. You're right, loyalty is something I prize more than anything else. Gerald Stone lost mine some months ago and I'm going to tell you why."

"Okay, I'm listening."

"Do you remember Jeremiah Johnson?"

"Sure, Mountain Man. Odd code name, especially for someone who looked more like Denzel Washington than Robert Redford. Sad to hear about him."

"Well, unlike what you heard, it wasn't an accident," Andi said softly. "Jeremiah and I—well, let's just say we were more than close."

"I had no idea. I'm so sorry."

"Yeah, we worked hard to keep it secret. My husband Derrick never knew and neither did Jeremiah's wife. Considering all the crazy hours we both worked, it wasn't hard to conceal."

Andi looked off into the distance. "Jeremiah threatened to blow the whistle on a removal Stone ordered him to perform. Someone innocent, he told me. I tried to convince him to keep quiet, but he couldn't stand to see this sort of thing go on. Now, he's dead."

She turned and Jessi saw the pain in her eyes, the hurt, the loss.

"Stone denies he had anything to do with it, of course," Andi continued, "but I found out what really happened. The records are always there if you dig deep enough."

"True."

"I want to see Stone answer for what he did to Jeremiah," Andi whispered.

Jessi sat silent for a few moments and listened to the breeze blow through.

"Okay," she said as she leaned forward and intertwined her fingers. "Yes, I was sent into Eagle by Tripper McKenzie, but it's not what you think. It was never anything official. Tripper knew of the bad blood between Stone and the president. He thought having me in place within Eagle would make it easier to monitor things. Give the president some internal eyes, so to speak. He ended up going to Moscow before we could finalize our system, so I've been unable to speak to him confidentially for some time. He has no idea what I've uncovered."

Andi smiled. "Thought I'd pegged you right."

"What?"

"You're a crusader, Mary Magdalene. You can't stand to see the bad guys get away with things, just like Jeremiah. You're also damn good at hiding your true feelings and way, way too detail intense. Stone underestimates the hell out of you."

"What makes you say that?"

Andi looked around. "Well, when we were discussing Archangel's removal, he called you a — what was it now? — an impertinent know-it-all. I almost laughed out loud."

"That pusillanimous son of a bitch," Jessi said.

"He wasn't wrong," Andi said. "That's what led me to give you a call. After our conversation just now, I'm very glad I did."

Jessi stood up and adjusted her jacket. "Okay, give me some time to pull things together and call the Deputy Director. When I've pulled the trigger, I'll phone you and tell you about my vacation plans."

"Sounds good."

Jessi stepped backward into the darkness. She kept her hand on her pistol and took a circuitous route back to Jon's Explorer. She stayed behind a tree and watched the parking lot for several minutes before she hustled to the car, fired up the engine and headed back to the Interstate.

She was certain no one followed her, one of the advantages of Jon's property being in the middle of nowhere. She parked the Explorer in the garage and headed inside the main house. A pair of gym shorts and one of Jon's Red Sox t-shirts made her feel like herself again. She headed for the pool house out back.

Jessi had never understood why Jon had overbuilt everything at Great Falls. He was never one for spending money foolishly. The entire complex was like one huge hunting lodge, with six bedrooms, four baths, three living areas, a restaurant-style kitchen, plus a swimming pool and workout room. He had also built a secure panic room in the center with an independent power source, plus a security system and arsenal to rival Fort Knox. The pool house was an ostentatious add-on, probably suggested by a greedy architect or contractor to jack up the price.

Jon had never used the pool house as far as Jessi knew, even though they had spent many afternoons in the pool itself when the weather was nice. She unlocked the door, went to one of the cabinets in the breakfast area, pulled out three cardboard boxes, set them on the glass table there, and went to work.

It took her longer than expected to select the items she thought told the story in the most unimpeachable manner. She had been tempted to make some coffee, but instead got up and walked around the pool periodically to stay awake. Finally, she put the unnecessary items back in the cabinet, grabbed her selected papers and turned off the lights.

The night birds and nocturnal insects sounded loud as she stepped into the pool area. A three-quarter moon showed overhead, and shadows ebbed and flowed in the darkness outside the wooden fence. The glow from the footlights embedded in the concrete danced across her bare feet as she walked past. She took the wooden steps up to the main floor deck, went through the sliding glass door, laid her packet on the kitchen table, and headed upstairs.

It took her a little while to locate Jon's suitcases. She rifled through her drawers and the closet in the master bedroom, amazed at how much of her stuff had ended up there. If she ever had to take it back to her apartment in DC, there was no way it would all fit. It was not something she cared to contemplate.

It took her a few minutes to pack, but when everything was finished, she stripped down to her underwear and crawled into bed. She needed a few hours' sleep before she called CIA Deputy Director Kerr.

There would be no turning back after that.

CHAPTER 14

9:00 AM, Moscow Time, Monday, August 19, 1991

Boris Yeltsin had been President of Russia for exactly forty days. He had been awakened shortly after the state of emergency was declared and had been in full outrage mode ever since.

"Hold off, Tatyana. I've changed my mind," Yeltsin said as he finished his breakfast in the kitchen of his *dacha* in the Russian Federation compound.

"Seriously, Poppa?" His brown-haired daughter looked up from the typewriter at the other end of the table. Yeltsin's closest advisors were collectively known as *The Family* and his two daughters were nearly always present at his strategy sessions.

"We need to go stronger here," Yeltsin said. "We're going to demand a general worker's strike all over Russia."

"What you propose will be inflammatory, Poppa," Yeltsin's daughter Elena said from the opposite corner of the kitchen. "Have you forgotten the KGB troops outside?"

"They're commanded by a blockheaded coward," Yeltsin said. He rose and took his dishes to the sink. He spoke over his shoulder as he washed his hands.

"Kryuchkov couldn't make a real decision if his hair were on fire." Yeltsin smiled and ran his wet hand over the thick shock of silver-white atop his head. "Not that he has any hair anymore." He turned around and looked at his assembled staff.

"I am the duly elected President of Russia," he said. "I am going to the Parliament Building to better lead the people."

Yeltsin walked over to his younger daughter and lowered his voice. "Tatyana, I need you to gather your mother, your sister, and her two little ones as soon as we leave. One of the bodyguards has an apartment on the outskirts of Moscow where he's offered to keep you all safe. Do it quietly, dearest, understood?"

The pretty young woman noticed her father's hand tremble as he took the typed statement from her.

"Yes, Poppa," she whispered. "I understand."

Lt. Colonel Greb Raushev of the KGB Alpha Group stood outside the compound's main gate and watched the growing activity through his binoculars. A sideways glance confirmed his men spread out in the grass on either side of the driveway. They had been on site since the wee hours of the morning and were supposed to have moved in and arrested Boris Yeltsin hours ago. Raushev had everything in place and was ready to move when Chairman Kryuchkov called and revoked the order.

Boris Yeltsin, wearing a bulletproof vest underneath his chestnut brown suit jacket, came out the front door surrounded by several aides, some of whom were armed.

"Colonel, what are they doing?" one of the men asked.

"Preparing to leave, Sergeant."

"They will have to exit via this gate, sir. Orders?"

"We let them pass," Raushev said. His gaze never left the motorcade as it approached the gate. "The Chairman has not responded to our requests. We have no orders to stop them."

Tasia stepped onto the sidewalk in front of the Savoy with her two escorts. An unseasonably cool breeze brought a chill to her bare arms and legs. She remembered storms were expected and wished she had worn nylons. She also regretted leaving her raincoat in the restaurant, but for what she and Jon had planned, it would be too restrictive. The white cloth bag on her shoulder contained her father's book, her identification papers, and every ruble she had. She had also brought along a pair of sunglasses. The overcast sky made them unnecessary from a practical standpoint, but the dark lenses in the gold-rimmed frames helped conceal her face.

Tasia turned north on *Ulitsa Rozhdestvenka* and resisted the urge to look over her shoulder. Foot traffic ran in all directions, and nothing appeared out of the ordinary. It was only a short distance to the end of the street, and from there she turned west onto *Pushechnaya Ulitsa.* The narrow one-way street housed nearly a dozen restaurants and nightclubs, all closed, but likely to reopen later in the day.

She scanned the rows of interconnected brick and stucco structures and found the recessed archway which led to the parking and delivery area. She stopped at the opening and her two escorts did the same. She took two quick steps forward and spun around.

"Comrades," she said with a coy smile that hopefully promised naughtiness. "Would you play with me?"

"What?" the closer of the two asked.

"Tag!"

She abruptly slapped the man's shoulder and bolted down the alleyway.

Tasia poured on the speed to reach the far end ahead of her pursuers. The long, fully enclosed parking area was empty except for two huge dumpsters a dozen or so feet from the entrance. She tossed her bag away, ran to the farthest one, hunched down along the white brick wall, and fumbled with the pocket of her dress. The burly KGB sergeant appeared within seconds. Fire was in his eyes, but he had not yet drawn his weapon.

"Woah!" Tasia said as she raised her left hand. "You are fast, big boy! That wasn't much fun."

"What the hell are you doing?"

Tasia stood up straight and looked at the man's face. His partner, a corporal with a flattop haircut, was nowhere in sight.

"Get moving," the KGB man said.

Tasia slashed the jagged neck of Kryuchkov's liquor bottle across the man's face. The slice through his eyeball sounded like a zipper pulled up fast. The bull of a man howled in pain and charged. Tasia slid to one side like matador, and the man smacked into the brick wall at full speed. He instantly bounced back, blood streaming down his face. "You are dead, bitch!"

Tasia sprang forward, arms crossed in front of her like a defensive lineman. She plowed into the KGB agent, and they hit the wall with a muted thump. She recoiled at the dark, jellylike substance that oozed from his ruined eye. She slashed at his neck with the makeshift dagger. His grip was too strong, and she missed, but carved a deep furrow into his cheek.

The man yelled again and violently jerked his head from side to side. The motion struck Tasia's hand, and her weapon fell to the ground. She tried to back away and retrieve it, but the KGB man stomped his boot on top of her cloth shoe. He slid to the side like a snake.

Tasia swung her fist at the man's nose. He expertly dodged it and reached into his jacket. She countered with her other fist and connected with his sternum. Shock and numbing tingles cascaded up her arm like she had punched the brick wall. She stepped back and shook feeling back into her arm.

Time slowed.

The man, blood and eye fluid streaming down his face, reached into his coat. It reappeared and she watched his Makarov track toward her. He offered a humorless grin as his finger tightened on the trigger.

What a stupid way to die, she thought.

A blur hit him from his blind side as he fired. Tasia felt the bullet zip past her arm. Jon pinned him to the wall and snuck an arm around the man's thick throat. The KBG agent grunted and choked, fighting the hold. Tasia heard the snick of what sounded like a knife. The KGB man's movements grew weaker, the sounds quieter. Jon's other hand reached around and slashed across the man's throat. Tasia watched the brute slam onto the pavement and twitch like a fish in the bottom of a rowboat. He went still after a few seconds and a dark spot spread across the back of his jacket.

"What did you do?" she said.

"Renal artery. Death is nearly instantaneous."

Blood covered Jon's front, camouflaged only slightly by the dark colors of his shirt and jacket. A thick, sticky redness coated his hands and the lower parts of his sleeves. A bloody, double-edged knife dangled from his fingers with casual familiarity. His eyes looked nothing like they had in the restaurant yesterday, or even a few minutes ago. A dry white coldness stared at her.

"Holy—" Tasia said. A shiver coursed down her spine. "You really are a killer, aren't you?"

Jon knelt, wiped both the blade and his hands on the corpse's jacket, then stood and inserted the knife into the front of his belt. He grabbed the body by the armpits and nodded for Tasia to grab the legs.

The dribbling blood made a red, wet line along the ground as they waddled together to the dumpster. Jon pulled open the metal lid and the two of them swung the body back and forth and vaulted it over the edge. They did the same for the other KGB man. Tasia's eyes flittered over Jon's front as they dusted themselves off.

"Get rid of the tie," she said.

Jon slid the blood-splattered piece of rayon out of his collar and tossed it into the dumpster. Tasia checked him over again, partially satisfied.

"I suppose if you stay close to me, we can conceal the stains somewhat."

Tasia scanned the second-floor windows as she and Jon walked away. Despite the pistol shot, they all remained empty and dark. She glanced at the two large puddles of blood where the KGB men met their ends. Yesterday, they had been her bodyguards. Today, she had orchestrated their deaths.

"Where's your friend's café?" he asked.

"About a block north of here." Tasia grunted as she picked up her bag.

"You alright?"

"Oh, like it matters. We need to get out of here."

Jon leaned over a planted a quick kiss on her cheek. Tasia could not have been more startled if he had slapped her.

"Lead the way, Lady Macbeth," he said.

CHAPTER 15

Approximately 10:00 AM, Moscow Time,
Monday, August 19, 1991

"Mr. President! KGB Chairman Kryuchkov is on the phone!"

"Route it to my desk," Yeltsin said to the nervous young aide. "Then grab whomever you can and cram them into my office. I want as many people as possible to hear this."

Yeltsin beamed with manufactured bluster by the time the hurried footsteps sounded in the hallway. He waited until everyone was in position, stepped in front of his desk, and picked up the receiver.

"This is President Yeltsin."

"Good morning, Mr. President," came the crisp reply. "I think you recognize my voice. It is a pleasure to speak with you this morning."

"I suppose it would be from your perspective, Comrade Kryuchkov." Yeltsin would not dignify the man by referring to his title. "Taking control of the entire Soviet Union is a daunting task. I hope your heart is healthy enough to take the stress."

"My heart is just fine, Mr. President. I wanted to inform you personally of the State of Emergency that was declared a few hours ago."

"I am aware."

"This new arrangement will mark a peaceful return to the type of governing which has served us so well in the past. The *GKChP* simply wants what is best for the Soviet people."

"I was unaware brute force was in the people's best interest."

"You do me the honor of being blunt, Mr. President," Kryuchkov said. "I will return the courtesy. The purpose of my call is to convince you that coming along with us would be in your best interest. No one wants bloodshed."

"Where is Mikhail Sergeyevich Gorbachev?"

"Where the news reports say, resting at his *dacha* on the Black Sea. I have no reason to lie about this."

"I want to speak with him."

"Mr. President, you must know that is impossible. The head of the Soviet Union is now Acting President Gennady Ivanovich Yanayev. I could arrange for you to speak with him if you like, but I assure you conversing with me would be much more profitable."

"Get to the point."

"My request is simple, Mr. President, and something I think you can live with. Keep silent, that's all we ask. We know you oppose what we are doing, and I respect your principles. The reality is the *GKChP* is in charge now. You can either work with us, or we will crush you."

"Comrade Kryuchkov, I delight in your directness. Please allow me some of my own." Yeltsin raised his voice so everyone in the room could hear. "No one in the Russian government will remain silent about what has taken place in our motherland this morning." Yeltsin's face flushed and he continued. "Russia is our mother, and she is not someone you can abuse any longer. You and your traitorous friends have roused Mother Russia's spirit of defiance! We will oppose you in every manner possible, do you hear me? Press releases have already gone out and will continue to do so."

A few seconds of silence preceded Kryuchkov's reply.

"You do realize, Mr. President, the army is moving into the city as we speak? A significant number of tanks are stationed near you right now. Do you want me to direct them toward you?"

"Send in the tanks whenever you like," Yeltsin said, his left fist above his head. "I will meet them at the doorstep. Me and all the people who still love Mother Russia!" He slammed the phone into its cradle.

Someone clapped, and others quickly followed. Yeltsin turned and saw the instigator was his vice president, Aleksandr Rutskoi. The tall war veteran, with his Hero of the Soviet Union medal displayed on his lapel, was all smiles beneath his large mustache. The room quickly filled with thunderous applause. Yeltsin raised his hands, and the room quieted.

"Friends! Vladimir Alekandrovich has just given us the greatest gift imaginable. You all heard it. He is afraid of us! I mean to exploit that fear. We will tear this unconstitutional coup d'état of his out by the roots!"

The applause resumed. Yeltsin knew the good feeling would not last long. He needed more people, more visible support—and fast.

"Aleksandr," he said to Rutskoi. "We need to get the word out. Set up a radio broadcast from here as soon as possible. I must tell the people of Moscow what we are doing as it happens. Start a phone network, too. Everyone is to converge here at the Parliament Building. Tell the people their president asks them to stand with him for freedom and the time is now!"

"What do you mean you lost her?"

KGB Lieutenant Hamilcar Zarax of the *Mokryye Dela* sat behind the wheel of his KGB sedan and picked at the dry, irritated skin under his thin mustache. He and his men had waited for days for the traitor to run, and when she finally did, they had all choked.

"They were no longer visible by the time we made it outside," came the voice through the hand radio. "We're not sure which direction they took."

Idiot, you were supposed to be prepared, Zarax thought. "We saw them turn west onto *Pushechnaya* when they came out of the hotel," he said. "They cannot be very far in front of you. Head in that direction."

"Then what?"

Pushechnaya dead-ended just a block away at *Neglinnaya*, which ran north and south. Which way would they head? Either direction was a reasonable possibility. He was just about the tell the men to turn south when the radio spoke.

"We found her. Heading north on *Neglinnaya.* Her red hair is easy to spot. She's quite a bit ahead of us, but I don't see her escorts. A tall man is beside her."

"That would be the *Amerikanski* boyfriend. Get in close and stay there," Zarax said. It seemed impossible for this woman to have slipped away from two highly trained KGB men, but he had been warned she was both bold and clever. Also, the American was supposedly highly dangerous. Zarax suddenly had a very bad feeling. "Those are all shops or restaurants along there, so she must know someone. Keep an eye on them, but do not approach until we get there."

Zarax started the car and looked for an opportunity to pull out. "The technician and I will relocate north of *Rozhdestvenka* and move toward you. When she enters one of those storefronts, radio us. We'll block the back exit while you two watch the front. Whichever way she comes out, we'll regroup and encircle them. Remember, non-lethal capture is the order."

"Confirmed."

Tasia held Jon's hand as they pushed through the crowds along *Ulitsa Kuznetskiy.*

"We don't have time to linger," Jon said as he scanned behind them.

"This will be quick, I promise. You can take the opportunity to wash up. I need to warn you about Sivilla. It's a virtual guarantee she'll come onto you."

"Are all you Russian women sex maniacs?"

Tasia smiled. "Sivilla certainly is. Even in primary school, she would lift her skirt for anyone who caught her fancy. Trust me, there were loads of them. She was an actress for a long time, and I suspect a prostitute at one point, but she's gorgeous so you'll be flattered."

Tasia removed her sunglasses and put them in her bag as Jon reached for the café door. The little bell attached to the top of the lintel rang as they entered. The aroma of butter, dill, and breakfast meats invaded Tasia's nostrils, mixed with the steam of hot tea and the odor of over-varnished wooden floors. The café had a lively bustle to it, with a large number of customers in line at the counter. More sat at the square wooden tables near the front.

Sivilla stood at one of them, hands on the chairbacks of two elderly gentlemen who seemed engrossed in her every word. Short, dark hair curled around her ears, and she wore a scandalously short, form-fitting silver dress that accentuated both her breasts and behind. She caught sight of Tasia as her story concluded and her lovely face broke into an animated grin.

"Sweetheart!"

She ran forward, heels clapping along the dark wooden floor, and caught Tasia in a fierce embrace. The two of them spun each other around for several moments.

"We need to talk, dear heart," Tasia whispered in her ear. "In the back, away from the windows. My, uh, friend here needs to use the washroom."

Sivilla glanced at Jon and smiled. "Come on."

The three of them elbowed their way through the crowd of customers, in the opposite direction of the counter, to a wooden door at the back. "You can wash up in the kitchen, big fella," Sivilla said as she pointed to a door along the opposite wall.

"Surely there's some high-powered dish soap in there somewhere," Tasia said. "Come see us when you're more presentable."

Jon nodded and left. The two women entered the tiny office which was filled to the ceiling with stacks of canned foodstuffs and cardboard boxes. A tiny desk sat along the wall, but both it and its chair were piled high with papers. There was nowhere to sit so Tasia simply stood.

Sivilla stepped in close and ran her fingertips across the huge bruise on the side of Tasia's jaw. "What the hell happened?"

"Vladimir."

Sivilla let loose a string of curse words that seemed to go on for nearly a minute. Then she spit on the floor. "When will you listen to me?" Her hands cut through the air as she talked. "I don't care if he is Yuri's father or your boss, nothing is worth what he does to you, sweetheart!" She crossed her arms beneath her breasts.

"I'm listening now, dear heart," Tasia said. "I'm sorry it's taken me this long." She looked at her friend and wondered if her fears were visible. "I can't tell you what's happened because the less you know the better. Trust me, I've done some terrible, terrible things today, and need to get out of Moscow as fast as possible. There's no turning back now."

"I don't care what you've done, sweetheart," Sivilla said as she touched Tasia's cheek. "I only want you to be free and happy. You never have to worry about my support, just tell me what you need."

"Couple of things, actually," Tasia said. "First, my jaw hurts like hell. I need whatever pain reliever you have around here."

Sivilla pointed to the desk. "Big bottle of aspirin in the top right drawer. What else?"

"I need that packet I gave you."

"You told me it was important."

"It is, now more than ever."

"Alright, it's here somewhere."

Tasia helped herself to a handful of aspirin and some cold tea from the corner of the desk while Sivilla dug through the stacks of paper. She handed Tasia the taped-up, oversized envelope just as Jon opened the door. His shirtfront and jacket were sopping wet, but the bloodstains appeared far less pronounced. Tasia was confident they could board the train without undue attention. Sivilla pursed her lips and let her eyes shamelessly roam over Jon's large frame.

"Glad to see, sweetheart, when you finally picked one, you made sure he was beautiful!" She stepped over, placed her hands flat on Jon's wet chest, stood on her tiptoes and brought her face within inches of his. "Do you have a name, comrade, or should I call you Lucky Guy?"

Jon hesitated. "Ivan Drago."

"You have a beautiful princess here, Ivan," Sivilla said and nodded in Tasia's direction. "Pure sexy ass royalty, in my mind. You'd better treat her right."

"Guaranteed," Jon said.

"Right answer, comrade." Sivilla patted his cheek, lowered her hands, and took two steps backward. "She's the truest friend I ever had, and we've been through a ton of crap together. I said it was mistake when she first got involved with that *zhopa*, Kryuchkov." She rolled her eyes and stuck out her tongue. "She was nursing a broken heart at the time. Some foreign guy she had met in France."

"Really?" Jon said.

"Oh yes, whatever happened over there tore her up something bad. Cried herself to sleep for weeks. Her heart was so soft and tender in those days."

Tasia, caught off guard by her friend's admission, blushed a deep red.

"It can be again," Jon said with a smile.

"True enough," Sivilla said as she moved aside some papers and leaned against the desk. "Sweetheart told me the two of you are leaving. Don't know how you managed it, but you should be congratulated on convincing her to complete what I had her start back in the day. I was the one who persuaded her to accept the consequences, as painful as they were, and tell that evil creep he couldn't have her anymore."

"That price was too high, Siv," Tasia said. "I'm only realizing that now."

"Don't you dare talk that way," Sivilla said as her eyes darkened. "He would have killed you if you'd stayed and you know it. You and I needed to find a way to keep you alive back then, just like you and Ivan do now."

Tasia smiled and brushed a stray lock of hair from her eyes. "We really do have to go."

Sivilla stepped forward and took Tasia's hands. She swung them back and forth as if they were children again and she wanted her friend to come play one last time. "Alright, one more question. Serious now. When will I see you again?"

"I have no idea, Siv," Tasia said. "I promise to contact you as soon as it's safe. Remember, if anyone asks, you haven't seen me."

"Got it," Sivilla said. "Treat her right, Lucky Guy."

Tasia and Sivilla gave each other tight hugs, then kisses on each cheek. The three of them left the small room and weaved through the crowded café floor to the front door. Sivilla waved them goodbye, and they stepped through the door.

Tasia donned her sunglasses again. The bag on her shoulder felt slightly heavier, and that comforted her. She led them toward the entrance to the Kuznetskiy Most Metro Terminal across the street. They were halfway there when two men—one tall, the other thin—stepped out from behind a stone archway. The tall one reached into his jacket.

"Jon!" Tasia shouted.

Jon yanked her off the street. Two other men came up behind them and one grabbed her arm.

"Good night, General."

Something jabbed into her back. The man let go of her arm and Tasia felt like she had been set on fire.

Everything went black.

CHAPTER 16

Approximately 11:00 AM, Moscow Time, Monday, August 19, 1991

"Gotten any sleep, Dick?" Tripper McKenzie set down his coffee cup and spoke into his Embassy phone connection to Washington, DC.

"Hopefully soon," Dick Kerr said with a yawn. "It's three thirty in the blessed morning over here, and I'm running on fumes. Been sending your intel up to Scowcroft in Maine. He heard about the thing a few hours ago on CNN. What's the latest?"

"Tanks are all over the city. A huge number of them are watching the Parliament Building and Yeltsin. There's also a large group moving in on Red Square. Several hundred tanks and several thousand troops as best we can tell. Hate to say I told you so."

"Yeah, yeah," Kerr said. "Still, from our perspective, does any of this really matter? Life seems fairly normal over there from what you say."

"Well, the trains still run on time, if that's what you mean. We just heard Yeltsin's called a press conference. Foot traffic over there has grown steadily as the morning's gone by."

"The president doesn't think much of Boris Yeltsin. We're going to be hard pressed to convince him to do much of anything if he's the focal point."

"Don't underestimate the guy," Tripper said. He heard Kerr yawn again on the other end.

"We're in a wait-and-see pattern, at least for now," Kerr said. "Keep feeding me updates. Scowcroft tells me the president's worried if we weigh in too soon, we might piss off whoever comes out on top. It's essential we pick the right horse here. What else?"

"The princess operation."

"You were going to extract the two of them this afternoon, weren't you?"

"Yeah, but I can't get over there now because of all the tanks in the streets. Also, Jon didn't check in with me this morning."

"Damn," Kerr said. "You think they've been made?"

"Maybe. At this point, I think we need to prepare for two possibilities."

"Which are?"

"I've briefed the guards out front to be on the lookout for them. Our contingency plan was for Jon to get the general over here by any means available. At this point, that likely means on foot."

"And the other one?"

"If they don't show up here, or contact us soon, they're probably already dead."

Jon opened his eyes. It was hard to think. He needed to gauge his surroundings.

Back seat of a car. In motion, can't tell how fast. Someone warm beside me. Likely Tasia, but she's not moving. Front seat is quiet. Stay still.

He closed his eyes and tried to take stock of what had happened.

Groggy, extremities tingling. Stun gun of some kind. Jaw hurts, sharp pain on the side of the face, sore all over. Likely from falling to the concrete. Possibly received a few kicks.

He flexed his fingers and toes. Everything seemed to work. His awareness slowly grew. Handcuffs bit into his wrists. His shoulder holster was still in place. From the weight, it was empty. His belt was still around his waist. If he could slip out one of the small knives in the back, the handcuffs should be easy enough to open. He cracked his eyelids into tiny slits and quietly set to work.

Two men sat in the front seat. The taller one was behind the wheel. A thin, wispy one occupied the passenger seat. No partition divided the front of the vehicle from the back. Jon felt sure the back doors would be locked, but for what he had in mind, it would not matter.

Four men had ambushed them. Where were the other two? If they were in a second car behind them, that would make things tough.

Tasia stirred and the driver looked into the rearview mirror.

"Where are your escorts, bitch?"

Tasia groaned. "What are you talking about?"

"Don't play stupid with me! The two KGB men who walked out of the Savoy alongside you, where are they?"

Keep them talking Tasia, Jon thought.

"We, uh, eluded them," Tasia said. "It wasn't hard."

"Like hell!" the driver said. "Those were elite Ninth Directorate men. What happened to them?"

Jon opened his eyes, smiled and looked into the driver's reflected face. "They encountered Archangel," he said in Russian.

The driver became visibly upset. "Alekhin, radio Kostin and Patrushev. Tell them they need to retrace the route on foot. Archangel's killed them both!"

"Yes, Lieutenant." The thin man picked up a hand radio from the center console. Jon worked his cheeks back and forth to build up saliva.

"You traitorous whore!" the driver yelled. "Killing our own men! I ought to pull over right now and blow your brains out, orders be damned!"

"My methods will be more appropriate, Lieutenant," the thin man said with a hand over the radio's mouthpiece.

"What does that mean?" Tasia asked.

The lieutenant snorted. "Alekhin here is one of our most talented technicians. He has some special surprises in store when we reach the safehouse."

"I will need to verify the facilities are ready," the skinny man said as he set down the radio. "My instruments haven't been sterilized yet either."

"Not a problem," the lieutenant said. "The *mudak* needs to verify the papers in her bag first."

The turd? Jon thought. *That seems an odd code name for their boss.*

"You should feel honored, General," the technician said as he leaned over the armrest. "I've been given unlimited time to work on you. First, I shall shave every follicle of hair from your beautiful body. Then I'll rub you down with alcohol from head to toe." The little man's eyes lost focus and his voice took on a dreamy lilt. "I will start at the bottoms of your feet and work my way up. My scalpels are very sharp. It will take me hours to cut away your entire epidermis, but I need no respite when working on a beautiful specimen like you. Strip by strip, piece by piece, slice and peel. You will bleed to death, of course, but rest assured you will remain awake the entire time, thanks to the drugs we'll administer. The best part is when I finish with your face. You'll see the results yourself."

Jon felt Tasia tremble beside him. *Almost out of time*, he thought. The handcuff sprung open with a click.

Jon thrust his body upward. He jerked his head from side to side and widened his eyes. Foamy saliva spewed from his mouth. He fell back to the seat and bounced up and down.

"Dammit!" the lieutenant yelled. "He has a cyanide capsule!"

"Pull over! Pull over!" the technician ordered.

The driver sped up, then yanked the wheel over. The car bounced up and down and Jon heard the noise of something rough and raw underneath them. The driver hit the brake and slammed the car into park. The skinny man leapt out and yanked the back door open. Jon's shoulder landed hard on gravel, and he rolled onto his back, convulsing wildly with spittle dribbling down his chin.

"Get it out! Get it out!" the lieutenant yelled.

The little man straddled Jon's waist and attempted to force his fingers past his clenched teeth. The lieutenant extended his right arm over the back seat, silenced Makarov at the ready.

Jon slashed upward in an X motion and sliced through the technician's carotids with his small razor needles. Blood sprayed in all directions.

Tasia's teeth tore into the KGB man's exposed wrist at the same moment he pulled the trigger. The silenced shot flew wild. The technician fell to the ground, hands at his throat. The lieutenant brought his free hand around and pounded the crown of Tasia's head. She let go of his wrist and dropped to the floorboard.

Jon charged and drove the large razor knife into the lieutenant's left eye. The man jerked and twitched, firing another round into the roof. Jon held fast until certain the grisly job was complete. The Makarov fell to the floorboard. Jon pulled the blade free and shoved the corpse against the door.

"Tasia! Tasia, are you alright?"

Tasia exploded into a fit of Russian profanity. Jon could not understand most of it, the words came so fast. Blood covered her teeth and chin and spewed in all directions as she yelled. She rose up and spit toward the lieutenant's body. She took a breath, turned, and spat at Jon.

"You lousy, American sonofabitch!" she yelled. "I thought you were committing suicide on me!"

"I know, Tasia, I know! I'm sorry! I'm sorry!"

"Damn you, Archangel!" She rattled the handcuffs behind her back. "Get these things off me!"

"Sorry I'm late, doctor," Yuri said as he took off his newly cleaned trenchcoat.

The oversized space had no windows. The harsh white light from the industrial fluorescent tubes mounted in the ceiling made the room appear bright as midday. The blue-and-white checkered tile on both the floor and the walls, plus the white porcelain sinks and countertops, gave the room the impression of being one massive public bathroom. The antiseptic odor of ethyl alcohol overpowered all other smells.

Yuri handed his coat to the shorter of his two attendants and walked to the operating table in the center of the room. "I presume the subjects have not arrived yet?" he asked.

The balding older man in blue scrubs and rubber gloves raised his thin glasses.

"Comrade Zolotov? I was not aware you would be here, young man."

"I would advise you not to patronize me, doctor," Yuri said as he unclipped his belt holster from the small of his back.

The doctor raised his hand to his mouth and coughed. "I meant no offense. My apologies."

Yuri put his Makarov and belt holster into the hand of the taller man behind him. "I'll repeat my original question, doctor. Are the subjects here yet?"

"Not yet. I expect them shortly."

"Good." Yuri circled the operating table and yanked on its leather straps. He turned and fingered the variety of scalpels and other medical instruments on the adjacent metal cart.

"Where are the medical gowns and gloves, doctor?"

"In the upright cabinet along the wall." The doctor motioned with his hand. "May I ask why you need them?"

"You may not, actually," Yuri said, "although I will tell you anyway. I intend to assist you with the castration of the American agent."

"That is really not necessary—"

"You're trying my patience, doctor."

"Comrade Zolotov, you are not medically trained. I would prefer—"

"What you prefer doesn't matter." Yuri looked at the two agents standing along the wall near the door. "Why do people keep telling me what they prefer?" Neither man spoke; they only smirked.

"Let's start over," Yuri said. "I will tell you how things will go, and you will comply without comment. Am I clear?"

"Yes, Comrade Zolotov," the doctor said with a nod.

"Our task is simple," Yuri continued. "The American is to be castrated as soon as he and my mother arrive. The operation is to be performed without anesthetic with the subject awake and aware."

"It will be impossible to keep him still without sedation."

"The table restraints will suffice. Also, my mother is to witness the castration. My men will hold her down if necessary." He motioned toward the two men who had accompanied him. "She needs to learn the bloody price of treason."

The doctor looked at his shoes. "I was told there would be only one subject today?"

"You are correct," Yuri said. "A technician will handle my mother's interrogation. He supposedly brings his own equipment. I plan to assist him as well."

"Very well, sir," the old man said. "You will need to put on your gown and scrub up. We will also need to be masked. I understand this American must not contract any subsequent infection."

"Correct again," Yuri said. "He is to be kept alive and, in a condition where he can publicly stand trial. I also wish for him to witness at least the bulk of my mother's interrogation. Is that a reasonable possibility?"

The door slammed open before the doctor could reply. A short, overly excited uniformed agent ran into the room.

"Comrade Zolotov!"

"What?"

"The agents with the prisoners, sir." The small man tried to catch his breath. "They will not respond to our calls. We've checked the transponder on their vehicle, and it appears to be stationary."

Yuri's eyes widened and he snarled. "I told them not to underestimate that American!" He kicked the leg of the operating table. "Where is the vehicle?"

"*Butyrskaya*, just north of *Ulitsa Suchchovskiy*."

Yuri pointed at the doctor. "You remain here." He turned to the men along the wall. "Yushin, grab my weapon and coat. We need to go."

CHAPTER 17

11:30 AM, Moscow Time, Monday, August 19, 1991

Jon found the key in the lieutenant's pockets and promptly removed Tasia's cuffs. She rubbed her wrists, stepped out of the car, and looked around.

They were parked in a dilapidated grass-and-gravel alcove inset within a four-story warehouse of some sort. The main highway sat only a few yards away, but the alcove was so deeply recessed, the heavy traffic going past could not see them. The building had no windows on this side. The only entrance was a rusty iron door with a large sign in Cyrillic lettering that read *Keep out! Ring bell for deliveries.*

The two of them picked up the technician's body and stuffed it into the trunk. They left the lieutenant where he was. They retrieved Jon's Makarov, along with his spare ammunition, as well as Tasia's bag with all its contents. Her sunglasses were nowhere to be found, likely lost when she fell onto the pavement. Jon locked the car and Tasia checked him over. His face and front were literally drenched in the technician's blood.

"Come here, you bloodthirsty American murderer," she said as she untied her scarf.

"Tasia don't be like this. I did what was necessary to save our lives."

"I know that, *govnyuk.*" She rubbed the rapidly crusting blood from his face and neck with the scarf.

"So *shithead* is my new name now?" he said in English.

"Only because I can't think of anything worse," Tasia said in Russian. She rubbed his face harder. "I'm not ready to forgive you for making me think you were abandoning me by dying."

"Tasia, you should know I would never do that."

"Should! Yes, I damn well should!" She licked the dry portion of the scarf in hopes some saliva might help. The blood splatters were simply too large and too obvious. Clever positioning was no longer a viable option for them to walk the streets unnoticed.

"Come with me," Tasia said.

A small gas station stood on the other side of the brick fence next to them. Tasia led Jon across the parking lot to the wooden dumpster pen along the wall.

"Stay here," she said, "and don't kill yourself while I'm gone."

Tasia went into the store and bought two large bottles of Sitro lemonade and a bar of lye soap. She asked the bored, greasy attendant for the key to the outside restroom. Thanks to a rough and thorough scrubbing, which Tasia enjoyed far too much, Jon became generally presentable within a few minutes, although sopping wet.

"Come on, we need to get away from here," Tasia said after she returned the restroom key. The lemonade, plus her exertions with the soap, had made her feel a thousand times better.

"Where exactly are we, sweetheart?"

"Don't call me that," Tasia said. "Only Sivilla gets to use that word." The two of them turned in a general easterly direction. "We are still in the city, believe it or not. Moscow is enormous. *Ulitsa Butyrskaya* runs alongside us. Industrial area, fairly busy road. *Mendeleyevskaya* Metro Station is just a short distance south."

Tasia looked both ways.

"We can take the Gray Line to *Chekhovskaya.* It's only one stop to the embassy from there. If we cut through a few alleys in this direction." She motioned to the left. "We're less likely to be seen."

"They'll be coming after us, you know."

"That's why we need to move fast."

Yuri knew what had happened when he saw the blood on the gravel. It had taken much longer than expected to find the car. KGB vehicle transponders were generally accurate, but the tanks and troops in the streets had created an enormous number of traffic problems.

"Try the doors," Yuri said as the wind flapped the edges of his trenchcoat. His men wore civilian clothes with light vinyl jackets.

"Locked, sir," Yushin said.

"Force them." Yuri glanced at the large rainclouds overhead. "We need to hurry."

They worked the doors and trunk open and discovered the bodies. A light sprinkle began. Yuri pulled out his handkerchief and held it over his nose and mouth.

"No rigor mortis," Yushin said. "This happened not long ago, sir."

"Damn," Yuri said. "Alright, presuming they're headed for the American Embassy, what's the most logical route from here?"

"*Mendeleyevskaya* Metro Station," Golovkin said. "It's only a short distance south."

"Still, quite a way for two people walking," Yuri said as he looked into the distance. "Yushin, take the car and get to *Mendeleyevskaya* as fast as you can. You have a general idea from which direction they'll come. Golovkin and I will pursue them on foot."

The one called Yushin glanced at the two corpses. "Sir, this American is apparently much more dangerous than we realized. Shouldn't we call for assistance?"

"No one could get here quickly enough in all this traffic," Yuri lied. He was not about to share his prize. "Let's go."

Tasia had just purchased their Metro tickets when Jon noticed a squat, dark-haired man in a vinyl jacket scanning the crowds.

"Tasia, careful. Look toward the far entrance doors. Do you recognize him?"

"Yes," Tasia said. "Dmitri Yushin with the *Mokryye Dela*. He took part in the suppression attempt in Lithuania back in January. A known killer and very, very good at it."

A voice over the loudspeaker announced the arrival of the next train. "That's ours," Tasia said. "We need to get down to the platform."

The main lobby at *Mendeleyevskaya* was huge, with inlaid stone tiles and high marble archways. Unfortunately, it was not overly crowded. If Jon and Tasia stepped into the open, the KGB man was sure to see them.

"I have an idea," Jon said. "Duck your head inside my jacket."

"I won't be able to see."

"You know how to dance?"

"Better than you, I'll wager."

"Pretend we're dancing and I'm leading."

"I suppose I can follow this one time."

Jon gently pulled Tasia's face to his still-wet chest and the two of them moved in sync into the lobby area. He slipped in among a large family on their way to the departure platforms. Yushin stepped toward one of the far stairwells as Jon and Tasia entered their own. The arriving train's brakes screeched, as they stepped onto the packed platform. Jon scanned the crowd to locate the KGB man. The two men locked eyes as the train's doors swished open.

Jon grabbed Tasia around the waist and lifted her off the ground. He held her tight to his chest as they plunged through the oncoming sea of bodies. The two of them stepped inside the crowded train car and the doors slid shut behind them.

Jon set Tasia down and turned. Yushin stood only inches away on the other side of the glass. Jon glared in defiance as the *Mokryye Dela* man reached into his jacket. The train started to move. Jon raised an eyebrow when the thickset KGB man pulled out a radio. The train picked up speed and the platform disappeared from sight.

Jon turned back around, and Tasia snaked one arm around his waist. "Love that lye soap, *govnyuk*. Makes you smell all fresh, clean, and sexy." She rubbed her nose along his still-damp collar. "I might have to forgive you for scaring me half to death earlier. How about I strip those filthy wet clothes from that amazing body of yours later and give you a nice hot bath?"

Jon met her eyes. "Yushin saw us board the train. He was talking into a radio as we pulled away."

Tasia's smile vanished. "Our destination is obvious," she said.

CHAPTER 18

A few minutes before noon, Moscow Time, Monday, August 19, 1991

The train had barely departed *Mendeleyevskaya* when the inevitable finally happened.

"Mother Russia!" someone yelled.

A buzz spread through the tight passenger compartment. Even though there was hardly room, the crowd backed away to get a better look at their famous comrade. Tasia could feel everyone's eyes upon her, so she turned to face the people, smiled broadly, raised her arm, and waved. Applause rippled through the compartment.

"I am delighted to be with you this morning, comrades!" She raised her voice to be heard over the noise of the train. "Thank you for remembering me!"

"We love you, Mother!" someone said from the crowd.

From one of the seats along the far side of the car, a *babushka* stood up. Barely four feet tall, the old woman wore a long peasant's skirt and headscarf. Her gnarled hands clutched a large, embroidered cloth bag.

"Mother," the old woman said in a clear voice. "You must do something. Our government has been stolen from us. We will follow you, Mother! Save us!"

Multiple voices repeated the old woman's words. "Save us Mother!" someone else said. "We need you!"

"Comrades! Friends!" Tasia yelled as she raised both hands. "You are correct! Traitors and thieves have stolen our country from us!" The rumbling of the crowd grew louder as she spoke. "I stand for you, comrades, and for the people of Russia! We must not allow this to happen!"

Shouts of agreement echoed back and forth.

"Mother! President Yeltsin has asked us to come to the Parliament Building! Many of us are headed there now!"

"Did you hear that, friends?" Tasia yelled. "President Yeltsin is leading the resistance! We must join him! Mother Russia calls on everyone who loves our beautiful country to follow her!"

The crowd murmured their approval. The *babushka* who first stood began to chant, and others quickly joined in. "Mother Russia! Mother Russia! Mother Russia!"

Soon the chanting filled the entire compartment.

"I'll be damned," Jon whispered in English.

"Get ready, *govnyuk*," Tasia whispered into his ear. "These wonderful Russian patriots are about to escort their mother all the way to the United States Embassy."

In the hallway of the Russian Parliament Building, a panting young aide ran toward Boris Yeltsin.

"Mr. President! Mr. President!" he said. "T—there are troops outside. They appear to be converging on this building."

"How many?" Yeltsin asked.

"At least ten armored personnel carriers. Perhaps a dozen tanks. Maybe more."

"How many people are out front?"

"Fifty or sixty, as near as we can tell."

"Comrades," the Russian president said to his surrounding staff. "Let us take a walk outside."

The doors on the arriving train at *Smolenskaya* Metro Station swooshed open and Tasia stepped onto the loading platform amidst chants and cheers.

"Mother Russia! Mother Russia! Mother Russia!"

She clicked her heels together, raised both hands into a Y and threw back her head as if to announce to the world a member of the Russian royal family had arrived. Applause from the platform quickly joined in with the chants from the train. Tasia pointed toward the marble steps. Her followers fell in behind her.

A wave of intense euphoria washed over her. Was this what real power felt like? A tremendous zeal for the wellbeing of her fellow countrymen consumed her heart and spirit. How could this be something evil? She understood why men like Kryuchkov might crave it, but why did it have to poison them? She suddenly knew what she was meant to do. This was the moment she was born for, the moment she had suffered all those years to achieve. For the good of her people, she would act. Mother Russia would save her children.

Smolenskaya's lobby area was a massive space. A huge concrete dome gleamed high above the marble floor as hundreds of people came and went at varying levels of hurriedness. An alcove containing an enormous white-stone *bas relief* dominated the main wall. Well over twenty feet high, it depicted the struggles of the Communist revolution, complete with cannons, flags and charging workers. Tasia marched across the floor, knocked over the rope in front of the depiction and stepped in front of its marble base so everyone could see her. Her followers gathered around.

"People of Russia!" The building's structural acoustics acted like a natural amplifier. Her voice boomed throughout the space. "Friends, comrades, and patriots!" She raised her arms. "I am Mother Russia!"

Everyone stopped. All eyes were on her.

"Our country has been stolen from us! President Gorbachev has been taken prisoner and traitors have seized control. President Yeltsin is our only hope! He needs us, friends, and the time is now! Follow me to the Parliament Building!"

She mimicked the scene behind her and pointed toward the front exit. It seemed as if everyone there was hers to command. The mob took on a life of its own as more and more people joined the exodus for freedom. Tasia led the way and rammed open the ornate wooden doors that led to the brick pavement circle out front. A tremendous number of people followed behind her. The chanting began again.

"Mother Russia! Mother Russia! Mother Russia!"

A light rain was falling. Tasia pointed north and set off along the wide sidewalk that bordered Garden Ring Road, the main thoroughfare that encircled the city. The chants behind her echoed up and down the street, despite the traffic noise next to them.

Tasia heard Jon speak to some of the people around her and suddenly he and three burly men she did not know picked her bodily off the ground. They raised her onto their shoulders, and she swayed slightly in the wet breeze. She caught her balance and waved not only to the crowds behind but also at the long line of cars sitting still beside her. Horns honked in support while the chants grew louder. Hundreds of people joined in from all directions. Tasia shook her hair into the breeze, a red banner for them all to follow.

They reached Kalinin Avenue, and she directed them toward the river and Boris Yeltsin.

Yeltsin strode out the front doors of the Russian Parliament building, a copy of his appeal to the citizens in his hand. Half a dozen aides scampered behind him like frightened mice. One of them carried the mid-sized version of the Russian flag he had asked them to retrieve. The white, blue, and red Imperial flag was a replica of the one the people carried when they toppled the Tsar in early 1917, months before Lenin and his Bolsheviks came to power.

"Mr. President, you cannot be out here!" an aide yelled. "The danger from snipers!" Yeltsin pretended not to hear. Several other aides grabbed his arms. "I am curious," he said as he shook them away. "I must see what is happening out here."

Yeltsin felt a surge of energy from the tiny crowd that swarmed around him as he moved down the steps. A light drizzle fell from the grey clouds. He buttoned his brown suit jacket, more for the cameras than against the raindrops.

A harsh and oily grind of metal gears grew louder. A T-72, twelve-wheeled, olive-green behemoth led the way. Two others were behind it. People lined the roadway, some waving small tricolor Russian flags. Yeltsin reached for one with a smile and a nod as he passed. A few of his aides followed, but most stayed on the steps.

The front tank moved toward him. The bore of its main cannon pointed down.

There is no way they will run over the President of Russia, Yeltsin thought. *There is simply no way.*

The enormous metal monster lumbered closer as Yeltsin stopped at the edge of the roadway. He looked forward without blinking, the small flag held up beside him. A screeching noise, so loud it hurt his ears, erupted directly in front of him. The barrel of the forty-five-ton death machine's main cannon halted only feet from his face. In the distance, he heard chants but could not make out what they said.

The sixty-year-old Yeltsin took a breath. It was imperative he portray the image of calm. His opponent had just blinked, and he was not about to waste the opportunity. The Russian president reached for the step bar and with a grunt clambered to the top of the tank. Several nearby men joined him. People surrounded the tank from all sides within seconds.

Yeltsin handed his flag to someone and reached into the open hatch. He shook hands with the tank's commander, turned, and shook the hand of the young dark-haired soldier at its mounted machine gun. More people climbed atop the tank from all sides.

Yeltsin stood upright and turned to face the cameras. A sea of humanity surrounded him. Thousands had filled the space from every direction where moments before there were merely a handful. The chants on the ground grew louder. Someone unfurled the Imperial Russian flag next to him.

A smile on his face, the Russian president raised his fist into the sky and shook it twice.

Jon saw Boris Yeltsin, along with maybe a dozen others, on top of the tank a few hundred feet in front of them. He smiled when the Russian president took up the *Mother Russia* chant and directed those around him to do the same. He pulled Tasia down from the men's shoulders as her people flooded the area around them.

"Tasia!" he shouted in her ear. "Yeltsin looks like he's about to speak. This is our chance. The embassy's just a couple hundred yards up the hill."

"Let's move then," she said.

Jon grabbed her hand and the two of them made their way through the tightly packed crowd. Tasia's celebrity status had worked in their favor so far, but as attention turned toward Yeltsin, they became vulnerable again.

The crowd thinned as they approached its edge, but Jon stopped short a few seconds before they completely broke cover. Three men in different colored trench coats, with tight buzz cuts and flinty faces, leaned against the iron-spiked fence that bordered the back side of the embassy. Jon pivoted right and headed toward the opposite corner, careful to stay surrounded by as many people as possible.

Hands clutched tight, the two of them moved slowly inside the periphery of the crowd. The KGB men watched Yeltsin with evident interest as the Russian president spoke from atop the tank. The Embassy gates stood over the rise. Jon quietly edged their way out of the crowd. A heavy breeze blew in from the river and everyone looked eastward to keep the rain out of their eyes. All three KGB men turned their heads at the same time and locked onto Tasia's red hair.

"Run!" she shouted.

Hands still together, Tasia and Jon leapt forward at sprinter's speed. The KGB men ran to cut them off.

"Make for the gate!" Jon yelled.

The two of them ran into the street along the Embassy's side entrance. The KGB men ran in a straighter line, giving them the shorter distance. Jon poured on the speed. Tasia was a half-step behind. The KGB men were barely feet away.

"Open the gate! Open the gate!" Jon shouted in English as they came within range. "American citizen! American citizen!"

The mechanical gate cranked open. The two of them ran for the crack and Jon slid through, but he lost Tasia's hand, and she fell face first onto the pavement. Jon turned. She was laying half inside, half out. Two guards with M16's ran toward them from the gate shack.

The KGB man with the brown coat grabbed Tasia's legs and pulled. Jon saw her eyes go wide as she tried to dig her fingernails into the pavement. He leapt over her like a gazelle and punched the KGB man hard in the mouth. He went down like a felled tree.

The other two KGB men raised their fists, but Jon snarled and shook his clawed fingers at them, ready to tear their throats out. The wolf inside him was out for blood and it undoubtedly showed. Tripper McKenzie's voice yelled somewhere behind him.

"Get back in here, Jon! She's safe now!"

Out of breath, Jon sucked in oxygen and looked at each standing KGB man in turn. The taller one wore a blue trenchcoat, the shorter one tan. A crowd had formed along the fence. Both Embassy guards appeared on each side of him, their rifles sending the unmistakable signal no further trouble would be tolerated. Jon raised his hands slightly and walked backward. His teeth stayed bared, and his eyes focused on the KGB men until he was inside the gate.

"I—I'm—Jonathan—Cole," he said to the two guards beside him.

"We know, sir," one of them said. "Mr. McKenzie told us to watch for you."

"Thank God for Tripper." Jon wheezed as he caught his breath. He turned around and saw Tripper helping Tasia across the lot to the Embassy doors. He looked back at the crowd.

The smaller of the KGB men helped up the man Jon had punched. The taller one, with a sour-looking face and sandy brown hair, came within feet of the gate. He stared at Jon with disgust and spit on the pavement. Jon stepped to the fence. Neither of them blinked.

"It's over," Jon said in Russian. "She's with us now. Time for you to move on."

"No way, American," the man said. "You think you're in control now, but you're wrong. She will not live out the night in there, I assure you."

"Sounds like empty talk to me."

"You keep thinking that, American," the man said. "The KGB always cleans up its loose ends."

CHAPTER 19

A few minutes before 1:00 PM, Moscow Time,
Monday, August 19, 1991

Tasia's hands were scraped and bleeding when Tripper McKenzie helped her through the Embassy doors and into its main reception area. A well-dressed man with a square white haircut and equally square eyeglasses walked toward her with several young staffers trailing behind.

"Mr. Acting Ambassador," a beaming Tripper said as they met in the middle of the marble floor. "Let me introduce Major General Anastasia Aleksandrovna Zolotova, head of the Special Investigations Directorate for the KGB." He turned to Tasia. "General, this is Chargé d'affaires James Franklin Collins."

"Mr. Collins," Tasia said in English as she extended her hand. "It is an honor to meet you." Collins took it and she winced slightly.

"It is my pleasure, General," Collins said, slightly bowing. "Welcome to the United States. Please, permit me to offer you more comfortable surroundings."

"Thank you," Tasia said. She looked around and was about to ask where Jon was when she saw him walk through the door behind them. She deliberately stayed where she was until he caught up. She reached for his hand and looked back at Collins.

"We're at your service, Mr. Collins. Please lead the way."

Collins led the small group through the spacious lobby, then to an open flight of stairs. Tasia was sore from her fall and leaned slightly on Jon as they walked up. They entered a large conference area on the second floor with a high ceiling and a crystal chandelier. Ornate blue-and-gold benches lined the walls between the arched windows, and a long mahogany table with cushioned chairs dominated the middle of the room.

"Make yourselves comfortable," Collins said. He sat at the head of the table while several staff members joined them. 'We've got refreshments on the way up."

"Thank you," Tasia said as she eased herself into one of the chairs. She glanced sideways at Jon who sat next to her. "Both of us are quite exhausted."

"Mr. Collins, I'm Jonathan Cole."

"You've done both the general and your country a great service, Officer Cole," Collins said. "Your dramatic entrance makes me think we'll hear about this on the diplomatic front."

"I'm afraid it's worse than you think, sir," Jon said. "We had to remove four KGB operatives to get over here, not to mention holding off three others at the gate. I had a rather tense conversation with one of them. He told me the general would not live out the night in here."

Tasia's head jerked around.

"Empty threats," Tripper said.

"I'm not so sure," Jon said. He laid his hand atop hers, but it did not make her feel any better. "The KGB goon was smug, rubbing my nose in something."

Collins sharply inhaled. "General, it seems you are a hot commodity."

"I can explain why," Tasia said. She reached for her bag on the floor, pulled out the taped-up, oversized envelope Sivilla had given her and laid it on the table. "This packet contains pages of financial transactions which show billions in Communist Party funds transferred outside the Soviet Union into foreign accounts. These destination accounts are not government or intelligence-related, but personal."

"Soviet golden parachutes," Tripper said.

"I do not understand that reference," Tasia said, "but I think you are correct. This documentation confirms these personal accounts belong specifically to Vladimir Kryuchkov, Boris Pugo, and several others."

"Good God," Collins said.

"So much for the good of the people," Tripper said.

"The KGB has tried to kill General Zolotova three times already," Jon said. "She was also assaulted by Vladimir Kryuchkov himself earlier this morning and fell outside a few minutes ago." He glanced over at Tripper. "She could use some medical attention."

"We'll get someone up here right away," Collins said. He nodded to one of the staffers who hurried from the room.

"Mr. Collins, I do not wish to seem ungrateful or difficult," Tasia said. She tried to keep her voice even, but the reality of her situation was beginning to set in. "But with everything that has happened to me, coupled with Jon's conversation at the gate, I am more afraid for my life than ever."

"Let me give you some comfort on that, General," Collins said. "Our security here at the embassy is the finest in the world. We have the most sophisticated electronic systems, as well as large numbers of highly trained personnel whose sole job is to keep everyone here safe. I promise you, nothing, absolutely nothing, is more important to us than your safety."

"I thank you for those kind words, Mr. Collins," Tasia said, "and I am certain every one of them is true. Nevertheless, I strongly request you remand me to the United States proper as quickly as possible. Given the growing crisis all around us, I will never feel completely safe in here while Vladimir controls the world outside your gates."

"We have a method to get you there, General," Tripper said.

"I'm glad to hear that, Mr. McKenzie," Tasia said as she squeezed Jon's hand. "In the meantime, I would like to request Officer Cole remain with me at all times. Please understand my trepidation and do not take offense."

"Not to worry, General," Collins said. "We will work hard to prove our trustworthiness. Ambassador Matlock has recently retired, and Ambassador Strauss has not yet arrived, so the ambassadorial suite is currently unoccupied, if a little bare. I can offer you that space as a secure residence while you're with us. Also, if we can get your sizes and a list of your other needs, we will send out for some clean clothes and personal items for both you and Officer Cole."

A sharp knock sounded. The conference room door opened before Collins could respond.

"Sorry for the intrusion, sir," a young staffer said. "Andrei Kozyrev, the Russian Minister of Foreign Affairs is downstairs. He asks if you can come to the Russian Parliament building right away. President Yeltsin wants to speak with you."

Deputy National Security Advisor Robert Gates thanked Jim Collins for his call.

"Take care over there, Jim," he said. "We're watching the situation very closely. Expect to hear back from us quickly."

Gates hung up the phone, punched in the extension for the White House switchboard and asked to be connected with Air Force One. His boss, Brent Scowcroft, sounded calm as usual.

"Brent, the text of this letter Boris Yeltsin gave Jim Collins is clear. He's asking for the return of Gorbachev to power. This is not some countercoup or hidden agenda we're not seeing. The boss has got to be okay with us going along with this."

"Sounds like a remarkable change of events," Scowcroft said. "A couple hours ago, Yeltsin's movement seemed about to wither on the vine."

"It very nearly did. Collins told me even as late as when Yeltsin stepped out of the Parliament Building, only a small number of supporters had gathered there. When the tanks moved in though, an enormous number of people suddenly arrived out of nowhere, all chanting and marching to join Yeltsin's cause. Their enthusiastic support is what the cameras captured. If it weren't for that last minute arrival, the pictures the world is seeing now would look very different."

"CNN has a repeating video of Yeltsin on that damn tank," Scowcroft said. "Thanks to that image, support for him is growing exponentially."

"It's in the homes of most of the folks in Moscow too," Gates said. "Collins and crew are picking it up off the airwaves over there. Brent, I think we need to go stronger here. It's time to throw the dice."

Gates waited while Scowcroft considered. The president had made a cautious statement a few hours earlier. The images of Yeltsin on the tank, though, surrounded by massive cheering crowds, had changed everything.

"Alright, Bob," Scowcroft said. "I'll speak to the president. We should be back in Washington shortly."

"What do you mean they got away?"

Boris Pugo grabbed the ornate brass clock on his desk and hurled it with both hands at the oil painting on the opposite wall, one of the few early copies of Boris Kustodiev's *The Bolshevik* from 1920. The springs and gears of the clock exploded; the metallic crash echoed up and down the halls of the Soviet Interior Ministry. Pugo jumped to his feet before the sound faded.

Yuri quietly stood, uncertain what he would do if the Interior Minister actually assaulted him.

"Sir, this is to our advantage," the young man said with a raised voice.

"Oh no, boy!" Pugo came around his desk, index finger raised. "Your traitorous mother is at the US Embassy now. The Americans have all her proof against both me and your father."

"So?" Yuri said. "All they have are a bunch of complicated financial documents and my mother's words. It will take time for this to become any real threat. The *GKChP* is in full control now. It's a matter of perspective going forward. One that stems from whoever controls the political narrative."

Pugo glared at him.

"I understand the United States just made a stronger statement against us?" Yuri said. "Surely this was expected at some point. The press conference you are preparing is the real battlefield now, sir. You and my father will win the struggle there, no matter what Boris Yeltsin does. While that moment holds the world's attention, I will have my mother removed right under the Americans' noses."

"What?"

"We have an embedded operative inside the US Embassy. My mother's actual defection jeopardizes our intelligence operations on a near-global scale. Her death without delay is more imperative than ever."

"I've been telling you that all along!" Pugo said.

"Our operative will remove both my mother and her American lover this evening," Yuri said. "In the dead of night so we do not jeopardize his position. Regarding yours and my father's personal issues, without my mother's testimony, the papers she brought over can easily be denied as a propaganda falsification on the part of the Americans. If they attempt anything at all without her, which is doubtful."

Pugo's eyes burned with barely dampened fire. "You've had a number of chances to do this, boy. Why should I think this time will be any different?"

"If I may be so bold, sir," Yuri said with a deliberate edge of impertinence. "Do you have any choice?"

The old Latvian stood up straight, crossed his arms and smiled. "You are more like your father than I gave you credit for."

"I will take that as a compliment, sir."

Ten minutes before 6:00 PM, Moscow Time, Monday, August 19, 1991

Boris Pugo entered the press center auditorium in the Soviet Ministry of Foreign Affairs building with a confidence he had not felt in some time. The *GKChP* needed to project the image of being in charge and working for the good of the people tonight, and Pugo was more than ready. He wore his finest grey suit and dark blue tie which his wife Valentina had specially selected for the occasion.

The room filled with press correspondents as Pugo made his way down front to the long, cloth-covered table. He had carefully selected the attendees for the event and filled slots with as many loyal correspondents as possible who would give the *GKChP* the fawning coverage he desired.

The original plan had been for Pugo and Kryuchkov to sit on either side of Yanayev so they could field any hard questions in a natural manner. They had prepped the acting president with a special signal of them rustling their papers to let him know when to direct questions to them. Unfortunately, Pugo had to rework all that thanks to Kryuchkov's traitorous former mistress. Makeup could not conceal the deep red scars on the Chairman's cheek. Kryuchkov simply could not appear on camera, even with a bandage, without drawing unwanted attention.

Pugo never understood why Kryuchkov had raised that woman so high, or why he seemed to equivocate whenever she appeared. She was surely nothing more than a punching bag to him anymore. The KGB Chairman had been rumored to be impotent for years.

Yanayev, looking tired and listless, sat in the center of the table and Pugo took the seat to his right. Although the acting president's grey suit and white striped shirt appeared pressed and well-fitting, he had pulled the front portion of his hair to one side in a ridiculous attempt to cover his bald spot.

Oleg Baklanov of the Central Committee took the chair to the left of Yanayev, with Vasily Starodubtsev, Chairman of the Peasant Union and Aleksandr Tizyakov, president of the Association of the State Enterprises in the chairs on the other side. Kryuchkov and Pugo had agreed to keep Marshal Yazov out of sight tonight to avoid any appearance of a military takeover.

The press secretary at the end of the table called the event to order, then turned everything over to Yanayev. Pugo could not smell any alcohol on the man's breath.

"Ladies and gentlemen, friends and comrades," Yanayev began. "I address you today at a moment crucial for the destinies of the Soviet Union and the international community..."

The words were good. Yanayev stayed on script, and while the man was never exceptionally energetic, he made sense. Pugo wished he would keep his damn handkerchief in his pocket when the cameras were on him.

Yanayev finished his opening statement then opened the floor for questions. The first came from an American correspondent from *Newsweek.* The woman asked the expected one about Gorbachev's health which Yanayev skillfully answered. She then asked about the presence of the tanks in the street, and Yanayev remained unflustered by her directness.

The next question was a preselected one from *Pravda,* where both Yanayev and Tiziakov glowingly spoke of Gorbachev and *perestroika* as if they were actually supporters of the thing. A few more questions came from some foreign correspondents, who tried to veer the discussion into difficult territories, but Pugo defused their inquiries himself to keep everything on track. He began to think they might come away with a complete and total victory.

A young woman wearing a teal-and-white checkered dress approached the microphone next. Pugo stared at her for a moment. She seemed familiar, but he could not place her.

"Could you please say whether or not you understand last night you carried out a coup d'état?" a young woman asked. "Which comparison seems more apt to you? The comparison with 1917 or 1964?"

Pugo had to struggle to keep his mouth closed. He suddenly remembered who the woman was; a reporter with the *Nezavisimaia Gazeta*, one of the newspapers his forces had shut down earlier in the day. She must have snuck into the room.

Yanayev gave an anemic denial. Pugo rustled his papers in the prearranged manner, but Yanayev ignored him. The acting president went off script and attempted to change the subject, but the young reporter pressed her advantage. Soon other reporters hurled inflammatory questions like grenades and all Yanayev could do was wave his hands with hysteria. Flash bulbs throughout the room captured the ridiculous moments for all the world to see.

Pugo watched everything he had so carefully planned disintegrate before his eyes. He finally wrested control away from Yanayev and attempted to right the ship, but it was too late.

The feeding frenzy had begun.

Vladimir Kryuchkov watched the press conference on television in his office at Dzerzhinsky Square. The event ended and he threw his empty whisky glass against the wall in disgust. His fingers went to his cheek and brushed over the three raw, red-rimmed scratches.

Damn that woman.

CHAPTER 20

8:00 PM, Moscow Time, Monday, August 19, 1991

A phone in a quiet, grey cubicle at United States Embassy buzzed and a man in his early forties with wavy blonde hair picked up the receiver.

"Fifty-nine, twenty-nine, seventy-two, ninety-six," a voice said in English.

The man hung up the phone and stood. His hands slightly trembled as he reached for his blue suit jacket on the coat rack behind him. He grabbed his keys and ID and hurried out of the room.

He walked a few blocks from the embassy and stopped at a payphone amidst the hordes of people along *Konyushkovskaya Ulitsa*, not far from the Moscow Marriott. The voice on the other end of the line spoke another numerical sequence, to which the man responded with his own series of numbers. More clicks sounded, and a new voice came on the line. It sounded like a child's, high pitched and squeaky.

"Mockingbird," the voice said in Russian. "I am activating you on direct authority of the Chairman. We have an urgent assignment for you."

Silence.

"Is there a problem?"

"No sir," the man replied in Russian. "This is simply unexpected. I cannot imagine anything worth risking my position."

"Your position is already at risk," the voice said. "I presume you know the identity of the woman who arrived there this afternoon?"

"Of course," the blonde man said. "I have sequestered myself at my desk to prevent her seeing me."

"Then you understand the urgency. She must be removed before she can be remanded to the United States. You, and others like you, will all be at risk if the Americans gain access to her knowledge. You need not worry about your cover. We have the means for you to carry out these orders which will keep you safe and in place."

"Very well, comrade," the man said.

"An operative is in your vicinity now with a package for you," the child-like voice continued. "In it you will find a pistol, noise suppressor, and a small electronic device. You are to smuggle these items into the embassy. I presume that will not be a problem?"

"I have a system for such things."

"Good. It is imperative this removal take place tonight. Do you know where the target is staying?"

"In the ambassador's quarters. They are currently vacant."

The child muttered something unintelligible. "You are to remove this woman using your silenced pistol while she sleeps. Also, it is possible an American agent will be in close proximity."

"I believe he's staying in the suite with her."

"That damn whore!" The sound of the child swearing jarred the operative, and he resisted a smile. "Alright, you will need to remove him first. He is extremely dangerous, so take no chances. Once he is dead, removing my, that is, the female traitor, should be easy enough."

"What you propose is dangerous, comrade. Access to that area is monitored by video surveillance."

"The device in your package is a low-level EMP device," the voice replied. "Carry it in your pocket and activate it prior to entering any area with electronic surveillance. All video signals will produce static while you are within one hundred feet of them."

"Will not the people monitoring the feeds notice this?"

"Perhaps, but it is unlikely they will understand what is happening. You will need to move quickly. We are also providing you with a pair of rubber gloves and a small vial of liquid. The gloves can be placed into any toilet along with the liquid. They will dissolve completely and can be flushed away. The vial can be rinsed out to remove any traces of the dissolvent and the EMP device has a lever on the bottom which will melt its electronics. You can throw both items into a public trash receptacle once your assignment is complete."

"What about the weapon?"

"Leave it in the room with the bodies. It makes a statement we want clearly understood."

"They will know someone on the inside did this."

"Very much so," the child said. "We want them to be afraid. Your length of service should keep you above suspicion as long as there's no physical evidence, and your alibi is properly prepared. Now, give me your exact location."

Two tall men greeted Jessi at the entranceway of CIA Headquarters and escorted her through its labyrinthine hallways. They eventually arrived at an unmarked wooden door and ushered her inside. Deputy Director Dick Kerr sat at the head of a small table. She looked around the room and saw no windows or mirrors, but assumed someone was still watching.

"Please sit down, Officer Bolton," Kerr said without expression.

"Thank you, sir." Jessi had worn her best jacket and skirt combo with a teal satin blouse and black heels. She hoped the bandage on her nose would not create a negative image of her.

"You got my attention on the phone," Kerr said. "Now give me the details."

"Late last night I was approached by a confidential informant from within Eagle Group. This person informed me that General Gerald Stone is preparing to abduct General Zolotova upon her arrival in the United States and to remove Officer Jonathan Cole at the same time."

"You have proof of this?"

"My CI was present when these plans were created, and confirmed this information came directly from the general's own mouth."

"So, at the moment, all you have is hearsay?"

"Regarding the general's immediate plans, yes. But as I told you over the phone, I have written proof of over two-dozen similar removals, all on American soil, performed via General Stone's specific orders over the last two years. I have some of that proof with me now."

"Let me see it."

Jessi opened her satchel and pulled out a thick file folder. Kerr silently thumbed through the papers. The look on his face went from frustrated annoyance to intense interest and ended with astonishment.

"Good God," Kerr said as he closed the file. "Officer Bolton, I owe you an apology. It was only because of your connection with Tripper

McKenzie that I didn't brush you aside when you asked to speak with me. This information, frankly, is explosive. Is this all you have?"

"Not at all, sir. I have several boxes of documentation in addition to what you have there."

"I see," Kerr said. "This goes beyond the scope of the Company, I'm afraid. The president will need to be informed."

"I understand, sir. My immediate concern is for mine and Officer Cole's safety."

"How so?"

Jessi sat up straighter in her chair. "Several of the unauthorized removals referenced in those papers were performed on Eagle personnel themselves. All were people who'd threatened to blow the whistle like I've just done. General Stone has informants everywhere and will stop at nothing to prevent any Eagle operative testifying against him."

Kerr's eyes widened behind his large-rimmed glasses. "So, you're telling me, as bad as I think this is, it's actually worse? Eagle has committed revenge assassinations against US Government personnel?"

"Quite a few, sir. I have documentation on some of them. Much of it references targets by their code names, but with help from someone like me who knows Eagle protocols, they're easily translated."

"Go on."

"Given that General Stone has consistently removed potential whistleblowers in the past, I am very much in fear for my life. Based on what my informant told me, I fear for Officer Cole's as well. I'm asking for immediate protection for both me and him whenever he returns to the United States."

Kerr sat silent for a moment. "You're as bold as brass, Officer Bolton," he stated. "Apparently, brave as hell, too. I can see why Tripper thinks so highly of you. Your clearance level prevents me from providing details, but I can tell you, what you've just given me is a gift from heaven as far as the president is concerned."

"Sir?"

Kerr leaned back in his chair. "President Bush has been looking for a quiet way to shutter Eagle ever since he took office. He doesn't want another Iran Contra fiasco. What you've just given me provides us with a solid legal means of closing down Eagle for good. On behalf of the president, I thank you."

"Uh, you're welcome, sir," Jessi said.

"Your exact contribution going forward will be for the president to decide. Regarding your protection request, however, that is very much within my authority to make happen."

"Thank you, sir."

"We'll have you stay here at Langley until we can get something set up with the FBI. This will be kept on a need-to-know basis to prevent word leaking out. We also need to devise some logical reason for your disappearance. We don't want to tip our hand to General Stone."

"I've arranged to take several weeks of vacation, sir," Jessi said. "I told folks I'm heading out to Denver to do some hiking."

The barest hint of a smile formed on Kerr's face. "One might call you overconfident, Officer Bolton."

"I try to be efficient, sir. What about Officer Cole?"

"Now that you've informed us of the General's plans, we have time to counteract them. Also, I see a unique opportunity to make a clean sweep with all of this, if I can convince the president. We'll have a better chance of getting everything right, though, if your CI can provide us with further details?"

"I can reach out," Jessi said. "My CI is rightfully cautious, but if we guarantee a safe and confidential connection, I expect they'll cooperate."

"Good," Kerr said. "I'll brief the president. Regarding Officer Cole, all I can tell you is that both he and General Zolotova arrived safely at our Moscow embassy a few hours ago. Even amidst the chaos going on in the streets over there, they should be safe enough for now."

A little after 2:00 AM, Moscow Time, Tuesday, August 20, 1991

It took Tasia a moment to catch her breath.

"Wow, you are something else, American lover boy!" she whispered in English. "Don't you ever sleep?"

"Not well," Jon mumbled, his face lost in the valley between her breasts. "Been a problem for a while."

"Sounds like you never feel safe." Tasia slid her fingers through his hair.

"Lot of truth to that."

"Well, you're safe here. The life-giving bosom of Mother Russia will protect you. Why not stay for a while? Fall asleep to the sound of my heartbeat?"

"I'd like that."

"Sleep now, darling," she whispered. "We're finally safe."

Tasia caressed his cheek and ran her fingers through his hair for several minutes. His body relaxed and breathing slowed. Satisfied, she allowed herself to drift off.

She had not been out long when the urge to go to the bathroom brought her awake. Gently, she slid out from underneath him and pulled her pillow under his head as he rolled over. Careful not to wake him, she planted a delicate kiss in the center of his forehead and swung her feet off the edge of the bed.

The huge ambassadorial bedroom was almost completely empty, with only a bed and a dresser which Collins' staff had acquired somewhere. The slap of Tasia's footfalls echoed throughout the space as she padded across the magnificent red marble. Her nakedness should have made her chilly, especially barefoot on the rugless floor, but she and Jon had laid intertwined for so long, the coolness refreshed her.

Tasia left the bathroom door open and the lights off. She made her way to the toilet but did not linger long. The pile of wet towels beside the tub served as a reminder of how she had fulfilled her promise earlier to give Jon a proper bath. She stepped to the sink with a smile and ran a warm spray of water over her hands.

She peeked into the bedroom from the doorway. The silhouette of a man stood at the far door. Some sort of weapon was in his hand, aimed at the bed. Her blood froze.

"Jon!" she screamed.

The man fired. A muted pop filled the air.

Tasia dropped her head and charged.

The man's pistol tracked toward her as she dove for his legs. A second pop sounded, and a bullet whizzed past as she smashed into him above the knees. The man's head hit the unyielding marble with a sickening crack.

Tasia recovered and straddled the man's waist. She seized the hand with the pistol, raised it, and smacked it against the floor. On the fourth impact the pistol skittered into the darkness. She grabbed his throat with both hands, and like some naked and enraged Hera descended from Olympus, smashed his head repeatedly against the tile. The man went still. Dark cranial blood spread out along the floor and brought her back to reality.

"Jon!"

Tasia rolled off the corpse and ran for the light switch. Jon lay curled in a tight ball on his side of the bed. Blood soaked the middle of the sheet.

Oh my God, he's been shot in the groin, she thought.

She ran to the bed, grabbed Jon by the shoulder and yelled in English. "Talk to me, Jon! Talk to me!"

Jon rolled onto his back with a moan. He clutched his left hip. Blood covered his hands.

"Talk to me!"

Jon opened his hands. An angry bleeding furrow about four inches long cut along the fleshy part of his hip.

"Burns like a son of a—!" he growled through gritted teeth.

Relief washed over Tasia like a wave on the seashore. Tears of joy filled her eyes, and she put her arms around his neck. "Oh, you big, beautiful *govnyuk*!" she cried.

CHAPTER 21

Approximately 2:30 AM, Moscow Time, August 20, 1991

Tasia called Tripper McKenzie, and the CIA Station Chief was struck mute for several seconds. She barely had time to pull on her borrowed satin robe before Tripper, in a white undershirt and wrinkled slacks, burst into the room along with two security men and three medical personnel.

Jon trembled as he lay on the bed, head in Tasia's lap. One hand grasped hers while the other clutched a blood-soaked bath towel against his wound. Tasia eased herself out from underneath him, gently slid a pillow under his head, nodded at the medics, and marched over to Tripper. The CIA veteran stared without blinking at the rubber-gloved body with the smashed skull at his feet.

"The man who tried to murder us," Tasia said as she adjusted the belt on her spruce-green robe. "His weapon is over there." She pointed to her right. "Fortunately, he stood too far back, and it was dark. The bullet is in that bloody mess of a mattress. Another is in the wall somewhere near the bathroom, I expect."

Tripper nodded, then squatted without taking his eyes from the corpse.

"This man is an American, General," he said. "A CIA veteran I've known for years. Why would he do this?"

Tasia's brow wrinkled as she stared at the corpse's face for the first time. It took her a moment to respond. "I have an answer for you, Mr. McKenzie, but I'm sure you won't like it. This man is KGB."

"What?"

"I knew him once. We planted him inside your government about a decade ago."

"That's impossible."

"I'm telling you we did."

"How the hell could you know that?"

Tasia shuffled her bare feet along the cold floor. "Because I was the one who assigned him."

A hush came over the room. Everyone stopped what they were doing and looked at her.

"All right General, let's have it," Tripper said as he stood up.

"I don't know who you think this man is," Tasia said. "But I knew him well from my time as head of the KGB Personnel Directorate. We were ordered to provide suitable personnel for the program that embedded him, along with others, into strategic positions within your government. His real name is Sergei Alekandrovich Subranov."

"Impossible," Tripper said as he walked around the corpse. "I've known Joe Telford for years. I've been to his house numerous times. I was the one who asked him to come over here. His wife Marjorie is supposed to arrive around Christmastime after she wraps up everything back home."

"I'm sorry, but this man never really was that person," Tasia said. "We created a life for him inside America designed to pass your background check procedures, plus trained him to defeat your polygraph screenings. I suspect even his wife has no idea who he really is."

Tasia touched Tripper on the shoulder, and when he turned toward her, she looked him in the eye.

"He was only supposed to gather intelligence," she said. "The long-term advantages of his concealed position were greatly valued by us."

"Yet killing you was important enough to risk that? Jesus Christ, what the hell's going on here?" Tripper sighed. "Okay, General, let's cut to the chase. How many others are there like him?"

Tasia sensed the discomfort in the room. "Dozens," she said. "At least those of whom I have direct knowledge. The program is still operating, as far as I know." She coughed to clear her throat. "I was told it had been wildly successful."

"Are you saying you can identify these infiltrating operatives?" Tripper asked.

"Not all of them, but yes, I could identify a great many."

Tripper sighed again.

"Alright, we need to sound the alarm to the folks back home. It's—" He looked at his watch. "—not even 8:00 PM there, so most of them should be easy enough to corral."

"When were you going to tell me Cole was shaking the sheets with our defector, Trip?" Dick Kerr said via the secure line from Washington. "I knew we shouldn't have rushed into this."

"Due respect, Dick, but we should be glad he was," Tripper said. "Otherwise, she'd be dead, and we'd have no idea how compromised we are."

"You're going to have to convince me on that."

"Joe had some kind of EMP device in his pocket. Definitely Soviet made, as was the silencer on his Makarov. He was also reported slipping out of the embassy last night shortly after eight and was gone for about an hour. We found a vial of some kind of dissolvent in his room, likely to get rid of the evidence. Everything adds up, I'm afraid. I have no idea what I'm going to say to Marjorie."

"Damn," Kerr said. "Gerald Stone was right. This is a disaster of nuclear proportions, Trip. We need to get that woman over here, fast."

"She's ready and willing. We just need to activate the hostile portion of the plan."

"Agreed. How do you see that working?"

"There's upward of a hundred thousand people in the streets right now. That makes for the perfect distraction. If you approve, we can have her on the road and out of the city within a few hours."

"Which brings me back to my original concern. Do you still believe Cole is the man to take her?"

"She'd have a fit if we tried to separate them. They've saved each other's lives multiple times now. Also, no one over here has anything close to Jon's skills and experience. We've treated the graze on his hip. It's next to nothing."

"Should you send some additional folks with them?"

"We'll have a car shadow them until they're clear of the city, but such a thing would stick out like a sore thumb in the ultra-rural countryside where they're headed."

"What about the general herself? She is KGB. Could this be something we're not seeing?"

"Not a chance. Her history with both Kryuchkov and Gorbachev is well known. I'm sure she's on the level, especially after what just happened. There's simply no way the KGB would risk an ace-in-the-hole asset like Joe Telford if all this was some kind of ploy. They're cagey and ruthless, but definitely not stupid."

"Long as you're sure. We can't afford to make a mistake. The stakes just got a hell of a lot higher."

"I know Jon well, Dick. Also, the general is tough as nails. She smashed Joe's skull with her bare hands when she thought he'd killed Jon. Never seen anything like it."

"Mama bear indeed."

"Their trip to the extraction point will be long, but not particularly difficult. They should link up with the *Kentucky* in about thirty-six hours."

"Alright," Kerr said. "You know your system, Trip. We're trusting you with something extremely important here. You've got my approval but plan it well and make sure they're ready."

"Guaranteed," Tripper said.

Shortly before 11:00 AM, Moscow Time, August 20, 1991

"Get that away from me, *govnyuk*!"

Barefoot in their new quarters, Jon wore only a clean pair of Soviet-made boxers. He held a metal tray filled with plastic squeeze bottles, a pair of scissors and half a dozen other items. "Tasia please! You know how recognizable you are on the street."

"I won't let you do it!" Tasia pulled her borrowed robe tighter and crossed her arms. "You Americans don't understand what a woman's hair is to us Russians. It's not only a symbol of our beauty and grace, but also our sexuality and fertility. The sacredness of Russian motherhood is literally tied up in our hair!"

"Sivilla had short hair."

"Oh, Sivilla is a damn French whore wannabe."

"Tasia, the KGB will stop at nothing to see you dead. You've got to let me cut and color your hair! I promise to do it gently."

"How about you let me gently circumcise that big fat *neryx* of yours, huh? You okay with that?"

"Too late and you know it. Dammit, sweetheart, I'm serious!"

"So am I, *govnyuk*, and I told you to stop calling me that." She stomped her foot and drew her eyes into tight little slits. "Taking scissors to my hair is not going to happen. It would take me years to grow it back." She pointed to the dark squeeze bottles on the tray. "That *basma* crap would be like putting glue in my hair."

"This is Clairol," Jon said. "Safe, gentle, and used by millions of American women every day. One of the staffers here uses it to cover her premature gray. Tripper talked her into giving this up for you."

"So, Tripper put you up to this?"

"No, it was my idea, but he agreed. I want to give us a fighting chance! Don't you trust me?"

Tasia recrossed her arms and swung her head to the other side. "That's not fair and you know it. Of course, I trust you. But that doesn't mean I'm going to let you touch my hair."

"Tasia, there are plenty of professional hair salons in Washington. One of them can have your hair back to its natural color in nothing flat. I'll find you one myself as soon as we get over there."

Tasia snapped her head back around. "Oh really? What would you know about women's hair care?"

Jon paused. "Fair enough," he said. "But I have, uh, a friend who does. I'm sure she would help you."

"Oh, a lady friend?" Tasia said as she tapped her foot on the carpet. "Do I need to be worried?"

Jon blushed a deep red. Tasia studied his face for a moment but when he did not say anything she let the question drop. "Alright, I'll let you color my hair." She raised her index finger. "But that's it! No cutting!"

"No cutting, I promise."

The two of them took off their clothes and Tasia cried huge tears when Jon applied the viscous black dye to her roots. Time seemed to stand still as he slowly worked the color down her hair with the applicator bottle, and Tasia gasped several times when he seemed to go too fast and missed spots. Due to the length and fullness of her hair, it took several bottles to do the job, and Tasia was concerned they would run out before it was complete. It took well over an hour for Jon to completely saturate her hair, and the two of them sat there in virtual silence as they waited for the color to fully develop.

Finally, they stepped into the shower together, and while Jon stood behind and rinsed her hair, Tasia watched the nasty black water slide down her belly, legs and feet. Jon turned her around, dragged her hair out of her face, and kissed her. Tasia put her arms around him and held on tightly as Jon reached for the shampoo to finish the process. After they dried off, Jon opened the bathroom door to let the mirror defog.

Her image slowly came into focus and Tasia nearly burst into tears again. Her beautiful red hair was essentially covered, but uneven bands of lighter and darker portions blotched up and down its length in hideous patterns, almost as if a child or chimpanzee had done the job. Tasia looked at Jon's reflection and saw his shock.

"*Govnyuk*, you are unbelievably inept." Tasia's voice broke as she shook her head from side to side. "I look like a can of black paint fell on me!"

"Tasia, I promise we'll get your hair back to its beautiful, normal red once we get to the States."

"Don't lie to me, Jon! It will not be that easy. I've had enough of people lying to me, do you understand? I need to know I can always get the truth from you. Can you promise me that—and mean it?"

"Alright," Jon said. "I promise. But we need to get moving. They're waiting downstairs to take the photos for our new papers."

Two hours later, they sat in the same conference room they had used the day before. Tasia felt like it was a lifetime ago.

"Well, that's different," Tripper said as he walked into the room.

"Oh, shut up," Tasia said.

She had pulled her newly colored hair into a tight ponytail with three equally spaced hair ties. The high collar of her black knit pullover completely covered the abrasions on her neck, and while the vomit-colored work pants were slightly baggy, the brown work boots were sturdy and good for walking. The whole package completed the picture of an unassuming, average Soviet citizen on the streets of Moscow.

"Put on a headscarf with some sunglasses and suddenly Mother Russia's hiding in plain sight," Tripper said. "We've got everything else ready." He handed them two beige envelopes. "Your new papers, courtesy of the best forger in Moscow. Guaranteed to pass even the most detailed inspection."

Tasia pursed her lips. "Mr. McKenzie, I must compliment you. Finely produced false papers like these have befuddled the KGB for some time now. Your forger may account for many of them."

Tripper motioned toward the end of the conference table.

"We've got you two windbreakers. Solid material, fairly heavy and a little on the large side. Should effectively conceal your shoulder holster, Jon. I've got a belt holster for you, General, along with a PSM like you requested. Extra magazines are in your jacket pockets."

"Perfect," Tasia said.

"There's a cloth bag here for each of you containing plastic jugs of water, bread, cold meats, and cheeses. We've got a stack of rubles for each of you which you should put in your pants. You probably won't need the foodstuffs today, but tomorrow's a long drive through the middle of nowhere."

"Got it," Jon said. He wore an outfit similar to Tasia's, but with a steel-colored flannel shirt, black boots, and a grey-linen newsboy-style cap.

"Jon, there's clean bandages, surgical tape, and antibiotic ointment in your bag," Tripper said, "plus a bottle of prescription-strength analgesics. The doc asked me to remind you to take them faithfully every four hours." He turned to Tasia. "We placed your father's book in your bag, General, like you asked. It's wrapped up well to protect it."

"Thank you."

"The little black plastic squares in your envelopes are your transponders to signal the *Kentucky*. Push the smaller button on either one about an hour ahead of reaching the extraction point and they'll send in the SEALs. Once you're in position, push the larger button and they'll come ashore and get you."

"That it?" Jon asked.

"Almost," Tripper said. "I've got something special packed into your bag, Jon. It's double wrapped in cotton rags, but please be careful. It's a big bottle of Very Old Barton bourbon for your host tonight."

"Really?"

"Yeah, Abagor Kadurin and his wife Ruslana. Abagor's a big fan. I've sent him some on occasion before. VOB is not the expensive stuff you favor, mind you."

"It's totally solid," Jon said with a smile. "No such thing as a bad bourbon."

"The Kadurins live on a farm northwest of Moscow," Tripper said. "Should take you a little over three hours to get there. Your envelopes have written directions to both there and the extraction point, along with maps that show safe locations along the way for fuel. You should both memorize those details before you leave."

"Will do," Jon said. "What else?"

"We've got a produce delivery due here shortly. The drivers are on my payroll, just like *Babushka* Sophia and her boys. You'll have to ride in the back with the cabbage and stuff, but they'll drop the two of you at one of their next stops. The Sheraton Palace Hotel along *Leningradisky* Avenue. It's about three miles."

"I know the location," Tasia said.

"Good. Two more of my guys will meet you in the parking lot. They'll have a Lada Riva for you, complete with a hidey-hole for your stuff. They'll follow behind in their own car until you're outside the city. Take the route laid out on the map to avoid the known checkpoints. Think that's about it."

"Trip, I can't thank you enough," Jon said. "Guess this is goodbye?"

"Maybe not for long, old fart," Tripper said. "After what happened last night, if the big boys don't recall me for incompetence, Cathy will scream to high heaven to get us back home. I'll probably see you sooner than you think."

The two men embraced and smacked each other soundly on the back.

"How rude," Tasia said when they finished.

"You two stay safe," Tripper said. "When you're ready, we'll head down to the lounge for a quick lunch before the truck gets here."

"Mr. President?"

An aide peeked into the unoccupied office where Boris Yeltsin had taken a moment off his feet.

"Come in, Nikolai," Yeltsin said. "Taking a moment of pause."

"Mr. President, General Lebed is here. He's asking to see you."

"Give me two minutes." Yeltsin said.

Yeltsin remembered Major General Aleksandr Ivanovich Lebed was not a man usually kept waiting. A veteran of almost every Soviet military conflict of the past decade, Lebed was second in command of all Soviet Airborne troops and the direct commander of the 106th Guards Airborne Division, which surrounded the Parliament Building at that moment.

"General," Yeltsin said as he entered the small conference room on the second floor. "A pleasure to see you!"

"Mr. President," Lebed cautiously said.

"Please, be welcome," Yeltsin said as he sat down at the large wooden table. If bad news appeared on the doorstep, it was often befuddled by a cheerful attitude.

"Mr. President, I am committing a breach of regulations by coming here," Lebed began, "although I do so with the knowledge and blessing of my commander, General Grachev. The presence of so many of our Soviet citizens compels me to speak with you personally."

Yeltsin interrupted. "Will you join our cause, General? We would welcome you with open arms."

Lebed's eyebrows rose.

"You have my respect and my personal sympathy, Mr. President, but I am a soldier who has taken an oath. Thirty minutes ago, I received orders to withdraw my troops from around the Parliament Building. I presume you understand what that means, Mr. President?"

"I do indeed," Yeltsin said.

"Please, Mr. President," Lebed said. "Consider the lives of the men and women you have called into action around you. Surrender and send them home. It would only take the release of a few guided missiles, and this building would go up with the brightness of the noonday sun. The fire would burn so hot the people inside would jump out the windows to escape it."

"General, I know you to be a good man," Yeltsin said. "Honest in speech and concerned to do the right thing. I, however, am the duly elected president of Russia and as such, I issue you a counter order to leave your troops where they are. The people deserve a chance. You know the illegality of what is being done here, and of the bloody judgment of history that will descend upon everyone involved in a potential massacre like you describe."

"I'm afraid history is written by the victors, Mr. President," Lebed said. "Sometimes our laws and rules are all that separate us from the beasts. Unless you're willing to declare yourself Commander in Chief of all our Armed Forces, I am unable to follow your orders."

Yeltsin considered the words. *Such an action would take time and effort to make a lawful reality. Lebed has to realize that. What he suggests, for the moment at least, is a step too far.*

"Very well then, Mr. President," the general said. "I will begin withdrawing my men as soon as I return."

"Thank you for coming, General," Yeltsin said. "I hope we meet again under better circumstances."

"Agreed, Mr. President," the general said as he rose to leave.

Yeltsin sat in the quiet and attempted to discern what he should do concerning the attack he now knew was imminent. He called a staff meeting and forlornly travelled the halls to the conference room. He took his place at the head of the table and opened his mouth to give them the bad news.

"Mr. President!" Another of his aides disrupted his thoughts.

"Yes, what is it now?" Yeltsin asked.

"Mr. President, there's an international phone call for you! It's President Bush of the United States! He wants to speak with you!"

CHAPTER 22

Approximately 5:30 PM, Moscow Time, August 20, 1991

Yuri sat and stared at the wall. Mockingbird had not reported in. Anger boiled his blood.

How lucky can this woman be?

The phone next to him rang. He picked it up.

"Comrade Zolotov?"

"Yes, this is he."

"Lieutenant Drozdov with the Personnel Tracking System. I have some important information I believe you will want to hear."

Yuri had never ordered the PTS to stop monitoring his mother's whereabouts. He was both delighted and puzzled to learn she had left the American Embassy and was headed north. He quickly called Boris Pugo who agreed to escort him to see Kryuchkov.

Dozens of uniformed personnel of varying services, ranks, and duties scurried about the Kremlin situation room when Yuri and Pugo arrived, although most were KGB. Dozens of officers sat with headsets at communication stations, relaying orders and receiving reports. Kryuchkov stood in the center of the storm, between two huge map tables in the middle of the room. One showed the USSR in total, the other Moscow and the surrounding area. Colored markers dotted the maps to represent the various units in place. Red for KGB, blue for Interior Ministry forces and green for regular military.

Yuri stood at Pugo's side as the two men approached Kryuchkov from behind. The KGB Chairman had obviously slept in his wrinkled suit.

"Vladimir, we need to speak with you," Pugo said.

"Boris, the *GKChP* meeting is not for—" he checked his watch, "—another two hours."

"I think you will want to speak with us now," Pugo said.

"I will decide who I speak to and when," Kryuchkov said as he turned around. "You need to—Yuri? What are you doing here?"

"We have an urgent matter to resolve," Pugo said.

"What matter?"

"Your bitch."

Kryuchkov's eyes narrowed.

"Boris, I do not have time for this. Operation Thunder is scheduled to commence at midnight. Bush just held another press conference and condemned our actions. Others are following suit. Why in the name of Karl Marx should I waste my time with this worry of yours?"

The ambient noise in the room suddenly dropped.

"Mother has left the United States Embassy and is headed north," Yuri said. "We have an opportunity to end this."

In the many encounters with his father over the years, Yuri had witnessed the man display many emotions. Controlled pride and subdued encouragement were the most common, occasionally red-hot anger, and on a handful of awful occasions the worst thing possible, disappointment. Until now, though, he had never seen astonishment in those eyes.

"For the love of all that is human, Yuri," Kryuchkov said. "You cannot be serious? Your own mother?"

"Vladimir, the security of the Soviet Union is at stake," Pugo interjected as he stepped closer and lowered his voice. "All we are asking is that you allow us to redirect one KGB stealth squad." He raised his finger. "Only one, that's all. We can order them to pursue your woman to wherever she stops and quietly and permanently remove this threat before it's too late!"

"We, Boris?" Kryuchkov said. "We?"

"Father, she has betrayed you!" Yuri said. "She weakens you whenever she is around, something I have never understood!"

Kryuchkov stared at him again. Yuri straightened his back and brought his feet together in a formal, at-attention stance.

"It's gone beyond us now, Vladimir," Pugo said. "If the Americans gain access to her knowledge, our entire intelligence apparatus will be in jeopardy. She must be put down for the good of the Soviet Union!"

All eyes in the room stared straight ahead. The noise level dropped. The air hung heavy with anticipation.

"A stealth squad is already deployed on the north side of the city," Yuri said. "If you will allow it, I can direct them remotely and liaison with the Personnel Tracking System to provide my mother's precise location."

Kryuchkov stepped into the open area of the room. He grasped his hands behind his back and gazed off into space.

"We do not have the luxury of time, Vladimir," Pugo said.

The KGB Director dropped his shoulders. "Very well," he said. "I authorize you to take command of the stealth squad in question. Give the details to the lieutenant nearest the door. Orders will be relayed within the next thirty minutes."

"Thank you, Vladimir," Pugo said. "You will not regret this."

"Don't be so sure, Boris," Kryuchkov said.

Jon and Tasia picked up their ivory-colored Lada without difficulty. Tasia followed a circuitous route out of the city, while her escort, another Lada, kept their distance but stayed in sight. She gave them a quick two-finger salute when they parted at the exit off the M-11 Highway.

The narrow road west was paved but became a rocky series of potholes before long. The little Lada held up well, although Jon looked pitifully cramped in the tiny front seat. At some point he drifted off, curled into an uncomfortable looking ball. Tasia could tell from his periodic tics and jerks his sleep was fitful. At one point, he seemed in such distress she pulled over and softly whispered a Russian lullaby into his ear until he grew quiet again. She did not wake him until they were about thirty minutes from their destination and had him move their weapons and holsters from the hidey-hole to their cloth bags.

The Kadurins stood on their front porch when the Lada pulled up. The man, Abagor, dressed in heavy tan overalls with an umber-brown wool shirt underneath, walked down the steps and motioned for Tasia to pull behind the house. She parked the Lada in the grass between the wire-and-metal clothesline and a huge cinderblock shed. A blue-and-white ZIL pickup occupied the open center section, balanced on both sides by two wooden whitewashed doors. Tasia caught a glimpse of farming equipment within the dark interior. The woman, Ruslana, dressed in a cornflower-blue dress, headscarf and apron, joined her husband at the car as Tasia and Jon stepped out.

"Welcome," Ruslana said. "Supper is almost ready."

"Thank you," Tasia said. "We're happy to be here."

The farmer's clean-shaven face had a weathered look, indicative of a lifetime of working outside. He extended his sun-burnished hand to Jon and then slightly bowed to Tasia with a thin trace of a smile. Jon grabbed their bags from the back seat. Tripper had mentioned the Kadurins would know nothing of Tasia and Jon's actual situation, only that they needed to escape from Moscow and stay overnight with them. His only caution was to not mention Tasia had been with the KGB.

"So, this farm is yours?" Jon asked as they walked through the grass to the front of the stone-and-mortar house.

"Well, I run it," Abagor said, a puzzled look on his face. "It is a community farm." The burly farmer spread his hands over the seemingly endless fields of almost-ripe wheat. "We are the breadbasket of the Soviet Union, my friend," he said with no small amount of pride. "The winters may be hard here, but the summer yields are always bountiful. If it were not for the damn wolves, we would have more livestock."

"Wolves?" Jon said.

"Yes, they've always been a problem. So are the damn boars. They get worse the further east you go, especially past the Volga. Fortunately, we've got Zver to protect what we have."

"Zver? A beast?" Jon asked.

Abagor laughed. "He's perfectly named if that's what you mean. Part wolf himself." He pointed at the field in front of the house. "Here he comes now." A fast-moving wave in the wheat headed toward them. "I must warn you both," Abagor said. "Do not make any sudden moves until we assure him you're friends. He tore the throats out of three thieves from Estonia about a year ago when they tried to steal one of our tractors and that's when he was practically a pup."

An enormous black and white furry animal burst out of the wheat field at high speed. Triangular ears swept back, wheat dust on his dirty coat, the Siberian Husky had to weigh well over a hundred pounds.

"Here, Zver!" Abagor said.

The huge dog did not appear to listen but instead zeroed in on Tasia, who stood off to one side with hands in the pockets of her windbreaker. Abagor and Ruslana shouted in horror when the dog plowed into her without stopping. Tasia lost her balance and landed flat in the grass. The husky put his front paws on her chest and licked her face. Dog slobber flew everywhere, and Tasia laughed almost hysterically from deep down inside.

"Never seen such a thing," Abagor muttered.

Jon stepped over and reached for Tasia's hand. She grabbed hold, pulled herself up, and rubbed the dog's neck with her other hand. The two of them walked back toward their hosts. Without warning Tasia leaned over, put both arms around Jon's neck and kissed him.

"What's that for?"

"I just realized," she said as she wiped her face on his jacket. "I can't remember the last time I laughed."

Jon smiled.

The huge husky followed at Tasia's heels. Ruslana called for him, but he ignored the command.

"Zver, go!" Tasia said and the dog obeyed and padded over to Ruslana who scolded him for bad manners. He seemed to tolerate the criticism but kept his eyes locked on Tasia.

"It seems Zver here has fallen in love with you, sweet lady," Abagor said as Jon and Tasia walked through the grass hand in hand.

The Kadurins brought their guests into their small house while Zver walked alongside Tasia like a puppy. The stone structure had running water and electricity, but only three rooms and a bath on the main floor. It did have a large and well-insulated second-floor attic space. Abagor said it was pleasant enough to sleep up there this time of year, but they could always turn on the large metal fan mounted in the back window if they wished.

Jon and Tasia both removed their jackets at Ruslana's insistence and Jon set their bags on the yellow linoleum. Tasia detected a curiosity in the farmer's gaze as she removed her headscarf but when he did not voice any questions, she said a silent prayer of thanks for the Russian virtue of minding one's own business.

The aroma of cooking cabbage filled the kitchen and dining area. Ruslana told everyone to sit at the aluminum table which she loaded with steaming dishes. Tasia was delighted to see the main dish was *golubtsy*, a savory beef and rice mixture inside cooked cabbage. It was accompanied by bowls of bubbling *solyanka* soup with huge slices of mushrooms and cucumbers in a salty butter-onion broth. Hot Russian tea and a long loaf of home-baked bread rounded everything out, and soon the only sounds were chewing and slurping.

"Ruslana makes the best *solyanka* in all of Russia," Abagor said after they finished. "It's been called the world's most perfect hangover cure. I've used it myself on more than a few occasions."

"That reminds me," Jon said. "We have a gift for you."

The farmer's eyes grew wide as Jon unwrapped the white cotton bundle. "I knew Tubman would not forget us!" he said. "Ruslana, bring some glasses!"

"Tub man?" Tasia said as she scraped the leftovers into Zver's huge bowl at Ruslana's direction. The huge husky assaulted the food as if he had not eaten for days.

"Tripper has a fine sense of historical irony as well as humor," Jon said. "Harriet Tubman was a former slave in the last century who helped runaway slaves from the South escape to freedom in the North. The system she created was called the Underground Railroad, which is what Trip has named his own system for getting defectors out of here."

"My knowledge of United States history is rather pitiful," Tasia said as she returned to the table. "I can tell you about the Battle of Stalingrad if you like?"

"My father fought at Stalingrad," Abagor said as he unscrewed the cap on the big bottle. "So did Ruslana's. If you are interested, I can give you a few tales."

"We are," Jon and Tasia said in unison.

The entire table chuckled as Abagor poured the liquor into the four glasses Ruslana had laid out. "I know Americans are supposedly decadent and lazy," he said, "but this liquid gold is something we Russians have never been able to duplicate." He drank the bourbon down in a single gulp, then poured himself another.

Ruslana sipped once from her glass, rose, and began to gather the plates and dishes from the table. Both Tasia and Jon pushed back their chairs to assist, but she politely asked them to remain seated. Abagor pulled his own chair closer to the black-iron woodstove that sat in front of a deep brick alcove and set the bourbon bottle on top like a holy relic. Once the table was clear, Ruslana turned on a small metal floor lamp beside a rocking chair along the opposite wall. She picked up a small basket and several articles of clothing from beside the chair, sat down, and began to hum while she sewed.

Jon and Tasia stayed at the table and listened to Abagor's stories of the great Soviet victory against the Nazi hordes. Zver never moved from Tasia's feet, and she periodically ran her hands along the soft fur on the big dog's neck. The level in the bourbon bottle dwindled steadily as the evening wound down.

"Abagor," Ruslana eventually said. "I'm sure our guests must be tired. We need to let them go on to bed."

"*Da, da*," Abagor said as he poured a small amount of bourbon into his empty glass. "I want just one more—wait! The radio!"

"Oh yes!" Ruslana said. "We need to hear what's happening in Moscow!" The small woman tossed aside the shirt she was mending and went to the large white box on the kitchen countertop. Static-filled murmurings filled the kitchen for a few minutes until a strong voice finally broke through.

"This is the Voice of America, now broadcasting with increased transmitter power from the Baltic to the Kamchatka Peninsula," the voice said in Russian. Moments later, the voice of Boris Yeltsin, using what sounded like a bullhorn, proclaimed himself the new Commander in Chief of all the Russian armed forces. His booming baritone sounded like a roar of defiance as he urged defections from the police, army, and KGB. The clip ended, and the announcer reported a large number of military and KGB forces had surrounded the Russian Parliament Building and an assault was expected at any time.

Abagor rose to his feet as if he had been stung.

"Bastard!" he shouted. "Damn Vladimir Kryuchkov and his KGB!"

"Abagor!" Ruslana rose from her chair and pointed a finger at her husband. Tasia did not believe the quiet woman could speak with such authority until it happened. "You need to apologize for your rudeness! These people do not need to be bothered by our problems!"

"No, please," Tasia said as she turned from side to side to speak to both her hosts. "I want to understand. Please tell me."

Abagor looked at the floor. "They killed our boy Andrei. He went to Moscow with some friends about a year ago and never came home. None of them did. We received word later that the KGB had arrested them. We made trip after trip to Moscow to get him released but no one would tell us anything. I know they killed him. I just know it." The man suddenly looked ten years older. He whimpered softly and shook his head from side to side.

Jon turned to Ruslana. "This is true?"

"We believe so, yes," she said. "We have no idea why. Our boy just disappeared."

"It was Vladimir Kryuchkov!" Abagor shouted. "He's in charge! He's the one responsible!" The man swore with ferocity before he hung his head again.

"Abagor," Tasia said softly as she placed her hands on the older man's shoulders. "I too had a friend killed by the KGB. His name was also Andrei. They murdered him only a few days ago."

The big farmer looked up with tears in his eyes. "Ah, sweet lady. You understand a little. There has to be an end to this. For your Andrei and for ours. Evil men like Kryuchkov cannot be allowed to rule our country." He raised a finger into the air. "Gorbachev would never have allowed this!"

"Nobody knows what happened to Gorbachev," Jon said. "There's been no word about him for two days now. The rumors say he's dead."

"Oh, he's still alive," Abagor said. "Kryuchkov is nothing if not a coward."

"Yes," Tasia said. "You're right about that."

"Gorbachev will make it back somehow," the farmer said, "and a reckoning is coming with him. I pray to be able to see it. I want to personally tell Vladimir Kryuchkov he can kiss my drunken Russian ass for what he did to us."

CHAPTER 23

A few minutes before Midnight, Moscow Time,
Tuesday, August 20, 1991

KGB Colonel Kirill Gruzinsky parked the black GAZ sedan under one of the few large trees in the area. The three-quarter moon cast an eerie glow over the enormous wheat fields despite the cloudy sky.

“Hand me the night-sight glasses,” he ordered, and someone handed him a pair of oversized black binoculars from the back seat. He scanned the outbuildings first, then the main house. The lenses illuminated the landscape in an unnatural radiance. No lights burned anywhere on the property, nor could he detect any movement through the windows. A small Lada was parked in the grass behind the house. He lowered the binoculars and ran a hand over his slicked-back dark hair.

Why did this have to fall to me?

“Split team maneuver with flak jackets and night-sight equipment, comrades,” Gruzinsky said. “Bershov, you and Denikin will enter together through the front door. I will cover that entrance behind you. There appear to be only two vehicles here, one in the backyard and the other in the shed. Kasyanov, you will disable them both, then situate yourself to cover the back exit. When everyone is in position, I will give the order to proceed. Am I clear?”

The three men, dressed in night-black combat suits, grunted their assent.

“The traitor and her American lover are in one of two places, either the bedroom or the attic space. Russian hospitality should compel the occupants of the house to offer up their own bed for the night, but there are no guarantees. Remember these occupants are sheltering a known traitor and an American spy, so they’re under our kill instructions as well. Do not hesitate. Our orders are specific. There are to be no survivors."

The colonel looked at the house again through the binoculars. He would at least give her a quick death.

"Kasyanov, radio our exact location to the *mudak.* Remind him not to approach until we give the all-clear. We don't want daddy's little monster getting hurt, do we?"

All four men chuckled.

Gruzinsky hoped he would not have to see her face. *She was so beautiful. I want her memory to remain that way. She should have known better.*

The huge husky raised his head from the floor beside the bed and growled.

Jon's eyes flew open. The nap on the drive up had done him no favors. He had tossed and turned since they first laid down, unable to fall asleep, despite the pleasant coolness of the attic space.

"Tasia, wake up," he whispered in English as he shook her shoulder. The dog's growls grew deeper. "Something's out there."

Tasia stretched one arm out from underneath the covers. "Oh, go back to sleep. It's probably some wild animal roaming around."

"I don't think so, and neither does Zver," Jon said as he yanked the heavy patchwork quilt from her mumbling form. "We need to get dressed." He grabbed his shoulder holster from the table next to the bed and handed Tasia her PSM. "Take this and keep alert."

The two of them dressed in silence. Jon tried to attune his ears to the noises outside. Night insects were all he could hear. He pulled on his jeans and kept his eyes on the big dog, whose growls grew more and more frequent.

He took a full, deep breath. The cool night air invigorated him and energized the wolf inside. He reached over to Tasia as she pulled on her boots. His fingers stroked the length of her horribly colored hair. She brought his hand to her lips, leaned toward him and smiled. He sat on the edge of the bed and tied the laces of his boots.

A loud crash from downstairs fractured the silence. Footsteps pounded on the floor below them. The noise of suppressed gunfire erupted.

"Jessi!" Jon hissed. "We're under attack!"

"What did you call me?"

Jon ran to the attic door, jerked it open, and both he and the dog thundered down the stairs. The huge husky rocketed into the master bedroom and within seconds the sound of a man's yell mixed with his angry bark. Jon crouched low as something hit the floor in the other room. Gurgled screams mixed with furious roars and grunts as Jon peeked around the edge of the doorframe.

The stink of blood and gunpowder filled the air. Two shapes lay unmoving on the high wooden bed. Zver thrashed with something beyond the footboard. A human shape against the far wall moved.

Jon fired twice into the upright man's face. A splattering noise like a bursting watermelon told him he was on target. The standing man fell forward onto the bed at almost the same moment the screams from the floor ceased. The sounds of ripping and tearing flesh blended with the dog's frenzied snarls. Jon sensed movement behind him. He spun around, Makarov aimed for a headshot. The dim silhouette of Tasia's figure stood at the bottom of the stairway.

"Get down!" he whispered. "Call the dog!"

"Zver, come!"

The dog lifted his head at the sound of Tasia's voice. He attempted to drag the corpse on the floor over to her but was unable to turn the body as the room was packed with furniture. Jon moved near the bed as Tasia crawled to the doorway and called again. This time the big dog left the bloody corpse and padded over to her. Jon edged over to the body and examined it as best he could in the darkness.

"Helmet, body armor, night-sight equipment? Tasia, what is this?"

"KGB stealth squad," she whispered. "Elite killing unit."

"How many?"

"Standard grouping of four. The other two are likely covering the exits."

"They won't stay put for long after that commotion," Jon said. "Do they carry grenades or tear gas?"

"Not likely. They're not supposed to draw attention."

Jon hefted the long weapon on the floor beside the KGB man. "You familiar with this?"

"Yes, AS Val Integrated noise and flash suppression rifles. Standard issue for the stealth squads. Looks like this one has the twenty-round magazine."

"Okay, it won't be long before those other two storm this place." Jon removed the night-sight goggles from the body then handed both them and the AS Val to Tasia. "Get back upstairs and make sure Zver goes with you. Use the goggles and nail the man coming in from the back."

"On it," Tasia said. She hunched low and made her way to the staircase with Zver a few steps behind.

Jon holstered his Makarov and searched around the bed for the other AS Val. Fortunately it had fallen clear of the expanding pools of blood. He checked the action to make sure it was still operable, grabbed the shoulder strap of the man Zver killed with his other hand, and combat-crawled into the front room.

Colonel Gruzinsky whispered into his radio as he clicked from one channel to another. There had been an enormous uproar inside the house, along with a single unsilenced shot. Now there was silence, and neither Bershov nor Denikin were responding. The commotion sounded roughly like an animal of some sort, a guard dog perhaps. He should have expected that possibility. This was a farm. He switched channels again.

"Kasyanov! Report!"

"Holding position, sir. Awaiting your orders."

Gruzinsky could kick himself. He and Kasyanov should have moved in as soon as they heard the animal. He needed to put his reluctance aside. Two of his men may have just lost their lives because of his hesitation.

"Proceed with caution to the back door," the colonel said. "I will enter from the front. Make certain of your targets and fire as they present themselves."

Jon dragged the corpse past the open doorway. He laid the AS Val beside him, rose to a squat near the doorjamb and, with one hand on the dead man's belt and the other on his collar, hurled the body into the darkness. The corpse tumbled down the wooden steps, the sound echoing into the still night.

"You hear that?" Jon shouted in Russian. "That's your man, you KGB sonofabitch! He and his partner met Archangel!"

Jon scooped the AS Val from the floor and made a fast crawl into the kitchen. He barely squeezed into the brick alcove behind the iron stove before the front window of the living room exploded.

Upstairs, Tasia set her AS Val on the heavy metal trunk under the back window. She took a second to yank the screen off the huge metal fan and pulled the bulky night-sight goggles over her head. The backyard lit up and the sparse number of items made her target easy to spot. The man crouched behind a long row of firewood stacked against the shed.

Jon's voice came from the front of the house, followed by a crash of glass. Intermittent clinks, pops and crashes came from below and went on for what seemed like forever, one after another in rapid succession. The noise finally ceased, and the man in the back moved.

Tasia aimed the AS Val between the metal fan blades. The killing zone was only a few dozen feet long. If she missed, there would not be time for a second shot.

The man stepped into the open and she pulled the trigger.

Jon detected a squeak from out front. The corpse he had examined had an armored flak jacket that covered the man's chest and abdomen, so he needed to aim below that. A dark shape entered the doorway, and he fired.

The shot went high, and the bullet struck the man's body armor. The KGB man staggered from the impact, raised his own AS Val in Jon's direction, and fired.

The shot pinged on the iron stove near his head and ricocheted into space. His opponent took refuge behind the edge of the living room wall and Jon sent two shots into the plaster. The Russian crouched low, extended the muzzle of his AS Val around the corner and fired off two quick shots.

Jon yelped as brick fragments and mortar dust sprayed into his face.

Gruzinsky knew he had scored a hit of some kind when the American yelled. If Kasyanov would just show up, they could setup a crossfire and finish the bastard once and for all.

"Don't move, or I will blow the back of your head off."

Her voice sounded a little rougher than he remembered, but there was no mistaking it.

"Lay your weapon on the ground and slide it away from you." He hesitated. "I mean it!" she shouted.

Based on her voice, she stood in the doorway to the bedroom. *Too far back and a good line of sight, even in the dark.* If he tried to turn, she would fulfill her threat. Gruzinsky laid his AS Val on the rug and pushed it away from him, although not too far.

"Now, stand up!"

Gruzinsky raised both hands as he stood with his back to her.

"Hello, Anastasia."

"Kirill?"

"Yes. It seems I'm not getting lucky with you this time around."

"Oh, Kirill, why you?"

"Bad luck, I suppose. The knowledge in your head must not fall into the Americans' hands."

"Jon, get over here," she said.

The American clambered out from behind the stove, his AS Val pointed in Gruzinsky's direction. He seemed to favor his left side, but his hands were steady.

"I've relinquished my weapon, American," Gruzinsky said. "Anastasia, may I please turn around?"

The American barked *nyet*, but she overruled him. A huge dog sat at attention beside her. A set of night-sight goggles hung from her left hand by the strap. No doubt they came from one of his men. In her other hand she held what looked like a PSM, pointed at his head. At that range, even without the goggles, she would not miss.

"I presume my man in the back is dead?" he asked.

"I took highest marks at sniper school, Kirill."

"Then you realize I'm no threat to you. May I please remove my goggles?"

"*Da*," the American said.

Gruzinsky slowly pulled both his helmet and goggles from his head. He motioned toward the couch along the wall, and when the American said '*da*' again, Gruzinsky tossed the headgear onto it.

"You look the same, Kirill."

"So do you, Anastasia, except for your hair. I cannot quite tell what it is. Did you dye it?"

"Yes, I wanted to get out of the city alive."

"Your beautiful red hair is one of my favorite memories of our time together. I can still smell your perfume. *Red Moscow*, yes?"

"How did you find us?" the American said in a clipped voice. His Russian was good but not perfect.

"I don't think I want to tell you," Gruzinsky said. "Then you would have no reason to keep me alive."

"No one is going to harm you, Kirill," she said. "We're not coldblooded killers."

"She might not be, comrade, but I certainly am," the American said. "If you want to go on living, you'd better talk. I've pretty much figured it out anyway. You're tracking her, electronically somehow."

Gruzinsky looked from her, to the American, then back again, hands still in the air. "Look, I have wrestled with my conscience ever since I received our orders. My reluctance and hesitation have cost my men their lives. I am willing, if you are, to just walk away from this."

"You didn't answer my question," the American said.

"It would make me feel more at ease, Anastasia, if you both lowered your weapons."

"I do not give a damn about your ease, comrade," the American said. "Answer the question." *He is a smart one, this American. He knows how to keep back and will not relax his guard.*

"Anastasia, please?" Gruzinsky said.

She bent her knees, laid the goggles on the floor, and directed the barrel of her pistol away from him as she stood up.

"Jon, lower your rifle," she said.

"Not gonna happen, sweetheart. Answer the question, Colonel."

"Very well," Gruzinsky said, "if it will prove my good faith." He inched slightly toward her. His eyes watched the American. No reaction. *It needs to appear natural.* "Two years ago, Chairman Kryuchkov instituted a program to tag high-level government personnel who were deemed problematic, usually because of their top-secret knowledge or questionable loyalty. Those persons all had a small electronic device implanted in their shoulders, just under the skin."

"That is an emergency communication device," Tasia said. "In case of a catastrophic event like a nuclear attack."

"I'm sure that's what you were told," Gruzinsky said. He edged a little bit closer, very slight. Still no reaction from the American. *Careful, very careful.* "But the truth is very different. I only learned about this a few hours ago when I received my orders."

"Keep talking," the American said.

"The device is essentially inert until activated remotely," Gruzinsky said. "Once online, it transmits an electronic pulse every thirty minutes which is detectable via satellite anywhere in the world, similar to the way our vehicle transponders work. You can see the value of this in cases of kidnappings or attempted defections."

Gruzinsky turned his head toward the American and moved a little closer to her as he spoke. "Answer me this, American. Have you ever known any high-level defectors to survive long term after they escape the USSR?"

The American did not say anything. Gruzinsky moved ever so slightly again in her direction. *Almost there.*

"This is why what you are doing, Anastasia, is doomed to failure. Even if you make it to the West, we will still find you and remove you. Your only hope of staying alive is to come back with me."

"You're insane, Kirill."

"I promise you will not be harmed," he lied as he moved his foot a little bit closer. *Just a few more inches.* "I will protect you myself if need be. While prison would be a foregone conclusion, I can work to make sure your time there is short and relatively pleasant." *Almost there.* "Your American lover can even go free."

Gruzinsky moved his right foot forward.

The sound of the gunshot, even suppressed, still startled. The side of Gruzinsky's head exploded, and blood and brain matter sprayed into Tasia's face and down her front.

"Kirill!" she screamed.

The body collapsed. Zver barked but stayed at Tasia's side. Jon lowered his rifle.

"Why did you do that?" she shrieked as her eyes scanned the bloody corpse at her feet.

"I could hear him inching his way toward you."

"You bloodthirsty bastard! He was my friend!"

Tasia dropped her PSM and charged. She stepped over the colonel's body and slammed the heels of both her fists against Jon's chest. His rifle clattered to the floor. The two of them spun around in the darkness in an angry tussle. Wrath burned inside her, along with a storm of other emotions. She tried to slap his face, but he blocked her with his arm. He stepped to the side and grabbed her wrist. In a fluid, almost dance-like motion, he slid behind her and encircled her with his arms.

"Let me go!" she yelled. "Let me go, you murderer!"

Jon arched his back and lifted her, kicking and squirming, completely off the floor. Wild fury coursed through her body. Outrage demanded satisfaction. What kind of murderous monster is this man?

Jon stepped over the bloody corpse, strode into the Kadurin's bedroom with Tasia in his arms and stopped at the foot of the bed. Even in the dark, the site was gruesome. He gently lowered her feet to the floor but still held her tight.

"Look at them!" he shouted in her ear when she tried to turn away. "We ate their food, heard their stories! These were good people. Now tell me who the murderer is!"

"He was disarmed! He couldn't have hurt us!"

"Yes, he could! The corpse I examined carried both a sidearm and a combat knife."

"Let me go!"

Jon released her. She whirled and slapped him hard across the face. "Keep your filthy, murdering hands off me!"

She stared at him for several moments. His face did not move. His eyes seemed far away, even in the dark. She thrust a finger at his nose.

"You should not have killed him! He was a good man! You did not have to do that."

"I'm sorry, sweetheart," Jon whispered, "but I damn well did."

Tasia did not speak for several seconds.

"We have to go," she finally said as she wiped her eyes on her sleeve. "But this is not over, *govnyuk.* Our first problem is to do something about this piece of metal in my shoulder."

"We've got another problem too, I'm afraid."

"What?"

"I took a ton of brick shards in the face from the colonel's last shot," Jon said. "My eyes are bleeding, and I can barely see."

CHAPTER 24

A few minutes after midnight, Moscow Time,
Wednesday, August 21, 1991

"Mr. President, we need to leave. Now!"

Boris Yeltsin startled from a sound sleep in one of the Parliament Building's infirmary beds. The voice of his chief bodyguard, Aleksandr Korzhakov, roused him.

"What? Aleksandr? What is it?"

"The attack is beginning, Mr. President. We need to get you out of here."

"Out of here? Where?" Yeltsin rubbed his eyes, still half asleep.

"To the American Embassy, sir. We must get you downstairs. Please come with me."

Yeltsin and several other bodyguards, led by Korzhakov, walked down the hallway to the elevators. Sounds of gunfire echoed in the distance. One of the bodyguards carried the bulletproof vest Yeltsin had worn on and off over the past two days. The entourage paused long enough for him to put it on and within minutes, they were in the presidential limousine.

"Aleksandr, did you say we're going to the American Embassy?" Yeltsin asked as the limo moved toward the underground garage's exit.

"Yes, Mr. President. They have men at their gates who will hold them open for us. We have removed enough of our barricades to provide a clear route out. It's only about two-hundred-meters away."

"No, no, no," Yeltsin said. "This is not right. Stop now!"

Korzhakov told the driver to stop. "Mr. President, we talked about this," he said as he turned around from the front passenger seat. "You said fine when I told you about this plan earlier this afternoon."

"I know I did, Aleksandr," Yeltsin said, "but this is the wrong course. Absolutely wrong."

"Mr. President, please. Your safety is paramount."

"Not as much as what we are trying to do here!" Yeltsin yelled.

Thousands of supporters had taken up residence around the Parliament Building over the last two days. Yeltsin had called them all to him in an effort to show the world the Russian people were willing to fight for freedom. Homemade weapons and makeshift barricades surrounded them now, along with whatever his supporters could steal, cannibalize or create out of thin air.

Hundreds of police, soldiers and ordinary people had rallied to his call. He had walked through the crowds and spoken to many of them himself. He was the reason they were there. If they were willing to sacrifice everything for him, could he do any less for them?

"I will not abandon our people!" Yeltsin said. "I could never look them in the eye again if I ran away. Especially into the arms of the people we've been telling them to hate for the past fifty years! You might as well call Vladimir Kryuchkov right now and tell him he's won!"

Korzhakov nodded. Yeltsin knew he had convinced him, but the victory was hollow. There was no good solution to their predicament.

"Very well, Mr. President," Korzhakov said. "The final call is, of course, yours. May I at least urge you to take refuge in the basement?"

"That would be fine," Yeltsin said. "But I want constant reports from outside."

"Not a problem, Mr. President," Korzhakov said with an edge of bitterness in his voice, "as the old proverb says, bad news refuses to leave."

The conference room at the Kremlin was where Boris Pugo believed everything would be put to rights.

The spacious seat of power, with its enormous paintings of revolutionary icons, wall maps of vast vision and architecture of clean, straight lines was the ideal space to shed the last remnants of the bourgeoise West that Gorbachev had allowed to infiltrate their Motherland. Only plain, modern communism, like the square, functional furniture around the heavy oaken table, would rule from this day forward.

The legitimate power of the Soviet State, the *GKChP*, had convened to fulfill its purpose of solving the near disaster that Boris Yeltsin and his popular rebellion had begun. The attack was scheduled, and the outcome was not in doubt.

Pugo was proud to be one of the saviors of Communism. They all dared to dream, to remember and risk everything—to create a bright new dawn for the USSR with decisive purpose and bold, concrete action.

Pugo and the other members had met for about ninety minutes with several dozen related officials and press members before they sequestered themselves to solve their weighty problems alone. When they finally emerged, two and a half hours later, everything was not only worse but teetering on the edge of disaster. In Pugo's mind, only one man was to blame.

"Vladimir!" Pugo grabbed Kryuchkov by the arm in the wide hallway outside the conference room. Dozens of personnel sped around them on various missions of importance. "What the hell is wrong with you! Why the hell did you permit Yanayev to get away with that crap! Were you asleep?"

Acting President Yanayev had stunned everyone with a dramatic about-face, motivated by blatant cowardice as far as Pugo was concerned. During the closed-door portion of their meeting, Yanayev had read a ridiculously worded statement about how the *GKChP* would, under no circumstances, attack the Russian Parliament building, either now or in the future, even though he damn well knew the plans that were in place. If that were not enough, he then demanded the statement be released to the press.

"I had no idea he was going to do that," Kryuchkov said as he jerked his arm away.

"You did not speak up. You did not correct him. You did not say a damn word!"

"Neither did you!"

"You are the one who has influence over that blubbering idiot, not me," Pugo said. "I barely know the man. You and Pavlov were supposed to keep him in line. Since that drunken fool is in the hospital with a hypertension attack or whatever it is, the job falls to you!"

"What did you want me to do, Boris? Brow beat the Acting President of the Soviet Union in front of dozens of people?"

"Act like a leader!" Pugo said. "Dammit, Vladimir, can you not see what is happening here? This committee of ours is disintegrating right in front of us. Yazov is pissed as hell over Yanayev's betrayal, and I don't blame him. There is no doubt this is an attempt to force blame onto the military for whatever happens tonight." He folded his arms. "We only succeed if this is seen as a broad-based movement from within the legitimate Soviet leadership. Yeltsin has perhaps a hundred thousand people around him now. We have to spirit him away from here to regain control. We can only do that if we hold everyone together— and that requires you doing your part!"

Kryuchkov stared back at him but said nothing.

"It's her again, isn't it?" Pugo said. "That's why you're off your pins. You just want to stay pissed because your bastard and I made you give that removal order."

"You are talking about my son, Boris," Kryuchkov said. "I will thank you to refer to him in a civil manner."

"Can you please answer my question!"

"You had no business pressuring me into giving that removal order," Kryuchkov said. "I'm going to rescind it as soon as I can get to the situation room."

"What a weak-willed, indecisive coward you are!" Pugo said. "I am trying to save the Soviet Union and all you can think about is that damn woman!"

Pugo saw the punch coming but could not move in time. The impact knocked him two steps back. He licked his lips and tasted blood. People all around them stared.

"So, that's how it is," Pugo said, wiping the blood from his lip. "Well, I will not allow this ship to sink, even if I have to save it by myself. Do what you must, Vladimir. If that means burning in hell for letting this all fall apart, so be it."

The KGB Chairman stared at Pugo for a long moment. Finally, without a word, he turned his back and walked away.

Marshal Dmitri Timofeyevich Yazov's motorcade pulled up to the Ministry of Defense building on Arbatskaya Square in the midst of a downpour.

The Soviet Defense Minister waited for an aide to bring an umbrella and fumed. He knew a setup when he saw one. He would not let Yanayev get away with directing blame onto him for all this. Damn him and Kryuchkov both.

Yazov grew tired of waiting and opened the car door on his own. He brushed aside the multitude of aides around him and stormed across the concrete, up the steps and through the front doors. He shook the rain from his green cap and greatcoat as a timid-looking corporal hurried toward him. He handed his things to the little enlisted man, who gave him a crisp salute, took the cap and coat, and hurried away. The personnel before him parted like the Red Sea as he strode to the elevators.

The echoes of wet boots on the marble floor sounded much like the raging thunderstorm outside as the marshal's aides finally caught up to him. A quick, silent elevator ride up and the small party entered the huge operational command center on the sixth floor. The assembled personnel rose to salute when the marshal entered, but Yazov waved them off and stomped to the center of the room.

"Report," he said to his deputy minister, Colonel General Vladislav Achalov.

"M—marshal, sir," Achalov sputtered. "We have just received a report from one of the Taman Guard units. They were attacked."

"Where?"

"In the underpass below *Kalinin* Avenue. The pathway was blocked, and they were accosted by a barrage of Molotov cocktails."

A sinking feeling of dread came over Yazov. "Casualties?"

"Th—three civilians, sir. Two were shot by our men as they tried to retreat, another was crushed by the lead IFV as it tried to break out. One of our men received some significant burns. Two of the IFV's had to be abandoned at the scene."

Yazov stood silent for a moment. "General, I am issuing a command to all Army forces now engaged," the marshal said. "The order is to stop the attack."

"Sir?" Achalov said, a look of confusion on his round, tanned face.

"You heard me, General," Yazov raised his voice so all around him could hear. "Give the command to stop!"

Vladimir Kryuchkov entered the Kremlin situation room after a slight detour to guzzle two glasses of whisky. He slightly staggered and stopped at the console near the door.

"Orders were given earlier today to redirect a stealth squad away from Moscow," he said to the lieutenant seated there.

"Colonel Gruzinsky's squad, sir."

"Contact the colonel right away," Kryuchkov said. "He is to abort their operation and return to Moscow immediately."

"Yes, Chairman."

Kryuchkov lurched to the center of the room. The officer in charge was a haggard KGB brigadier in a sweat stained uniform.

"Situation," Kryuchkov said.

"The Army units are all pulling back," the officer said. "They say their orders came directly from Marshal Yazov."

Kryuchkov muttered something under his breath.

"We have also received word the Interior Ministry forces are refusing to continue—" the brigadier swallowed "—and—and—"

"And what?" Kryuchkov asked.

"Our Alpha Group commandos, sir. They, uh, claim the storms—the storms are making their helicopter landings impossible."

No one uttered a sound.

"Well, the operation has to be canceled then," Kryuchkov said, "for the moment anyway." He looked at the officer behind the closest console.

"Captain, get me a phone connection to Boris Yeltsin. He needs to know this is not over."

CHAPTER 25

6:15 AM, Moscow Time, Wednesday, August 21, 1991

The sun finally rose after what felt like an eternity of driving in darkness.

The journey from the Kadurin's farm had stayed nearly silent, mostly because Tasia was afraid of what she might say if she did not get herself under control. Her knuckles were white, her hands glued to the wheel of their appropriated KGB car. Zver lay stretched out in the back seat, their luggage and whatever they could salvage from the farmhouse was in the trunk.

Jon eventually fell asleep. It helped Tasia sort through her feelings knowing they were not about to break into an argument any second. The fact that she loved him was never in doubt. The fact she did not really know him bothered her more than she could comprehend at the moment.

A section of power lines broke away from the main road. Tasia turned after them into a long gravel driveway, hoping they might get lucky and find a sympathetic soul who would help them with the tracking device embedded in her shoulder.

The driveway ran for well over a mile and ended in a muddy gravel lot beside a large cinderblock building. No cars were present, nor were there any other structures or human activity she could see. Long flat fields of waving tundra grass spread out in three directions, bordered by an enormous lake whose shoreline began several dozen yards down the slope behind the building.

Tasia parked on the far side of the building, out of sight from the long access road. She rolled the windows part way down and ordered Zver to stay with the car. She hoped the huge husky would prove a reliable early warning system should anyone approach.

A tire iron from the trunk made short work of the padlock on the metal door. Tasia fumbled in the dark for a moment, found the light switch and flipped it. Dozens of florescent lights came on throughout the building and revealed what appeared to be an automated pumphouse, designed to constantly pull in water from the adjacent lake. A flood of running water a few feet below a concrete retaining wall filled most of the huge space. A windowless room just off the entrance contained a large aluminum table and four chairs, along with a filthy bathroom that smelled of sewage and gear oil.

Tasia had flushed out Jon's eyes as best she could before they left the farmhouse. She had looked closely and saw dozens of tiny abrasions all over his eyeballs and the surrounding skin. She had fashioned a crude blindfold from one of Ruslana's long aprons and hoped it would at least keep things from getting worse.

"Tasia, will you please talk to me?" Jon said in Russian.

"I don't have anything to say to you, *govnyuk*. You're a bloodthirsty killer and I suppose I've only now realized what that means. That's your solution for everything. Kill, kill, kill!"

"What would you have done? Tie him up and leave him there?"

"Yes! That would have been an excellent option."

"You're a naïve child. He would've put a bullet in your brain in two seconds—or sliced your throat open."

"Not Kirill."

"Yes, Kirill! I heard it in his voice. I've heard hundreds of voices like his. Killers just like me. Shooting him was the only sure way to keep you safe and I won't apologize for it." He paused. "You can boss me around on anything else, but I draw the line at endangering your life, sweetheart."

"Stop calling me that!"

Tasia stomped into the small bathroom and slammed the door. The noxious odor inside nearly made her gag, so she hurriedly took care of her business. She emerged a few minutes later shaking water from her hands.

"I am grateful to you," she softly said.

"I know," Jon said. "Are you sure you want me to do this? I'll have to work completely by touch. Once we're aboard the *Kentucky*, they could remove the device far more efficiently, and with anesthetic."

"I don't want that horrid device inside my body a second longer. I'm mad it never occurred to me they could track me with it. We still have a long way to go, and God knows how many they'll send next time."

"You're the boss, sweetheart."

Tasia managed a weak smile. "Damn right I am."

She unpacked the bundle of materials she had brought from the car, spread them out on the table, grabbed Jon's hands and moved them to touch everything as she named it. "I've laid one of the bed sheets over the table. The other one's folded up beside you in the chair. Here's a needle already threaded from Ruslana's sewing kit. Next, there's the bandages, surgical tape, and ointment from your bag, plus the bottle of bourbon."

"Shame to waste good bourbon like this," Jon said as he shook the bottle back and forth. "I've got the small razor knives in my belt. I suppose we're as ready as we'll ever be." He touched her on the sleeve. "Take off your jacket and bra and lay face down on the table here. Put your hands together above you and rest your head on them."

Tasia pulled off her windbreaker. She wore nothing underneath except her newly purchased bra. The cheap thing was, of course, too tight and she winced at the rubbed-raw places on her side and underneath her breasts as she pulled it off. She had washed most of the blood and gore out of her top before they left the Kadurin's farm and spread it over the car's back seat to dry. She laid down and Jon probed her upper back with his fingertips.

"I found it," he said after a few moments. Tasia cringed as he pinched the edges of the device. "Slightly larger than a half dollar. There's an indentation next to it, likely the original incision. Give me a minute."

Tasia heard Jon rip the folded bed sheet into strips and felt him lay them across her bottom. "Bite down on this," he said as he put a rolled-up piece of sheet into her mouth. "It's going to hurt with no anesthetic, so feel free to yell if you need to."

"*Da, Da, Da.*"

Tasia bit down on the sheet when Jon poured some of the cold bourbon over the upper portion of her back. She heard him rub his hands with it, then felt his fingers press her skin near the device.

"Here goes."

Tasia grunted as the razor sliced into her skin. The pain was sharp but manageable. She felt the warm blood roll down her bare back and shivered from the cold metal underneath her as she tried to hold herself steady. Jon dug around inside the incision, and she winced.

"You're doing great, sweetheart," Jon said. "Give me a few more seconds."

Her flesh made a sucking sound as Jon pulled the small circle through the incision. Abruptly, it popped free.

"Got it," Jon said.

He tossed the device onto the edge of the table and Tasia felt him grab the needle and thread. It took him a few minutes of fumbling to sew the wound shut.

"I'll need to clean and disinfect the area with the bourbon before I bandage you up," he said when finished. "Fair warning, it's gonna sting."

"Just do it."

The alcohol-soaked cloth touched the wound and Tasia screeched. She sputtered a string of Russian obscenities while Jon washed the blood from her back. He patted her dry with a fresh piece of sheet, applied the antibiotic ointment, then taped a clean bandage to her shoulder.

"The stitches are good and tight." He put his hands on her bare shoulders to help her up. "Be careful when you use your right arm for a while."

Jon leaned forward and blindly sought out her lips. Tasia thought he looked ridiculous, a child playing blind man's bluff. She took his stubbled-covered face in her hands.

"Here, *govnyuk*."

She opened her mouth to receive his. The kiss was warm and heartfelt. "Still mad at you, but suppose I'll get over it," she whispered as she ran her finger along the exposed portion of his jaw. "I owe you an apology."

"Not necessary. I understand."

"You were right about Kirill," she said. "I didn't want to admit that. It cut me deep to realize he wasn't who I thought he was. That was on top of me realizing you aren't the person I thought you were either. Everything in my mind about you and me and our future together was suddenly in jeopardy, and it scared me. I took it out on you and I'm sorry."

She laid her head against his chest.

"Hey, we're together," Jon whispered as he put his arms around her, "something I never dreamed could actually happen. We get to start over, and I won't let anything jeopardize that."

He ran his fingers down her spine, slipped beneath her underwear, and caressed the upper portion of her behind. Tasia shivered, drew a deep inhale, then reached around and gently pulled his hand out of her pants.

"Careful, *govnyuk*," she whispered. "Much as I'd love to make love to you right now, even on this dirty concrete floor, we can't spare the time." She patted his bicep then reached for her bra. "Surely my top is dry by now." She looked at the bloody metal disc on the table as her fingers fastened the bra's clasps and tugged it into place. "You think that thing's still operational?"

"Don't see why not."

"We need to leave it fully functional." She gingerly pulled the straps over her shoulders and flinched when one brushed across her bandage. "Since they're tracking it, we can dead end their pursuit right here."

"Brilliant, boss lady," Jon said with a smile.

"I have another brilliant idea," Tasia said as she grabbed her windbreaker. "We need to find some paper."

11:00 AM, Moscow Time, Wednesday, August 21, 1991

Boris Pugo arrived at the Ministry of Defense building the same moment as Vladimir Kryuchkov. Each eyed the other, but neither spoke as they ascended the steps and entered the reception area. Scores of uniformed personnel scurried about like worker bees as the two men walked to the bank of elevators. A few minutes later, a young captain escorted them into the operational command center. Marshal Yazov stood on a raised dais above a well-lit map table with several of his generals. Morning stubble covered his usually immaculate, craggy face.

"Thank you for coming, comrades," he said as the two men came close. "This way please."

A nearby conference room provided a private space where the three conspirators could talk without being overheard.

"Do you really think giving up is the proper course, Marshal?" Pugo said. "You yourself said our country needs strong decisive action by those committed to the Soviet revolution. Did we misunderstand you?"

Yazov looked from Pugo to Kryuchkov and back again.

"We no longer have the luxury of acting as we would wish, comrades. Too many civilians have risen against us. If troops remain in this city, more bloodshed is inevitable. All it would take is for one tank to be set afire and the forty shells inside it would kill dozens of people. I will not permit this insanity to continue."

Pugo took a sharp intake of breath. "Marshal, you know as well as I do, Yeltsin is the real problem here. Capture him and spirit him away from the city and this all goes away."

"Maybe before last night," Yazov said, "but Bush, Major, Mitterrand and all the others have backed Yeltsin this morning. We are the usurpers now. Any force we employ only strengthens that image." The marshal took a step backward. "Only one power is strong enough to turn this around, and that is Mikhail Sergeyevich Gorbachev."

Kryuchkov and Pugo looked at each other.

"What?" Pugo sputtered. "Are you insane?"

"Far from it, Comrade Pugo," Yazov said. "I am preparing to fly down to Crimea shortly to see Gorbachev. I am going to beg his forgiveness, and hopefully bring him back to Moscow. His presence is the only thing that can defuse this popular uprising Yeltsin has initiated. I'm offering you both the opportunity of joining me."

"Do you think Gorbachev will just forgive and forget?" Pugo said. "He could have us all shot!" The Interior Minister looked over at Kryuchkov. "Vladimir, say something!"

Kryuchkov rubbed the three long scratches on his cheek.

"Marshal, you raise some valid points," he said. "Yeltsin now holds the keys to the people. You are correct, we need someone stronger to overcome him."

Pugo moved to within inches of the KGB Chairman's face. "Vladimir, this is ridiculous. Gorbachev has been held hostage for three days now, along with his entire family. If we let him loose, he will destroy every one of us in the blink of an eye!"

The Interior Minister stepped backward and looked at both Kryuchkov and Yazov with fury.

"We need to stay the course! We need more committed troops who are unafraid to arrest Yeltsin. If we can do that, it will send a signal to the world we are still in charge. Anything less is cowardice!"

Yazov crossed his arms over the many medals decorating his green uniform. A sly smile came over the military man's face.

"Thank you for your kind offer, Marshal," Kryuchkov said. "I will indeed accompany you on your flight to Crimea. I have a proposal the president should find appealing." He turned to Pugo. "Boris, will you come with us?"

"You're both out of your minds," the Interior Minister said as he turned on his heel, strode to the door, and slammed it behind him.

1:15 PM, Moscow Time, Wednesday, August 21, 1991

Boris Yeltsin walked down the Parliament Building steps into the early afternoon sun.

"Aleksandr," he said to his vice president as they strolled amidst the jubilant crowds. "What are we hearing about that blockhead Kryuchkov?" He noted both of them wore the same sets of clothes they had been in since Monday.

"I was just informed he and Yazov are preparing to fly down to Crimea," Rutskoi said. "Multiple sources have confirmed it, so it's likely true."

"I guarantee you it is," Yeltsin said. "Once Kryuchkov lost control of his war hounds, the only way out was the coward's."

Yeltsin stopped for a moment to shake a few hands. Rutskoi followed behind him and did the same.

"Aleksandr, I smell blood in the water and surprisingly it's not ours," Yeltsin said as soon as they cleared the edge of the crowd. "I think it's time to press our advantage."

"What do you have in mind, Mr. President?"

"I am going to call Air Marshal Shaposhnikov," Yeltsin said as he waved to some supporters. "He has been on our side since this all started. You and a few others, plus as many armed troops as we can find, need to get into the air as soon as possible. It seems Mikhail Sergeyevich is now the key to everything. We need to make certain he ends up in our pocket."

"I'll start putting together a delegation right now, Mr. President," Rutskoi said. "We can be ready as soon as the plane is. Is there anyone you want to accompany me?"

"Yes," Yeltsin said as they turned to walk back inside. "Call the American Embassy and see if Jim Collins will go. It might be helpful to show Mikhail Sergeyevich who the Americans are willing to support in all this and by implication who they are not."

A blood-encrusted metal disc lay in the center of the long metal table. Under it lay a tattered piece of paper with the words *"Screw you, KGB"* written in big Cyrillic letters.

"He cut the damn thing out of her!" Yuri yelled as he stomped around the table.

They had found six bodies at the farmhouse. Yuri ordered the ones in the yard hauled inside and the doors locked. He had no intention of admitting this failure to his father. He could smooth over everything so long as he brought his mother and her American lover back to Moscow—alive if possible but dead if need be.

"Yushin, where do you think they're headed?"

"It's not Leningrad after all. I'd say the coast."

"A water extraction then," Yuri said. "Damn Americans."

"What are they driving, sir?" Golovkin said.

"Whatever they left the city in."

"No, I don't think so. A Lada Riva sat in the yard behind the farmhouse with flattened tires."

"The farmer's truck?" Yushin asked.

"Still in the shed, also with flattened tires."

Yuri pointed his finger at Yushin. "Get on the satellite phone to Dzerzhinsky. If they are in a KGB car, there's a transponder in it. Find out which one the stealth squad was issued and get its location."

"That may take some time."

"I know that!" Yuri said. "The western coast is still hours away. We can head in that general direction and zero in on them as the data comes back. My mother thinks she's safe now, so they will keep to a sedate speed while they drive though unfamiliar territory. If we move fast, we can still overtake them."

The three men hurried toward the door.

"She will not escape us again," Yuri said.

CHAPTER 26

6:30 PM, Moscow Time, Wednesday, August 21, 1991

"Are we there yet?" Jon said in English with a chuckle as Tasia put the black KGB car in park.

"Guess I should get used to speaking English," she said as they stepped out of the car.

Jon zipped up his windbreaker. "Cold up here."

"We're much further north than Moscow. Your friend Tripper was smart to give us jackets with some weight." Tasia walked around the car and took Jon by the hand. "Let's take a look at those eyes, *govnyuk.*" She had him lean against the edge of the trunk and untied his blindfold. "Do they still hurt?"

"A bit."

She removed the cloth. "Go ahead and open them."

"Well, I can see." Jon shook his head and blinked multiple times. "Everything's a little blurry, but definitely clearer than this morning. The light hurts a bit, so good thing it's overcast. I can manage."

"Good," Tasia said as she laid the cloth on the trunk. "I'm tired of doing all the work. Keep those fingers out of your eyes, *govnyuk*, or I'll smack your hands."

"Yes, Mother."

Jon looked around. Logi was a location so small it did not qualify as a town. Two hours south along the coastline from St. Petersburg, the rocky peninsula thrust into the Gulf of Finland like a forgotten and feral child left to fend for itself. The area had no commercial developments, no significant infrastructure and nearly no people. One road led in and out, and that dirt and gravel pathway barely deserved the name.

A tiny seawater cove lay a few dozen feet down the slope, surrounded on both sides by dense clusters of tall, arrow-straight pines.

Oversized rocks dotted the tan and sandy ground around them. Cobalt colored rainclouds stretched along the horizon.

"Smells like rain," Tasia said.

"Hopefully we'll be gone before it hits."

"How long before your people get here?"

"Soon. I pushed the pickup button a few minutes before you parked and sent the standby alert well after we should have been within range."

Tasia slightly swayed as a strong breeze blew in from the water.

"You okay?" Jon asked. "I can grab some of those pills?"

"No, just a little stiff from all the time in the car." She looked at Jon's waist. "How's your hip?"

"Manageable. I won't be running sprints anytime soon."

Tasia opened the car's back door and Zver jumped to the ground. "Are you sure they'll let him come with us?"

"I'll insist," Jon said as he grabbed their bags, "and so will you. Flash that beautiful smile and no man on earth can say *no* to you."

The two of them plus Zver walked to the edge of the water. The waves churned in response to the incoming storm. Tasia eased herself onto a large rock embedded in the sand. Zver took up station on her left as Jon eased himself down on the other side.

"What's going to happen to me?" she asked. "We never really talked about it."

"No need to worry." Jon laid their bags on the sand, folded his hands and rested them on his knees. "We're not the KGB, you know."

"You're right about that. I've never seen an organization as incompetent as your CIA. I have no idea why we were ever afraid of you."

Tasia pulled the rubber bands from her ponytail and shook her hair into the wind. "I hope this woman friend of yours is smart enough to help me fix this nasty color job."

"No need to worry. Jessi's smart in all sorts of areas."

"Is that her name? Jessi?"

"Yeah, short for Jessica."

"Is that so?" Tasia stood up, walked behind the rock, and crossed her arms. "Didn't you promise not to lie to me, Jonathan Cole?"

Jon stood up and turned around. "Yeah?"

"You called me Jessi back at the farmhouse when the stealth squad attacked."

"No, I didn't."

"*Govnyuk*, I'm neither deaf nor stupid. You don't speak a woman's name you barely know at a moment like that. That's also why you blushed when I asked if I should be worried back at the Embassy. You're involved with this Jessi, aren't you?"

Jon stared at her with his mouth open. He was caught, and there was no way out now except the truth. His expression apparently telegraphed his feelings. Tasia's face flushed a deep red.

"Oh my God, you are!" Her shoulders fell and she dropped her arms by her side. "Are the two of you married?" Her voice cracked like breaking glass.

"No, we're not married."

"So, when were you going to tell me?" Tasia asked as the wind blew her blotchy hair about her face. "Or were you?" Her eyes turned misty. "Would she have just shown up when we got off the plane and kissed you right there in front of me?" She grit her teeth. "God, I can't believe I've been so stupid. I just presumed—and look where it's gotten me." She raked the hair out of her eyes.

"Another defeat for Anastasia, huh?" she said in Russian. "Why would God torture me like this? I've literally given up everything, and all I get in return is *have a nice life and see you later*?" She threw her hands into the air. "Yeah, the sex was great, sweetheart, but it's over now!"

"Tasia don't talk like that! That's not remotely true and you know it."

"I don't know anything of the kind, Jon. This is the second lie of omission you've foisted onto me. How many others are there?"

"I was going to tell you. I just—well, hadn't figured out how."

"Do you love her?"

He turned away and looked out to sea.

"Answer me dammit!" she yelled.

"Stay where you are!"

Zver growled as Jon spun around. Yuri stood at the top of the slope, a smug smile on his face. Two men flanked him with short-barreled submachine guns aimed and ready. Jon told Zver to stay as he raised his hands.

"Yuri?" Tasia said as she looked up the hill.

"It's over, Mother," the young man said in Russian. He skidded down the hill and stopped a few feet from them. "In the name of my father and the people of the Soviet Union, I arrest you for treason. You and this American assassin will come with us."

"My God, Yuri. What's the matter with you?"

"You are a traitor, Mother," the young man said as he raised his chin. "Caught in the act of defecting to our American enemies." His eyes narrowed. "Take out your weapons and lay them on the ground."

"Yuri, in the name of—"

"Now!"

Jon and Tasia gingerly withdrew their pistols, bent forward, laid them on the hard-packed sand and raised their hands as they stood back up. Yuri reached down, picked up each pistol in turn and flung them into the Gulf.

"Yuri, what are you doing?" Tasia said. "You practically begged me to escape to America. You even made the arrangements. You told me staying alive was all that mattered and now you want to shoot me?"

"The *mudak*," Jon whispered as he remembered the name the *Mokryye Dela* men mentioned in Moscow. "Tasia, I think we've made a horrible misjudgment about what's going on here."

"Shut up, *govnyuk*."

"You should listen to him, Mother," Yuri said. "On your knees, both of you!"

Jon and Tasia knelt. The foamy surf soaked their pants and shoes.

"It's been you from the beginning, hasn't it?" Jon shouted. "Your own mother! You were the one who tried to have her strangled. Then you sent the *Mokryye Dela* after us in Moscow. The assassin at the embassy too? The stealth squad?"

Yuri's face morphed into a frightening leer.

"Mother, you have been a millstone around my father's neck for years now. You sap his strength. You demand, and you insert yourself into his business. You distract and turn him away from his duty to the State. That had to end."

Jon glanced over at Tasia. Tears clouded her eyes.

"Y—Yuri?" she said. "I cannot believe—how could you hate me so? All I've ever done is love you."

"Liar!" He slapped Tasia across the mouth with the speed of a striking snake. "Love me? What an insane statement. It was Father who cared, never you. I've only seen you maybe a dozen times since I was six!"

"Because of him!" The rising winds caught Tasia's hair from behind and blew it around her face. "That's how he controlled me! Unless I submitted to his perverted desires, he would deny me access to you. Do you understand what that meant?"

The expression on the young man's face seemed to harden with her every word.

"I would beg him! Plead with him to let me see you! The answer was always the same and so was the price. You have no idea the filth he would demand I do. But, you're right, I could only take that for so long. I had to break free, and it cost me dearly. It kept me from you all those long, long years. Only since you've been on your own can I see you without going through him—but now I'm little better than a stranger to you." She shook her head. "Baby Boy, I am your mother. I love you more than you can possibly imagine. You cannot want to kill me." She paused as if unable to speak the words out loud. "You cannot be that much of a monster!"

"You are the monster, Mother! A whore who uses the wantonness of her body to seduce any man who catches her eye. A succubus that drains life and vitality." He turned toward Jon. "The only reason I haven't gunned you down already is because I want to present this American to my father alive for a public trial."

Yuri stepped in front of Jon and bent down so their eyes were level.

"Do you know what we do with foreigners who come over here and screw our mothers?" He kicked Jon hard in the crotch.

Jon dropped to the sand like a felled tree. His hands reached for his groin. He could not see, nor breathe, nor think. The agony controlled him, and he rolled back and forth in the choppy tidewaters, trying to ease the torment.

"Yuri stop!" Tasia yelled.

"Give me one good reason!" the young man shouted back. "Why shouldn't I pound these prize genitals you think so much of into a bloody pulp?"

Tasia did not speak for several seconds.

"Because—he might be your real father," she finally said.

Yuri's mouth opened and closed several times. His eyes widened in anger. "How dare you! How dare you malign my father!" His shout echoed like an angry ghost amidst the rising winds. "I ought to shoot you right now!"

"Give the word, sir," the taller *Mokryye Dela* man barked from the top of the slope.

"I'm not lying!" Tasia raised her hands higher. "I do not know for certain who your true father is. You can call me a whore again. I suppose you'd be right."

Jon could barely see. His vision was blurry and the pain in his gut burned hot. He rolled onto his side where he could see Tasia's profile above him. Her breathing sounded hard and ragged. She was obviously in a high emotional state, but he could not tell if it was with anger, sorrow, or something else entirely.

"Jon and I fell in love in late August of sixty-eight," she said. "When I left him to come back home, it was only a matter of weeks before I became involved with Vladimir Kryuchkov. You were born severely premature that following April."

"So?"

"Did you ever ask why? In all these years, have you never wondered?" Spittle flew from her lips as her face turned red. "It's because this man you revere beat the absolute hell out of me when I was seven and a half months pregnant! I went into early labor and nearly bled to death to bring you into this world! If it weren't for Sivilla, I would have surely died in the weeks that followed." She let out a moan as her tears flowed. "Oh, my baby boy, please don't do this. You're better than this, I know you are."

Yuri's eyes narrowed again. "They call you Mother Russia," he said with a venomous smirk. "You are an insult to Soviet motherhood, an abomination of a woman. I think your corpse will serve just as well."

"Hold right there, comrades," came a voice in Russian from the trees. "We have you in our sights."

Two men in blue camo appeared on the crest of the hill, rifles trained on the backs of the *Mokryye Dela* men's heads.

"Place your weapons on the ground, comrades, and no one gets hurt," said the voice from the trees.

The *Mokryye Dela* men may have been killers, but they were far from stupid. They laid their submachine guns on the ground in front of them.

"Now step aside."

The men in blue quickly retrieved the guns, ejected the magazines, cleared the chambers, and slung everything into the choppy sea.

"Step back, young comrade," the voice said. "One twitch and we will light you up, I promise."

Spray from the incoming storm blew across the tiny cove. Yuri swung his head from side to side. After several tense seconds, he finally moved back and raised his hands. The man who had spoken stepped out from the trees, hurried to Jon and helped him to his feet.

"Ramirez, sir, Navy SEALs."

"Glad to see you," Jon squeaked. A fourth Navy man approached from the other side to help Tasia up.

"How badly are you hurt?" Ramirez asked.

"I can walk," Jon whispered, still bent over with hands on his crotch.

"We've had eyes on you since we got close and saw you were in difficulty."

"Understatement of the year," Jon said as he tried to stand up straight.

The other SEAL's assault rifle was trained on Yuri. "We need to move, sir," he said.

"May I have a minute?" Tasia said in English.

"A brief one, ma'am," Ramirez said. "We need to get out of here before the storm hits."

Tasia stepped forward. Zver attempted to go with her, but she ordered him to stay.

"Don't get too close, ma'am," the other SEAL said.

"The very problem from the beginning," Tasia mumbled. "Yuri, I'm sorry I failed you," she said in Russian. "You are completely correct. I am a disgrace to Soviet motherhood."

Yuri lowered his hands and let them hang loose at his sides.

"I have to leave now," Tasia said as the winds grew more intense. "Due to all I've done these past several days, coming back is no longer an option."

She looked over at Jon then back to her son.

"I don't know how or when, but somehow, I will return to you when it's safe. I want to at least try and repair the damage I've done. It really is my fault. Had I only been stronger, able to endure more, I might have been there when you needed me."

The first raindrops fell onto the wet sand around them.

"I will not ask your forgiveness," Tasia said. "Only you can decide if that's possible. I told you the truth today, whether you believe me or not. Please think about it. I am so sorry for my many mistakes as a mother. Please know I've loved you through it all." She paused and sniffled. "Even if you didn't love me back."

She stopped speaking. Yuri said nothing.

"This is goodbye then," she said. "I love you, Baby Boy. I'll see you again one day, I promise."

She turned and walked down the slope. Ramirez and the other SEAL near the shore turned their weapons on the *Mokryye Dela* men to allow the SEALs at the top of the slope to make their way down. Jon stepped to the side to give Tasia room with Zver.

"No! No! No!"

Yuri produced a pistol from somewhere and fired. The bullet slammed into Tasia's back and propelled her forward. She fell face first into the water.

"Tasia!" Jon yelled.

The two SEALs near the shoreline opened fire. Bullets riddled the young man's chest. He fell back onto the sand as Zver slammed into him. The huge husky tore into the boy's flesh like a buzzsaw. The SEAL team tracked their weapons toward the men at the top of the slope. Both Russians raised their hands higher and yelled "*Nyet! Nyet!*"

"Hold!" Ramirez shouted, fist in the air.

Jon dropped to his knees and raised Tasia's face out of the surf. She choked for a second, then spewed brackish seawater out of her mouth.

"Tasia! Tasia!"

Jon drew her mouth to his ear. She was breathing. Her eyes were closed, and her head hung loose like a rag doll. An angry contusion marred the left side of her forehead. One of the SEALs helped Jon pull her onto the shore. Blood soaked the back of her jacket.

"Step back, sir," the SEAL said. "I need to stop the bleeding. We've got to get her able to travel."

"I can help—"

"Step back!" The SEAL's voice permitted no argument and Jon backed away. He turned and looked up the hill. Zver still viciously attacked the boy's corpse.

"Zver! Come!"

The dog did not respond so Jon stepped closer.

"Come on boy," he said in Russian. "It's over, you got him."

The huge husky raised his head. Blood covered the front of his snout and teeth.

"Come on," Jon said again. Zver looked at the corpse one last time before he padded over.

"Good boy."

Jon looked at the bloody lump of flesh on the sand. The dead boy's eyes stared skyward, toward the storm clouds. His open mouth seemed about to form a word. Vibrant red blood stained the front of his yellow trenchcoat, and Jon could see multiple bullet holes in his upper chest. Most of his throat had been torn away; his head barely attached.

Jon limped over and closed the dead boy's eyes. He studied the facial features but could not see clearly enough to make out precise details. He picked up the boy's pistol from the sand, flicked the safety and inserted it into his shoulder holster.

"Yushin," Jon said in Russian as he turned toward the shorter *Mokryye Dela* man. "You should take this boy's body back to Moscow. I promise we'll allow you to collect him without interference."

"Hell with you, American." The stocky KGB man spit on the ground. "That boy was an evil piece of filth. The damn wolves can have him. His whore of a mother is a corpse too, so we could care less what you do with her. Get the hell out of here and leave us alone." Both Russians turned and walked over the crest of the hill.

Lightning bolts split the sky as the full force of the storm made landfall.

Half a continent away, a line of black ZIL limousines entered the long, densely landscaped entryway that led to the Soviet presidential compound known as Foros.

Vladimir Kryuchkov sat in the back seat of the first car in line. Marshal Yazov sat beside him. General Yuri Plekhanov, head of the KGB Ninth Directorate and the man in charge of presidential security, sat in the front seat with the driver.

Kryuchkov stared out the window as the limo crawled up the winding concrete drive. The enormous villa consisted of multiple buildings erected on high stone bluffs above the Black Sea. The main house was known as the Sunrise Building due to its eastward orientation. Kryuchkov remembered the scandal of cost overruns to construct the place, but Gorbachev had won out. Times had certainly changed.

"Give me a moment, comrades," Plekhanov said as the limo approached the iron gates. "I need to clear our way for entry."

"I don't see anyone out here," Yazov said as the car stopped. "Where's your security, Plekhanov?"

"If you could see them, Marshal, they wouldn't be much good, would they?" the tall white-haired general said as he opened his door.

Kryuchkov leaned forward in his seat. That was a stupid response to a serious question. Something did not feel right, so he lowered his window. Four uniformed men appeared from the bushes on either side of the gate and pointed Kalashnikovs at Plekhanov's long frame.

"What? You are not letting the head of security through?" Kryuchkov heard Plekhanov say.

"We are under direct and irrevocable orders from the President of the Soviet Union, Mikhail Sergeyevich Gorbachev," one of the guards said. The man's assault rifle stayed aimed at Plekhanov's chest. "Absolutely no one is to pass this gate without his explicit permission."

"Especially you," another of the soldiers said.

"We are prepared to use deadly force to obey these orders," the first soldier said. "We advise you not to test us."

Kryuchkov thought he saw the old general blanch.

"There is no need for such measures," Plekhanov said as he raised his hands. "I have with me Defense Minister Yazov and KGB Chairman Kryuchkov, along with several others. We urgently request permission to see the president."

"You will back your cars down the driveway," the first soldier said as he gestured with his weapon. "You will park at the Guest House at the bottom of the hill and will be contacted there regarding your request."

Inside the Sunrise Building, Mikhail Sergeyevich Gorbachev, in a wrinkled business shirt and casual slacks, looked up from his polished oak desk as his personal secretary, Anatoly Chernayev rushed into the room. The sixty-year-old Soviet president felt twice that age.

"Mr. President," Chernayev said, nearly out of breath, "Kryuchkov is here. So is Yazov. They request permission to see you."

Gorbachev put down his pen. "Request?" he asked.

"The guards at the gate threatened to shoot them," Chernayev said with a huge smile under his trimmed white mustache. "They're stewing down at the Guest House. I urge you, Mr. President, please do not admit them."

"Don't worry, Anatoly," Gorbachev said as he stood up. "I have no intention of doing such a thing. The BBC says Yeltsin's delegation is on its way here even as we speak."

The Soviet president walked to the large window and gazed out at the Black Sea, hands clasped behind him.

"Call down to the Guest House personally. Speak only to Kryuchkov. Tell him to restore my communications with the outside world. Then and only then will I speak to him."

"You will?"

"Of course not," Gorbachev said as he turned around. He smiled for the first time in four days. "Let me know when outside communications are restored."

Mikhail Gorbachev was in charge again less than an hour later.

His first call was to the Chief of the Soviet General Staff, Mikhail Moiseev, to tell him no orders were to be accepted from any of the coup leaders from that moment forward. Also, he said, the delegation on its way from the Russian Federation was to be allowed to land without interference. Seconds after Gorbachev hung up the phone, Chernayev rushed back into the room.

"Mr. President!" he said. "President Bush is on the line!"

Gorbachev smiled again. "Get my translator up here right away. George's voice is one I will be delighted to hear."

CHAPTER 27

9:15 PM, Moscow Time, Wednesday, August 21, 1991

"*Kentucky*, this is the *Refuge*. Request permission to dock."

"Granted, *Refuge*."

It had taken the small sub the better part of two hours to navigate around the sunken wrecks that dotted the sea floor of the Gulf of Finland. Its mothership rested on the bottom in a relatively shallow safe spot to await its tiny offspring's return.

Jon stroked Tasia's wet hair as she lay in the combat stretcher, covered with a blanket and propped on her side. Zver rested his head next to her. They were all soaked to the skin from the heavy rains that had buffeted their rubber raft as soon as they left Logi's rocky shore. It had taken what seemed like forever in the blowing spray to reach the barely visible submersible a few hundred yards offshore.

The *Refuge* was a prototype submersible designed to conduct rescue operations at sea. Unlike its predecessors—the Mystic and Avalon, which could only conduct operations underwater—the *Refuge* could also function on the surface as well. It held a maximum of twenty-four occupants in addition to its four-person crew, so there was plenty of space to accommodate both the SEAL team and the rescuees.

The team medic's field dressing had staunched Tasia's bleeding quickly enough, but Jon worried about organ or spinal damage. He was afraid to ask questions, mostly in fear of the answers, so he kept his anxieties to himself.

Tasia drifted in and out of consciousness and muttered words Jon could not understand. In Russian, he whispered into her ear she was safe, and everything was all right. Her normally pale skin had taken on a deathly gray pallor.

A sharp metallic bang signaled the submersible had successfully docked with the nuclear submarine, and after a moment, the pilot declared the seal secure. One of the SEALs rose and turned the wheel of the large circular hatch embedded in the floor, exactly opposite an identical one in the ceiling the team had used to board the sub from the surface. A burst of light entered the small, semi-dark chamber as Ramirez moved in close and spoke to Jon.

"Sir, it's time."

"What?"

"We're here, sir. We need to take her."

"Take her?"

"Yes, sir. The medical team is below. I sent the *Kentucky* an emergency signal when we boarded. They know we've got wounded."

Jon never looked up. "I can't leave her."

"Sir, our medical team is the finest in the Navy. She'll be in good hands."

"I can't let her go."

"Sir, we need to get her into surgery. I promise, you can see her as soon as it's safe to do so."

Jon stayed silent for a long moment.

"Okay," he said finally. "But I want to help."

"If you could hold onto the dog, that would help a lot."

Ramirez and another of the SEALs made sure the stretcher's straps were secure before they gently lifted it. Zver whined as they lowered Tasia down the ladder feet first. She mumbled slightly in response to the movement but never opened her eyes.

"Easy, boy," Jon said as they watched her descend. "We'll hand you down in a second, but I need to go first."

They cleared the passage, and Jon mounted the escape ladder and climbed down. His feet touched the deck, and he looked to his left. Tasia's stretcher lay on a gurney with three medical personnel around it.

"Sir!" came a voice from above. "We need you to call the dog."

"Zver! Come on boy, it's alright."

The dog seemed skittish as he looked down the hole, but seeing Jon was apparently enough. The SEALs lowered him down the ladder, back paws first.

"Good boy," Jon said as he grabbed the dog around the abdomen. The big husky made no protest as Jon lowered him to the deck. The medical team wheeled Tasia's gurney away and the dog looked up at Jon and whined.

"Sorry boy," he said as he rubbed the dog's ears. "We need to stay here."

Jon did not notice the officer behind him until he nearly bumped into him. "Oh, sorry, sir."

The dark-haired young man with the two silver bars on his lapel smiled. "Not a problem," he said. "Francis Bacci, Ship's Chaplain. Welcome aboard the *Kentucky*."

"Thanks." Jon noticed the chaplain corps insignia above the man's right uniform pocket. He raised an eyebrow at the accent. "Bronx?"

"Little Italy," Bacci said. "My grandfather came over from the Old Country back in the Twenties."

"I had probably the best dinner of my life in Little Italy," Jon said. "A restaurant on Arthur Avenue, near 184th Street."

"Dominick's, sir. Grew up not far from there. It's one of the very best."

"Awesome place. Sorry about our four-legged surprise here."

"Well, it's unexpected, but we'll make it work. Thankfully, Captain Riegel is an animal lover. He sent me down here because we heard there was trouble ashore. Do you need medical attention?"

"No, I can walk off one kick to the gonads," Jon said. "If I'd have taken any more, I might take you up on the offer. Got some brick dust in my eyes earlier today but think I'm okay."

"We can get your eyes looked at if you need to. If you'll follow me, we'll get you to some quarters." Bacci extended his hand down the narrow passageway. "We'll keep you informed, I promise."

The young officer led Jon and Zver down a series of tight corridors and several ladders before he finally stopped outside a cabin in the officer's section. "We've cleared this space for you," Bacci said as he opened the door. "Your canine friend should be able to lay on the floor beside the bunk."

"Thanks, Chaplain," Jon said. "How long?"

Bacci's face took on a serious look. "I couldn't say. She's got the best medical team in the Navy."

"Yeah, I've heard that."

"Seriously, Doctor Rogers has an enormous amount of surgical experience with trauma wounds like hers. If anyone can save her, he can."

"It's that *if anyone* part that worries me."

"Are you a praying man?"

Jon almost laughed out loud. "God abandoned me a long time ago, Chaplain."

"With respect," Bacci said. "God never abandons any of his children. We often walk away from him, but it's never the other way around."

Jon sighed and slapped his thighs. "I wouldn't know where to begin."

The young chaplain smiled and motioned at the bunk. "Mind if we sit for a minute?"

"Sure," Jon said, and the two men sat down beside each other. "I suppose I really do need to talk to someone. The possibilities here are eating me alive."

"You love her, don't you?"

It took Jon a second to realize the truth of the question.

"Yes, I do. They say love at first sight is a myth, but I can attest it's true. I've wanted to spend my life with her ever since our first touch. Damn me for an idiot, I could never tell her I loved her."

"Don't be too hard on yourself. So many of us never say what we feel. We go through our lives just presuming, and it's moments like these that remind us of what's really important. Take this as a gift, an opportunity."

"A missed one, it seems. Maybe she would've come with me all those years ago if I could have said those three little words. I've always wondered. Then, out of the blue, I get the chance to be with her again, and dammit, I still can't say them. Now, she's in there dying on that operating table, and she'll never know that I—"

Jon hung his head.

"I suspect she knows more than you realize," Bacci said. "Love is so much more than what we say."

"No, she needed to hear me say it. We were arguing on the beach before everything happened. She thought I loved someone else, but I don't. Those can't be the last words we speak to each other."

"Don't write that future just yet. Hope is a powerful force and so is prayer. When you feel the most powerless, that's when they make the most difference. I suspect you'll get your chance soon enough."

Jon looked sideways at the young man. "You're awfully easy to talk to, Chaplain."

"Part of the job description," Bacci said as he stood. "I'll send over some dry clothes and food for both you and your four-legged friend here. Just ask for me if you'd like to continue our conversation later."

4:00 AM, Moscow Time, Thursday, August 22, 1991

The plane carrying Mikhail Gorbachev and his family, along with Aleksandr Rutskoi and the Russian delegation, touched down at Moscow's Vnukovo airport without difficulty. Kryuchkov sat in the back, under guard, and stood when the plane finally parked.

"Mr. President, it's time," he heard Anatoly Chernayev say.

"Let Raisa and Irina go down with the children," Gorbachev said. "I want them in the cars first. I'll speak to the press afterwards."

Kryuchkov watched Raisa Gorbacheva make her way to the exit. The Gorbachevs' daughter, Dr. Irina Virganskaya-Gorbacheva, had to assist her mother as the Soviet First Lady had apparently lost the use of her right hand the day before. Dr. Gorbacheva's husband descended next, along with their two small daughters. Mikhail Gorbachev then exited amidst shouts of reporters and dozens of reflected flashes. The members of the Russian delegation waited for Gorbachev to finish his statement and depart before they disembarked.

Only Kryuchkov and his two guards remained.

Yazov had been taken to another plane and Kryuchkov had been shuffled to the back of this one as soon as he boarded. He had asked to speak to the president several times. He had so many things to say, so much to explain. The only words spoken to him for the entire flight came from one of the guards after he asked to speak to the president the fourth time.

"Will you please shut up!"

The larger of his two guards nudged Kryuchkov to the exit. The tarmac below was empty and a cool night breeze blew over him. When they reached the bottom of the airstair, he turned to the closest guard.

"Where are you taking me?"

Neither guard looked at him, much less responded. A few minutes later, a black GAZ sedan pulled up.

"Where are you taking me?" Kryuchkov asked again.

"You are under arrest, sir," came the reply. "Get in the car please."

The black KGB car drove off into the night and Kryuchkov wondered what was going to happen to him. He so wanted to call his wife.

A few minutes before 1:00 PM, Moscow Time, Thursday, August 22, 1991

Boris Pugo sat on the edge of his bed, hands in his lap, as he stared out the window.

The phone lay next to him. He had just placed the receiver back onto its cradle. The conversation had been brief. Viktor Ivanenko was the one who finally found him. Pugo wondered why they had not tried him at home to begin with. The rest of the plotters had all been arrested and spirited away. Only he remained, the last of the eight. The eight who only wanted the best for the Soviet Union. The eight who were guilty of nothing except failure.

Ivanenko told him they needed to meet. He spoke far kinder than expected. Pugo said only one word to him. "Come."

Pugo stood and walked to the ornate maple dresser against the wall. It had belonged to his mother, along with the rest of the bedroom furniture. He picked up the pistol he had pulled out earlier. He could not make up his mind until Ivanenko called.

"Boris Karlovich," came a voice from the bedroom doorway. "What are you doing?"

Valentina Pugo entered the bedroom she and her husband had shared for so many years. Her long cream-colored dress seemed more formal than usual.

Pugo sighed. "I think you know, my dear. They will be here shortly. I cannot stay."

"I know. Would you believe me if I told you I understood?"

"Of course. You know me better than anyone. You cannot be surprised at this."

"Not at all. I only want to tell you I'm coming with you. If your life is over, then so is mine. Until death do us part, remember?"

Pugo looked at his wife's face. She always was the stronger one.

"I will not ask if you mean it."

"You know the truth," Valentina said. She took off her eyeglasses and laid them on the dresser next to where the pistol had been. "I will go first."

Pugo looked at the PSM in his hand. It was small but accurate enough.

"Goodbye, my love," Pugo said as he rose from the bed. "I will see you on the other side." His hand shook as he pointed the pistol at his wife's chest.

Valentina closed her eyes.

Pugo pulled the trigger twice.

"I'm coming right behind you."

He inserted the barrel of the pistol into his mouth and pulled the trigger one final time.

3:15 PM, Moscow Time, Thursday, August 22, 1991

"Here are the lists you asked me to prepare, Mr. President," Anatoly Chernayev said as he laid several sheets of paper on Mikhail Gorbachev's cluttered desk in his Kremlin office. "These individuals are in the right positions of authority already and we can corroborate none of them supported the coup plotters."

"Let me see the KGB list first," the Soviet president said. "How many names do we have?"

"A total of ten, but the top three are the only real options."

Gorbachev looked over the names. "Anastasia Zolotova," he said. "Mother Russia herself. She would make a fine choice. Raisa always liked her. She's been fearless as head of the Special Investigations Directorate. She also has a compassionate heart, quite an unusual combination. Her famous face would ignite the press and send the perfect signal about how I want the new KGB to be viewed. I wholeheartedly approve."

"I was afraid you'd say that, Mr. President."

"Do you disagree?"

"Not at all. I was the one who put her name at the top of the list. The problem is we do not have the luxury of time. You need to make the appointment now, within the hour in fact, so we can make the press announcement."

"Agreed. So?"

"General Zolotova has disappeared."

"Disappeared?"

"Yes, no one knows her whereabouts. She was last seen being escorted under guard from Dzerzhinsky a little over an hour before the coup began."

"She was arrested?"

"We're not sure. It appears she and—well, the then-KGB Chairman—had some form of altercation in his office, so I'm told."

"The scratches," Gorbachev whispered. Kryuchkov had been on the plane. While they had not spoken, Gorbachev had seen the man's face.

"There are rumors of her leading a group of protestors at the Parliament Building on Monday, but we've not been able to confirm that. The only person we've not questioned about her is the former Chairman himself."

"And you will not," the Soviet president said with a hard edge to his voice. "Thank you for not mentioning his name. He no longer exists; do you understand me? Let the legal system deal with him."

"Of course, Mr. President. But we need to name the new head of the KGB now."

Gorbachev set down his pen and stared at the door. "I cannot help but think he had that poor woman killed. Something was always odd about their relationship. She deserved so much better. She was astoundingly brilliant, so beautiful, charming and full of life."

"We need a name, Mr. President."

"Very well," Gorbachev said as he glanced down at the paper in front of him. "Leonid Vladimirovich Shebarsin is next?"

"They told me he played tennis the day the coup started."

"I like a man who's not afraid to be himself," Gorbachev said. "I think he'll do fine."

CHAPTER 28

1:15 PM, Central European Time, Friday, August 23, 1991

Tasia heard voices.

A dull pain throbbed in her chest every time she took a breath. Something was in her nose. Her pulse pounded in her temples. Slowly, like cracking open the pages of a brittle book, she opened her eyes.

A white, fluorescent light hung close above her head. She blinked and tried to focus, but the room seemed to spin slightly. She lay in a bed, but the blinding light above her obscured the rest of the room. The air smelled both damp and metallic, overlaid with some form of antiseptic. The voices became clearer.

"Hello, Mercedes."

"Jon?" she croaked.

"Yes, I'm here," he said in Russian. His face moved into her range of vision and smiled.

"W—where am I?" she said. Her forehead ached and her mouth tasted like burned cotton.

"You're safe and going to be fine," Jon said. "We're onboard the *Kentucky,* in their Sick Bay."

Tasia's neck flushed with heat. "S—sick Bay? W—what happened?"

"You were shot, darling. On the beach at Logi."

"S—shot? H—how?"

"You're going to be fine," Jon said again as he took her hand. "The bullet punctured your right lung. They got it out without any problems, but your breathing will be a little uncomfortable for a while. They've got you on oxygen, plus antibiotics and some high-powered painkillers."

"My forehead hurts." She reached up and felt a large bandage around her head.

"You've got a concussion from when you fell. We think you hit a rock under the edge of the water. We need to let the doctor know if your vision blurs or you have difficulty concentrating. Periodic dizziness and headaches will likely be with you for a while."

She suddenly remembered, and a cold chill shot down her spine. "Yuri! My God! What happened to Yuri?"

Jon tightened his grip on her hand. "I'm so sorry, sweetheart." He paused. "It was Yuri who shot you."

"Yuri—shot me?" Tears welled in her eyes. *No. Not my Baby Boy. He couldn't have...*

"Yes. The SEAL team—well, they reacted. I'm afraid Yuri is dead."

Tasia thought she had misheard. "Dead? Did you say Yuri is dead?" A tide of understanding suddenly washed over her and quickly turned into a tsunami. "N—No! No, he can't be dead. He's just a little boy!" She wailed in agony and jerked her arms back and forth. "Don't lie to me, Jon! You promised not to lie to me!"

"Tasia, you're going to pull out your IV's."

"No, no! God, no! Yuri! Yuri! Baby! No!"

Someone said something in English.

"No, she doesn't need a sedative," Jon said. "Please, just give me a minute with her." He moved forward and gently took hold of her wrists. He held them beside her head on the pillow and laid his head on her chest.

"Cry it out for me, okay?" he whispered in Russian. "Let's cry it out."

Tasia's mouth gaped wide as Jon pulled her hands down and placed them on his shoulders. Her nails dug into the cotton cloth of his Navy sweatshirt. She could barely breathe.

"He's not dead," she mumbled. "He can't be. His whole life is ahead of him."

"I'm so sorry, Tasia," Jon whispered, his voice muffled by the cloth of her medical gown. "But he is dead. I was there."

"How?" she said. "Tell me how!"

Jon raised his head. "He was shot in the chest. Multiple times. He died almost instantly."

"You bloodthirsty murderers!" Tasia tried to jerk back and forth again, but Jon ducked his head between her breasts to keep her in place. "Kill, kill, kill, that's all you Americans know!" Her voice cracked. "First Kirill, now my beautiful baby boy!"

"Just cry, sweetheart," Jon whispered. "Just cry."

Tasia cried until her eyes hurt. Her fists pounded over and over again onto Jon's shoulders. It took a few minutes, but eventually her sobs slowed. Finally, Jon removed her hands, raised his head, and sat back in the chair beside the bed. Tasia sighed and stared at the grey-white wall in front of her.

"I'd almost come to terms with leaving him," she said as she wiped her eyes. "I had nearly a week to prepare before you arrived. I told myself Yuri was right and somehow, someday, I'd find my way back to him." She swallowed and adjusted the oxygen cannula in her nose. "Then he appeared on the beach and showed me who he really was."

Jon scooted his chair closer.

"He wasn't always like that you know," she softly said. She closed her eyes and conjured up an image of him in her mind. He was five and chasing butterflies, calling out for her to watch. "When he was little, he was brilliant. Always looking at everything, asking so many questions. He would say to me constantly, *I love you mommy*. His little voice still echoes inside my head."

She took a deep, ragged breath and opened her eyes.

"I still remember the day they took him from me. I had no idea how much Vladimir had manipulated me until that moment. I'd posed for the posters a year earlier and my life had become speaking engagements, photo opportunities, and event after event at the highest levels. It was all I'd ever dreamed of."

She turned her head to look at Jon. The corners of his mouth were turned up in a display of quiet sympathy.

"Vladimir said because of all that, we should send Yuri off to boarding school. I could better fulfill my duties to the State that way. He told me it was the finest education in the Soviet Union and would open many doors for him later in life. I was so trusting, so stupid."

She extended her hand and Jon took it.

"When Vladimir didn't come himself but sent four Ninth Directorate men, I knew something wasn't right. Yuri was so brave. He tried so hard to be a little man. When he looked out the back window and reached for me as they drove away, I suddenly understood the horrific mistake I'd made. I've seen that awful image in my mind countless times ever since."

She squeezed Jon's hand.

"I wish you could have known the real him before Vladimir corrupted him. If it hadn't been for his struggles being born, he would undoubtedly have been taller, more robust." She smiled and a warm feeling passed through her. "Like his father."

Jon's eyebrows shot up. "Really?"

Tasia blew out a wheezy exhale. "That's what I wish," she said. "I told the truth on the beach. I really don't know which one of you is his father." She squeezed Jon's hand again and kept her eyes on his face. "But I know who I want it to be."

"Our son then?" Jon said.

"Yes, our son," Tasia said as she turned her head back around and closed her eyes. "Can you imagine us raising him in America together? How different everything would have been?" Her voice broke. "Our little boy would still be alive."

She cried again. Jon did not say anything, but she felt him keep hold of her hand. Anger overtook her grief, and she jerked her hand away.

"That damn Vladimir!" She wrapped her arms around her chest and stared straight ahead. "That evil man destroyed our good little boy. In the end, he won again, didn't he?"

"Not this time," Jon said. "Kryuchkov's been arrested. They're saying he and the other conspirators will all be tried for treason. You won this time, Tasia. You got your revenge."

"There are no winners in this, Jon. There's nothing but dead bodies now, and one of them is our baby boy." She moaned and recrossed her arms. "I saved a huge wad of hair from his first haircut. Did I tell you that? It was platinum blonde. I attached it to a piece of leather and made it into a bookmark for Papa's book. I always wished they could have known each other."

She sat up straighter.

"I would run my fingers through it whenever Vladimir would refuse to let me see him. It was all I had then—now it's all I ever will."

She saw Jon swallow. "What?" she asked.

"Tasia, with all that happened—with you getting shot." He lowered his voice to just above a whisper. "I forgot to grab our bags."

Her eyebrows shot up. "You what?"

"We had to get you to the raft. In all that, I totally forgot. I left our bags on the shoreline."

Tasia's eyes shrunk with fury.

"You stupid—idiot—*govnyuk*!" she shouted with rage. "That was all I had! Everything of Papa. The only piece I'll ever have of my baby boy. My entire life was in that book, and you left it?"

She turned away and brought her hand to her mouth.

"Tasia, I'm so sorry—"

"Shut up!" she yelled and bit down on her knuckle. "Leave me alone!"

"Tasia, I—"

"Get out!" she screamed. "Get out! Get out! Get out!"

Jon stood and straightened his sweatshirt.

"Okay, I'll get out," he said quietly. "There's just one other thing I need to tell you."

"What?"

"I love you, Anastasia Aleksandrovna. I truly and honestly love you. You and you alone. I always have and I always will."

He left Sick Bay without another word.

7:30 AM, Washington Time, Saturday, August 24, 1991

"Officer Bolton?" the tall FBI man said. "There's a phone call for you. It's Tripper McKenzie from Moscow."

Jessi sat curled up on the couch with a bowl of oatmeal in the living room of her safehouse. Clad only in her blue silk pajama top, which admittedly revealed a little too much, she had taken the bandage off her nose to see the television better. The news anchors reported that under pressure from Boris Yeltsin, Mikhail Gorbachev had just resigned as the head of the Communist Party Central Committee.

"Morning, boss," Jessi said with a yawn as she took the phone.

"Well don't sound so excited. It's a new day, you know?"

"You're just a bundle of sunshine, aren't you?" Jessi said as she set aside her empty bowl and spoon. "I hope you'll tell me what's going on. No one at Langley will take my calls and I can't set foot outside of this nice suburban prison either. It is awesome, though, getting waited on hand and foot by these hot and handsome FBI guys."

Jessi drew her bare legs underneath her and waved at the bodyguard in the kitchen. She winked at him and the tall Bureau man with the sandy blond hair blushed.

"All for a good cause, Jessi," Tripper said. "Don't be too hard on Dick Kerr and the rest of the folks. A ton of crap is going on right now. You're safe and sound?"

"I'm fine," Jessi said as she pulled her hair out from behind her back and ran her fingers through it. "Will you please tell me where Jon is? He made it out of Russia okay, didn't he?"

"He did, although I haven't spoken to him personally yet. He took a wicked bullet graze to the hip and hurt his eyes somewhere along the way. He and the general made it aboard the *Kentucky*, although she was seriously wounded at the last minute."

"What?"

"Shot by her own son, I'm told."

"Holy hell."

"Yeah, it was pretty rough there for a while. The *Kentucky*'s scheduled to arrive at Holy Loch Submarine Base in Scotland before long. We'll fly the two of them to the States in a couple weeks when the general's better."

"Jon's with her now, isn't he?" Jessi said. "I mean, as in, really with her?"

"Yeah, Jessi, he is."

Jessi let go of her hair and switched the receiver to her other hand. "I knew it."

"I'm glad I didn't have to draw you a picture."

"This is so wrong, Tripper. I love him like you wouldn't believe and he goes and does this."

"I'm so sorry, lady, I really am," Tripper said. "I begged him not to do this. He should know how good the two of you are for each other."

"You'd think so."

"Let me give you some good news. The real reason for this call is something awesome, believe it or not."

"What?"

"Thanks to the information you provided, the president has asked us to put together an interagency task force."

"What for?"

"We're to lay a clandestine trap for General Gerald Stone and shut down Eagle Group for good."

"Holy crap."

"Yeah, it's happening. The Company will work in conjunction with the Bureau, with some support from both the DOD and the DOJ. It's a nearly unprecedented cooperation, actually. The best part is that yours truly has been tapped to head things up."

"Really?" The blond FBI man grabbed her bowl and spoon. She looked up at him, smiled and mouthed the words *thank you*.

"Yeah, a lot of things have changed in the last few days. Never could have foreseen this when we dreamed up your little infiltration mission."

"I should have called you long ago with what I found." She pulled her legs out from underneath her and stretched.

"Don't sweat that," Tripper said. "If I had any idea how things worked over there, I would have never asked you to go. You laid your life on the line for this, Jessi, and I'm riddled with guilt for putting you in danger."

"Neither of us knew what we were getting into." The bright September sunshine beamed through the window behind her and warmed the back of her neck. "I just listened, and when the rumors became more and more credible, I started quietly digging. Had no idea there were literally bodies buried, much less some of our own people."

"The president has taken notice of you because of this, Jessi. Your star is in ascendency. To circle back around, I asked for you to be my second-in-command on this task force and got an instant approval. If you'll agree, that is."

In her mind, Jessi could see Tripper's wide grin even though he was in Moscow.

"What do you think, Miss Smarty Pants?" Tripper asked with the nickname he had given her when she first started with the Company. "You up for it?"

"You know it, boss. Tell me when and how."

“Well, that’s the hard part,” Tripper said. “We have to go fully dark on this one. That means I have to ask you to do something I know you won’t like.”

CHAPTER 29

1:30 PM, Washington Time, Tuesday, September 10, 1991

"Good afternoon, passengers," the voice over the intercom said. "Looks like we need to make a last-minute diversion, nothing to worry about. Andrews Tower is rerouting us over to Davison Airfield."

A buzz went through the small passenger compartment.

"Davison assures us they'll make ground transportation arrangements for all of you. Should add only a few extra minutes to our flight time as we make the adjustments."

The military transport banked to one side as the pilot made the course correction. The normal eight-hour flight from Laken-heath RAF base had taken longer than expected due to some difficult weather over the North Atlantic. Jon felt Tasia hook his hand in a vice-grip as the plane banked. Only after the Gulfstream IV aircraft touched down and taxied to its parking location did she let go.

"Oh, thank God," she said in Russian. "We're finally on the ground again. My stomach almost let loose on you several times there, *govnyuk*. I would have hated to ruin that snazzy new turtleneck and tweed."

"Me, too." Jon said in English. "Throwing up on this beautiful Scottish workmanship would be downright tragic." He kept his seat as the other passengers stood and prepared to deplane. "We're in America now, sweetheart. The English equivalent is *shithead*."

"It does have a bite, but the Russian is still better."

Tasia stood in her seat and slightly teetered. Jon tried to take her arm, but she jerked it away. "Give me the damn stick."

Jon stood, pulled a stainless-steel cane from the overhead compartment, and handed it to her.

"Concussions are funny things," he said as the two of them stepped into the aisle. "The doctors said you might get lightheaded from time to time."

"Blah, blah, blah," Tasia said.

"Davison is only about thirty miles from Andrews," Jon said. "Tripper might have beat us over here."

"He certainly got here fast."

"Well, it has been three weeks, sweetheart."

"Guess I'm stuck with you calling me that." Tasia looked him up and down as they reached the front of the plane. "Put on those sunglasses before we go outside. What did you call them? Beach breakers?"

"Wayfarers. Bruce Willis wears them."

"Who?"

Jon chuckled. "Yeah, there's going to be a million of those." He fished the black plastic sunglasses out of his jacket pocket and slipped them on.

"Remember what the eye doctor told you. Keep them on whenever you're in the sun."

"Blah, blah, blah," Jon said, and Tasia frowned. "I'm going to try Jessi again when we get to wherever Trip is taking us," he said. "I get the distinct impression she's been avoiding me."

"Can't say I blame her," Tasia said. "She has every right to hate both you and me. We've hurt her terribly and I'm having a hard time with that. I don't like being this homewrecking other woman. We need to find a way to make things right with her, Jon."

The two of them descended the airstairs one step at a time. The wind caught the rayon folds of Tasia's black-and-peach dress, and she gripped Jon's arm tighter. It took longer than expected to reach the tarmac.

"Do you see Tripper?" Tasia asked.

A man in a dark suit and mirrored sunglasses approached before Jon could respond. He was abnormally thin, with pale-pink skin, and nearly vertical teased-platinum hair. Jon did not recognize him.

"Mr. Cole?"

"Yes, I'm Jonathan Cole."

"My name is Smith. I presume this is General Zolotova?"

"Pleased to meet you, Mr. Smith," Tasia said as another gust of wind blew through. She reached up to steady her bun of still-blotchy dark hair.

"Welcome to the United States, General. We have a car for you."

Smith waved in the direction he wanted them to go. Jon followed the hand with his eyes and gently patted Tasia's arm. "Tripper McKenzie is picking us up," he said.

"Mr. McKenzie sends his regrets, sir, and said to tell you he'd see you later this afternoon." Smith motioned with his hand again.

"Alright," Jon said. "Guess there's been a change in plan."

Jon held onto Tasia's arm as Smith took them around the other side of the plane where two black Crown Victorias waited. A second man sat behind the wheel of the first car, with two more in the front seat of the second. All three wore the same nondescript black suits and mirrored sunglasses as Smith. All four had telltale bulges of shoulder holsters under their jackets.

"I'm glad you have a second car," Jon said. "We'll need it for our companion."

An electric luggage cart came around the back of the plane. The huge dog inside the plastic kennel jerked and jumped when he saw Tasia. Jon went to meet it, extracted a nylon leash from the storage compartment on top and clipped it onto the dog's black leather collar. The enormous husky practically dragged him the entire distance.

"Zver, sit," Tasia commanded. The dog sat, still and alert as if she'd pushed a button. Smith's pale lips tightened.

"We weren't told about a dog."

Well, there it is, Jon thought. Tripper knew about Zver. If these guys were legit, they would have been told to expect the dog. Jon still had the razor knives in his belt, but neither he nor Tasia carried any other weapons.

"He's the general's personal guard dog," Jon said. "Certified as lethal, so please be careful with your words and gestures. He'll need to ride in the back seat with her. As you can see, he won't stand to be parted from her. I'll ride in the front."

Smith scowled. "I'd planned on riding in the front with the two of you in the back."

"Well, shootee poo, Smith," Jon said with an exaggerated drawl. "Surely a bit of the unexpected isn't a problem?"

Jon kept hold of the leash and moved closer to Tasia. "Let me help you in, General," he said as he put his hand on the small of her back. He opened the car door and leaned in close to her ear.

"*Mokryye Dela*, sweetheart," he whispered and felt her stiffen. "Stay alert and follow my lead." He grabbed her seat belt, and she kissed his ear as he buckled her in. He noticed her grasp her cane like a broadsword as he stepped away and shut the door.

"So, where are we going?" Jon asked Smith after he placed Zver in the seat on the other side.

"Special secure facility near Langley, sir," Smith said. "The director's waiting for you both. He figured it would be the most private option."

"Sounds great," Jon said. "Let me grab our luggage." His smile morphed into a death's head grin as he turned away from Smith's sunglasses. "I'm definitely looking forward to seeing the director again."

"What do you mean the flight was diverted?" Tripper said into the hand radio as he stood on the tarmac at Andrews Air Force Base. A black panel van with tinted windows sat behind him with an FBI SWAT team inside. Two other such vans were strategically placed about the airfield, each hidden behind various large vehicles, all with orders to converge on their target from different directions as soon as the command was given.

"To Davison, sir," Jessi said from inside the terminal.

"Davison? How the hell did that happen?"

"We're not sure. Andrews Tower received the message out of the blue, but with all the proper verifications, they told me. Similar story over at Davison. By the time we found out, they were gone."

"Gone where?"

"They've got to be taking them to Stone, sir. I fear us leaking their arrival may have backfired. Stone's suspicious and paranoid about everything. He apparently sniffed out our trap."

"Or someone told him our plans."

"Oh, very possible. He has informants everywhere."

"Damn," Tripper said. "We spend all this time designing and baiting the perfect mousetrap and now you're telling me we're the ones who've been suckered?"

"Davison has the descriptions of their cars," Jessi said, "and the license plates of everyone going in or out are photographed automatically by the security system. The FBI can issue a BOLO with state and local law enforcement."

"Okay, make that happen. Get us looped in with those folks, then radio the SWAT teams and tell them to standby."

"Should we delay Phase Two?"

Tripper held the radio to his mouth for a second before he pressed the talk button. "No. In fact, make that call first and pull the trigger immediately. I've got a bad feeling about this, Jessi. I'm coming inside."

Jon confirmed Smith was lying within minutes of their departure. Langley was north of Davison via I-495 and they were headed south into rural Virginia. Sooner or later, someone would figure out what had happened, but Jon could not wait for help to arrive.

They were alone on a long stretch of heavily wooded roadway when the car slowed. A paved turnoff lay to the left, blocked by a louvered-metal gate that looked strong enough to stop a tank. The driveway was short. Only one car at a time would fit in front of the gate. The other would have to remain on the highway.

"You'll like the director, General," Jon said over his shoulder as they pulled up to the keypad mounted on an iron pole. "Straight shootin' standup guy. Am I right there, driver?"

"I suppose so," the man said as he hit the button to roll down his window. "A true American patriot, I can say that." He punched in a series of numbers and the black gate opened inward with remarkable speed. The driver moved forward and when they cleared the other side, the gate began to swing shut again.

"Stop! Stop! Stop!" Jon yelled as he threw his arms into the air. The driver instinctively hit the brakes, and Jon drove the large razor knife concealed in his palm into the man's ear like a railroad spike. The body jerked and spasmed in a dance of instant death. Zver went wild and Tasia did her best to hold onto him.

Jon shoved the corpse to the side to prevent it hitting the horn. Fortunately, the man's foot was still on the brake. Jon jerked the gearshift into park, reached for the dead man's shoulder holster and pulled out a 9mm Beretta.

"Get down!" he yelled at Tasia. "Into the floorboard!"

Jon hit the button to lower his window. He jumped out of the car, pulled his door all the way open, ran around behind it and rested his arms on the window frame in a two-handed firing stance. The gate began to reopen. If the other car's windshield was bulletproof, he would be in trouble.

It was not.

The glass spiderwebbed as Jon's two shots slammed into the driver's face. The car had yet to move as the gate had not fully opened, so Jon tracked left and put two more bullets where the passenger should be. He fired again at the center, hopefully where the third man might sit so he could look between the seats.

"Stay down Tasia!" Jon shouted as he slammed the door.

The huge stone gatepost made a perfect cover. Jon peered around its edge as the big gate began to close. The passenger side doors on the outside car flew open. Smith practically fell out of the front seat and onto the pavement, so Jon aimed for his platinum white hair. At that range, the 9mm bullet made an explosion of blood.

The man in the back seat came out firing, apparently uninjured. Jon pulled back just in time as two bullets ricocheted off the stone. A noise like a foghorn sounded on the other side of the gate. Tasia had apparently set loose the beast.

"Please be smart, boy," Jon muttered under his breath. "Don't come around this side. He'll shoot you down the second you round the post."

A howl, then a scream, came from near the outside car. Jon peered around the corner. The man lay face down on the ground with Zver's huge jaws locked onto the back of his neck. The big dog had apparently bounded overtop the car and knocked the man down from behind. Jon saw the man's Beretta in the grass, so he walked over and placed one shot into the back of his skull. Zver jumped as blood and brain matter sprayed in all directions.

"Easy boy, we got him," Jon said in Russian.

The big husky looked up and wagged his tail. His jaws dripped blood, just like when he had savaged Yuri's corpse on the beach at Logi. Jon had vowed that was a secret Tasia would never know.

"I got them all!" he shouted. "Are you alright?"

"Fine!" came Tasia's voice from the other side of the gate.

"Be there in a minute."

Jon searched the corpses outside the gate and found three more Berettas plus six additional magazines. He inserted two of the Berettas into the waistband of his slacks after he checked the safeties, then stuffed the magazines into the pockets of his tweed jacket. He trudged through the weeds to the other side of the gate with Zver at his heels. The other two Berettas were in his hands.

Tasia sat on the ground in front of the car with legs outstretched. She pulled herself up with her cane when Jon came around the side.

"What the hell is this?" she said in English. "Blood wet operatives here? These men are not Russians!" Brown dirt splattered the front of her dress, but she appeared unhurt.

"No, they're American," Jon said. "General Stone sent them after us."

"Stone? I thought we removed that maniac years ago."

"You tried. Several times, actually, but that man has more lives than a cat. He outfoxed our people by rerouting the plane."

"How incompetent of you! That crap would have never worked on the KGB."

"Tasia, listen to me. Take Zver out front on his leash. The police will eventually arrive. Surrender to them and tell them what happened."

Tasia looked down at the pistols in his hands. "What are you going to do?"

"Stone is either up this road already or on his way here now. I'm going to end this."

"Like hell you are! We're grabbing that damn car out front and getting out of here!"

"No way, sweetheart. We'll never be safe as long as that bloody bastard is alive. I'm going to finish what your people started and remove his ass, once and for all."

Tasia swung her cane like a samurai sword. The metal tip smacked Jon squarely between the eyes and snapped his sunglasses in two.

"Jesus!" he said as the plastic pieces fell from his ears.

"Now you listen to me!" Tasia pulled her cane back like a Louisville Slugger primed for the next pitch. "I've already lost my son to this bloodthirsty business. I refuse to lose you, too!"

"You're talking to Archangel, sweetheart. I guarantee you—"

Tasia's cane whacked Jon soundly on each ear in two swift motions. "I don't give a damn!" she yelled. "Drop the guns! Now!"

"Okay, okay!"

Jon laid the two pistols on the ground. His ears rang and blood streamed from his nose as he stood up straight again.

"You can keep the ones in the back of your pants in case we need them," Tasia said as she pointed with her cane. "Let's move."

Jon retrieved their luggage and drug it through the grass to the other side of the gate. Tasia stood at the edge of the highway like a prison guard, cane in one hand and Zver's leash in the other, as Jon drug each corpse, one by one, into the grass beside the far gatepost. Finally, soaked in sweat, he loaded their luggage into the trunk.

"Is that it?" he asked.

Tasia strode over to him. She tossed away the items in her hands, grabbed the back of his neck, and jerked his face close, nose to nose, so their eyes were only inches apart.

"Don't you know I love you, *govnyuk*?" she said with grit teeth. "Don't you ever try anything like that again!"

CHAPTER 30

5:30 PM, Washington Time, Tuesday, September 10, 1991

"Tripper McKenzie, I don't give a damn about your apologies or your lies," Tasia said in English. "If you want my cooperation, you'd better start telling the truth."

The windowless gray room at CIA Headquarters was just large enough for the four people inside. Tasia and Jon sat on one side of the small, metal table, Jessi and Tripper on the other.

"You're right, General," Tripper said as he smoothed the vest of his charcoal suit. "Thanks to Officer Bolton here, we knew General Stone planned to go after you. We would have been fools not to take advantage of that."

"You dare call the KGB coldblooded." Tasia smacked the tabletop with both hands and swung her head toward the far wall. "Murderous savages, each and every one of you."

"May I, sir?" Jessi asked.

"Go ahead," Tripper said. "You can't do any worse than me."

"General, I'm Jessica Bolton." Jessi wore a navy jacket-and-skirt combo with a lemon-colored blouse and block-heel shoes. "I presume Jon told you about me?"

"It took him a while to get around to it," Tasia said as she looked sideways at Jon. A large white bandage, held in place by surgical tape, covered his nose. "But yes, he did."

"I'm going beyond our mandate now, General," Jessi said. "You deserve to hear the complete and unvarnished truth."

"Now wait a minute," Tripper said.

"Please allow her to continue, Mr. McKenzie," Tasia said. "It's refreshing to learn someone on your side values such things."

"Strategically, sir, we absolutely require the general's goodwill," Jessi said.

"Call me Tasia, please."

"Alright," Tripper said, "but be careful."

"The truth is, uh, Tasia," Jessi said. "We screwed up, pure and simple. Specifically, it was me." Jessi drew her hands from her lap and set them on the table. "I designed the plan to use your arrival as a trap for General Stone. If things had gone as we intended, the two of you would have never noticed a thing. Unfortunately, we were outmaneuvered."

"That seems to happen a lot," Tasia said. "So where is this maniac now?"

"Still at large, I'm sorry to say," Jessi said. "Shortly before we picked you up, our task force raided Eagle's underground headquarters here in DC. All we found were empty file cabinets, wrecked computers, and closed bank accounts."

"I see," Tasia said as she leaned forward in her chair.

"We're interviewing Eagle's administrative personnel as we speak, plus going over the location where they tried to take you in Virginia. So far, we've no idea where General Stone is or what's happened to Eagle's millions in funding dollars. Thanks to the effectiveness of his sabotage, it'll take us months to piece together their operations and come up with a new plan. Both you and Jon are still very much in danger. It's imperative you trust us a little while longer."

"Trust you?" Tasia leaned back and laughed out loud. "Do you know how many times I've nearly gotten killed trusting you?"

"Tasia, you have to know your safety is vital to us," Jessi said. "What happened this afternoon was a serious underestimation of the enemy, I admit it. We can't change the past, but our eyes are wide open now. I'm asking you—" she hesitated for a second then looked at Tasia directly for the first time, "—as a personal favor to me, please give us another chance."

An uncomfortable silence filled the room. Tripper was the one to finally break it.

"Well said, Officer Bolton."

"Thank you, sir."

Tasia brought her hands under her chin and stared back into Jessi's brown eyes. She was acutely aware of how beautiful and apparently talented this American woman was, and her own sense of guilt at what she and Jon had done to her simmered just below the surface. For some reason she could not explain, Jessi's words and presence produced an unexpected sense of calm, trust, and comfort.

"Alright," Tasia said softly, "For you, Officer Bolton. I will do it for you."

"Call me Jessi, please."

"Okay—Jessi."

"How do you see this playing out, Trip?" Jon said. Due to the bloodstains on his tweeds, he had been given the opportunity to change clothes. He had pulled some wrinkled khakis and a tight-fitting black t-shirt out of his suitcase, along with the navy-blue windbreaker Tripper had given him in Moscow.

"We've got to get you and General Zolotova into a secure location," Tripper said. "Given the unreliability of things where Stone's concerned, something off the books is critical. We should have something set up in a few hours."

"What about Zver?" Tasia asked.

"He's downstairs," Tripper said. "Wherever we put you, we'll make sure it can accommodate him, too. He's quite the guard dog, it seems."

"Oh, you've no idea," Jon said.

"That should take care of the immediate stuff," Tripper said. "I do have some other news for you, General. Hopefully, it will redeem us a little in your eyes."

"What news?"

"Jim Collins has arranged for the financial documents you brought over to make their way to Boris Yeltsin's people. We've been told they will be used at Vladimir Kryuchkov's trial, whenever it happens."

"You told President Yeltsin I defected?"

"Give us some credit, General, please," Tripper said. "We've received confirmation through our sources the KGB believes you dead after what happened at Logi. We're not about to squander that advantage."

"Forgive me if I assume the worst," Tasia said. "You still have a long way to go to convince me of your organization's competence."

"We've not disclosed where the data came from, nor how we acquired it," Tripper said, "and we've scrubbed any tracks that could be traced back to you."

"Thank you," Tasia said. "Truly. I've dreamed of taking my revenge against Vladimir for so long, for all he did to both me and my son. Now that it's finally happened, it almost doesn't seem real."

"Oh, it's real alright, General," Tripper said. "I expect old Vlad won't see the light of day for a long time, if ever."

Tasia giggled.

"What's so funny?"

"You called him Vlad."

"So?"

"No one would have dared call him that. It would enrage him to hear you say it."

"Well for us Americans, the name Vlad conjures up images of Dracula. You know, evil incarnate, king of the vampires and all that. Kind of fitting, don't you think?"

"If you only knew," Tasia said.

"Think that's it for now," Tripper said. "We'll get you two someplace comfortable here at Langley while we complete your preliminary living arrangements. You'll sleep someplace safe tonight, I promise."

"About time," Tasia said.

"Trip, can I have a moment with Jessi?" Jon asked. He looked at Tasia who nodded back, then turned to Jessi. "If that's okay?"

"I suppose so," Jessi said without looking at him.

Tripper stood up. "General, let me take you down to the cafeteria. It's been a while, but I used to be able to whip up a nearly authentic Philadelphia cheesesteak with the stuff they had down there. Can I interest you in one of the greatest American delicacies of all time?"

The grounds along the eastern side of CIA headquarters consisted of several acres of woodland. The weather was warm, so Jon suggested he and Jessi take a walk along the footpaths that snaked through the area. The early-September breeze carried the aroma of dry leaves and dying flowers. Jon studied Jessi's now-neck-length hair with frank astonishment as they wound their way along the narrow, sun-spotted path.

"What in God's name did you do to your hair?" he asked.

"I got it cut," Jessi said matter-of-factly and shook her head from side to side.

"Jessi, you loved your long hair. You worked on it so much, kept it so beautiful. Now you've cut away—" He stopped and stared at the back of her head for a second. "—probably eighteen inches! Why would you do such a thing?"

"Cause I felt like it," she snapped as Jon caught back up to her. "Tripper told me about your rediscovered Russian soulmate back there, so it became my act of defiance. My personal pushback against you, her and this whole awful situation." She glanced at the bandage across Jon's face. "Looks like you're the one with the broken nose now." The corners of her lips slightly curled. "You sound like a choking chipmunk."

"Gee thanks." Jon thrust his hands into the pockets of his windbreaker. "Looks like you're all healed up now. The bandage, bruises, and swelling are gone. Back to beautiful again."

"Don't waste your time with flattery. It's not going to help."

"You know I didn't plan this."

"No, I don't know any such thing!" Jessi said without moving her gaze away from the path in front of them. "I can't stop hearing in my head what you told that Russian after you read the note she sent you. My whole world crashed and burned that day, and I don't think I'll ever get over it."

"I'm so sorry, Jessi," Jon said as he turned to walk sideways. "I know I hurt you terribly, and you certainly didn't deserve it. You're so perfect—you can do much better than me."

"Oh, no!" Jessi stopped and grabbed his arm. "You don't get to pull that self-deprecating, male-macho crap. I don't want anyone else, and you know it. Give me the truth for once, Jon. Why did you do it?"

"Alright," Jon said. "The reality is—I fell hopelessly in love with Tasia all those years ago. I didn't understand how powerful that was until we met again in Moscow." He looked down at his shoes. "Up against that, Jessi, you and I never stood a chance."

She let go of his arm. "Is that designed to hurt me?"

"Of course not. You asked me to be honest."

Jessi craned her neck toward the large oak branches above their heads. “I risked literally everything for you, Jon—my career, my reputation, even my life. I thought we had something special, something worth risking everything to save.” Her head swung around, and her eyes drilled into him. “Then you go and do this.”

She sped up and walked away. The trailhead for a lesser used, rougher pathway appeared on their right and she took it. Jon scrambled over tree roots and piles of leaves to follow. They moved along in silence for several minutes before Jessi finally stopped and allowed him to catch up.

“When you wouldn’t take my calls these past few weeks, it tore the hell out of me,” Jon said as he came alongside her.

“Good!” Jessi shouted, fists at her sides as she turned to face him. “You deserve to be hurt! You ripped my heart out and stomped on it!”

A flock of birds burst from their perches as she rushed toward him, eyes enflamed with rage. Jon kept his hands in the pockets of his windbreaker and stood stock-still as she pummeled his chest with her fists. Eventually she stopped, stared at him for a moment, then smacked him across the face with her open palm. Nearly a dozen times she slapped him, one hand after the other in rotation. Angry red impressions marred the skin along the edges of his bandage, and a trickle of blood dribbled down his nose. He did not move, did not say anything.

Jessi trembled for an uncomfortable few moments then closed her tear-filled eyes. Jon reached out to touch her shoulder, but she shoved his hand away. She turned her back without saying anything and walked away. Jon wiped the blood from his nose and went after her.

They continued in silence for several minutes until she stopped again and spun to face him. “Tripper ordered me to avoid contact with you,” she said. “We couldn’t let you in on what we were planning. That made everything worse, letting this fester.” She rubbed her eyes on her sleeve. “Now I have to watch you build a new life with another woman—in the house and the bed that only a month ago was ours.”

She sniffled and looked into Jon’s eyes. Her own were red. “I don’t want to hate you, you know,” she said. “I still love you. So much it hurts sometimes.”

“I still love you, Jessi.”

“Liar.”

"I mean it. Love's not something you can just turn off. What Tasia and I have doesn't change my feelings for you."

"That's ridiculous," Jessi said.

"It's the truth. Because of what we shared—and to atone for the terrible sin I committed against you—I want to make things right somehow."

"Don't think that's possible."

"Jessi, surely you can agree it's not right to leave things as they are. Everyone loses that way. You said you don't want to hate me. Whatever it looks like, can we at least try and make some kind of peace?"

"Peace, huh?" She looked up at the blanket of branches above them. "Wouldn't that be nice?" She shrugged her shoulders and let loose a deep sigh. "I suppose you're right, though. Leaving things like they are hurts me far worse than it does the two of you. And I have to be honest—" She brushed a lock of windblown hair from her face. Jon could not remember ever seeing her so beautiful. "I can't stand the thought of you moving on and forgetting me."

"Not possible," Jon said.

He reached for her hand, and she allowed him to take it. They stood there in silence for several moments, holding hands, eyes directed at the ground. Finally, she looked over at him.

"God knows, I have a hard time saying no to you," she said, "but I think you're asking too much of me."

"Please don't say that," Jon whispered. "Surely there's something I can do to get you to reconsider? I'm not asking for forgiveness, at least not yet. I know that will take time and may never happen. All I'm asking is a willingness to try and not hate me—or at the very least, not Tasia."

Jessi's eyebrows shot up. "Now that you mention it, there is something you can do. I will happily work on forgiving both of you—if you'll start receiving psychiatric care."

"What?"

"Don't act surprised. You know I love you way too much to watch you suffer as you do. You think you're hiding it, keeping it under control, but I see right through you. That's my price, Jon. Will you agree to my terms?"

Jon looked at her and frowned. "You drive a hard bargain, Jessica Bolton. Guess not being able to say no goes both ways."

"Damn right," Jessi said. "The VA has a program for folks with issues like yours. Post-Traumatic Stress Disorder is what they call it. It's a long road and would call for some serious commitment on your part."

"Sounds like you've done your research."

"Love is a powerful motivator. If you agree, I can have Tripper set things up. He would need to clear whoever you work with for classified access."

Jon gave Jessi's hand a gentle squeeze and a small smile appeared on her face. "Okay," he said. "I'll do it."

"I'm going to hold you to this, Jon. You don't get to wiggle out. I won't forget about it either."

"Never expected you would," Jon said. "Don't worry, I plan on holding you to your side of the bargain as well. How about the three of us go to dinner tonight? Say, AV's Ristorante Italiano on New York Avenue?"

"My favorite."

"Naturally," he said with a smile.

Jessi shuffled her feet. "Don't think I'm quite ready for that. I keep my promises, though. Can we take this slow?"

Jon nodded and she pulled her hand away.

"We should start back." Jessi looked up at the branches again as the early evening sunlight shone through. "I'll stop by Great Falls in the coming weeks and pick up my stuff. Probably bring Harry the FBI guy with me if that's okay?"

"Whatever you want," Jon said.

It was close to midnight when Andi Jenkins walked out of CIA Headquarters.

The investigative sessions had been grueling, but Andi was pleased everyone treated her like a partner and not a criminal. She had poured forth countless details all evening and would likely do so for many months to come. The world would probably never know about anything Gerald Stone had done, but at least Jeremiah might rest easier.

Fortunately, Derrick had handled everything with the kids, even with no notice. Despite their relationship problems, he was an excellent dad and a decent husband most of the time. Andi had never gotten over the guilt of her infidelity. She vowed Derrick would never know what she had done and worked hard to earn her worthiness back, if only in her mind.

The houses were all dark as she drove through her subdivision. Coming home this late was always a navigational challenge with so many cars parked along the street. Maybe they should think about moving. Sidney would go to High School in a couple of years so now might be the perfect time.

She pulled into the driveway, turned off the engine, and slipped back into her shoes. The house was dark. Derrick had apparently already gone to bed. The two nearest streetlights were out, although the ones further up the street were lit. She opened her car door, stepped onto the driveway, and started for the house.

"Hold right there, Delphi." Andi froze in place like a deer suddenly caught in the headlights of an oncoming car.

"Who did you tell?" Stone said. He wore a dark windbreaker and black turtleneck. His hands were in the pockets of his coal-colored slacks, so only the white of his head was visible.

"Unless you want me to take this inside in front of your family, I suggest you answer," Stone said. "McKenzie's task force was waiting for us at Andrews. I had to rework things myself at the last minute to circumvent them. The only people who knew our exact plans were you and the Daggers. So, who did you tell?"

"Please don't hurt my family."

"That's entirely up to you, Delphi."

"Mary Magdalene," she whispered. "I told Mary Magdalene."

"Well, I'll be damned," Stone said. "She really was McKenzie's spy."

Andi nodded. "What happens now?"

"I'm a man of my word," Stone said. "Nightjack."

Andi felt the needle jab into her neck. She remembered Nightjack's fascination with exotic venoms as she collapsed into the grass.

"Four good patriots lost their lives this afternoon because of this woman's treachery," Stone said as he stared down at Andi's corpse. "Leave her where she is. The night animals can have her."

"Archangel killed the Daggers, sir."

"He's next," Stone said. "I want him in agony for as long as you can sustain it when the time comes."

"Not a problem, sir."

"Good. The omega protocol seems to have been successful. We can continue operations in the cold with most of our assets still intact. Red Eagle makes the most sense for us to regroup and retool."

"Understood, sir."

"They'll keep a tight guard around that Russian general for a while," Stone said. "We'll have to wait a bit before we can acquire her. Let them relax and get complacent. We can use the time to better prepare."

"Yes, sir."

"When we're ready, we'll take care of Mary Magdalene," Stone said, "and Archangel."

The two men disappeared into the darkness.

THE END of *RED MOSCOW*.

Tasia, Jon and Jessi all return in

HISTORICAL NOTE

Red Moscow attempts to integrate the fictional story of Tasia, Jon, Jessi, Tripper, and Yuri into the real events which took place that fateful August in 1991. What really happened makes for good drama on its own, serving as a cautionary tale of catastrophic misjudgments and fortunate weaknesses.

Vladimir Kryuchkov was indeed the head of the KGB and one of the major movers behind the August coup. While his motivations and dialogue are mostly fictionalized here, his movements and the events he orchestrated are all shown as they really happened.

Kryuchkov and the other surviving conspirators were all imprisoned and later convicted for their roles in the coup. They were all released "on their own recognizance" on January 26, 1993, and received full pardons by the Russian Duma on February 23, 1994. Kryuchkov spent the rest of his life criticizing both Gorbachev and Yeltsin and in 1996 wrote a lengthy memoir entitled *Private Business* where he attempted to justify himself and his actions. (Unfortunately, it is not available in English.) Kryuchkov died in Moscow on 23 November 2007 at age 83 and is buried in Troyekurovskoye Cemetery in Moscow beside his wife Ekaterina.

Boris Pugo, by all accounts, genuinely believed Soviet communism was the best system of government possible. The events at the August 19th press conference are depicted here precisely as they happened. Video of the event is publicly available, although it is neither dubbed nor subtitled. A full English transcription of the dialogue, however, is included in the excellent book *Russia at the Barricades* by Victoria E. Bonnell, which also contains numerous primary accounts of many of the events that took place during those critical three days. If you watch the video of the press conference carefully, you will see Boris Pugo rustle his papers at the exact moment described here.

Vladimir Kryuchkov was not present at that all-important press conference and the reasons for his absence have been debated ever since. It is certain, of course, they had nothing to do with any scratches on his face.

The account of Boris Pugo's shooting of his wife and subsequent suicide is completely accurate as reported in the newspapers at the time. His wife Valentina did indeed behave as depicted here, and her aged father admitted the investigative officials into their home shortly after the shooting with the words, "Here is great misfortune." Valentina Pugo actually survived being shot by her husband but took her own life a few weeks later in the hospital. She left a scribbled note for their children which read "My dears, forgive us, we are leaving. Don't take offense." She and her husband are also buried in Troyekurovskoye Cemetery.

Gennady Yanayev served as the only Vice President of the Soviet Union and is chiefly remembered for his ridiculous performance at that infamous August 19th press conference. He did indeed try to "hedge his bets" at the final meeting of the *GKChP* on the night of August 21st when he tried to direct blame onto Marshal Yazov's forces, an action which ultimately destroyed everything for the coup plotters. After his pardon, Yanayev worked for the Russian International Academy of Tourism and passed away from lung cancer on 24 September 2010 at the age of 73. Like Kryuchkov and Pugo, he is buried in Troyekurovskoye Cemetery.

Dmitri Yazov made a videotaped apology for his actions, which was shown on Soviet television the night of August 22, 1991, in which he called himself "an old fool". In December 1991, while still under detention, he was convicted by the Lithuanian government for his role in the Vilnius suppression attempt that previous January, but the Russian government refused to extradite him. He accepted the pardon given to him in 1994 but made certain the record showed he admitted no guilt for his actions. After his release, and although officially dismissed from service, he remained active, serving as military advisor to the Russian General Staff Academy and later in the Inspectors General Service. He wrote several books, again none are available in English, and his 1999 memoir, *Blows of Fate: Memoirs of a Soldier and Marshal,* enjoyed some minor success. The last of the coup plotters to pass away, he died on 25 February 2020 at the age of 95 and is buried in the Russian Federal Military Memorial Cemetery outside of Moscow.

Although he would leave office wildly unpopular eight years later, Boris Yeltsin was definitely the victor of the events that took place that August. Much of his movements, thoughts and dialogue here come from his own book, *The Struggle for Russia*, published in 1994. While there were no chants of "Mother Russia" when Yeltsin mounted the tank in front of the Parliament building, his own account does tell how the crowds grew by enormous numbers from when he first came down the steps to when he turned around from atop the tank a few minutes later.

The events shown here at Foros on August 22nd were as Gorbachev himself described them in his book, *Memoirs*, published in 1996. His aide, Anatoly Chernayev, also described those same moments in his own book, *My Six Years With Gorbachev*, published in 2000. Gorbachev did name the successors to the posts of Defense Minister, Interior Minister and the KGB the day after his return, although Tasia's inclusion here is, of course, fictional. Gorbachev did name Leonid Shebarsin to head the KGB, and Shebarsin did play tennis the day of the coup, but he was removed three days later at Yeltsin's insistence. Vadim Bakatin assumed the KGB Chairmanship until its dissolution later that year.

A great source for what happened from the American perspective during those three days comes from Robert Gates' 2007 book *From the Shadows: The Ultimate Insider's Story of Five Presidents and How They Won the Cold War*. James Baker was on vacation with his wife Susan in Wyoming when the coup started, and President George H. W. Bush was at his family's vacation home in Kennebunkport, Maine. Brent Scowcroft was with the president the night of August 18th and did first hear of the coup via CNN.

Deputy Director Richard James "Dick" Kerr was in de facto charge of the CIA at the time of the coup, as the previous director William Webster unofficially retired a few weeks earlier and the confirmation hearings for incoming director Robert Gates were scheduled for September. Kerr had been presented with the Presidential Citizens Medal for his governmental service during the Gulf War a few weeks earlier on July 3, 1991. He was officially appointed as interim CIA Director days after the coup on August 31, 1991, a post he would hold until November 6 of that same year. Kerr was widely praised in government circles for his expert handling of the US response during those critical three days but would retire from government service the following year to pursue opportunities in the private sector.

No American ambassador was in residence at the US Embassy when the coup occurred, which left charge d'affairs James Franklin "Jim" Collins in charge as shown here. Boris Yeltsin would have used the empty ambassadorial suite—which Tasia and Jon use here—had he actually sought sanctuary at the embassy during the Parliament Building attack. President Bush's phone calls to both Boris Yeltsin and later Mikhail Gorbachev did occur as portrayed here. Jim Collins attempted to join the Russian delegation's flight to Foros at Yeltsin's invitation on the afternoon of August 21st but arrived at the airport too late and missed the flight.

The *USS Kentucky* was indeed brand new at the time of this story, having been sent to sea only weeks before the coup, on 13 July 1991. Her captain at the time was Michael G. Riegel, who may or may not be a dog lover, but her other crew members depicted here are fictional. The special dual-purpose submersible, the *Refuge*, is also fictional, but is an extrapolation of two very real deep sea rescue subs in service at the time, the *Mystic* and the *Avalon*, both of which are mentioned.

While the Code Forty-Seven Protocol shown here is fictional, the very unthinkable civil insurrection it was designed to counter did happen. *Russia at* the *Barricades* tells the story of how, to prevent the storming of their headquarters the night of August 22nd, the KGB offered the out-front statue of Iron Felix Dzerzhinsky, its founder, as a consolation prize to the mob of protestors. The crowds initially tried to demolish the statue by hand but were eventually persuaded to await the arrival of several cranes so the eleven-ton statue would not crash into the Moscow subway system. The Lubyanka building remained mostly dark during the removal process, although whenever an occasional light appeared in one of its windows, the crowd pointed and shouted until it went out.

Mikhail Gorbachev's return to Moscow did happen as described here, and his wife Raisa did suffer a stroke as a result of the events. Gorbachev's victory would prove short lived, however. The events of the coup had shifted popular support to Yeltsin, and being the canny politician he was, Yeltsin took every advantage of it.

Gorbachev attempted to establish a State Council of the Soviet Union on September 5th, hoping to bring the leaders of the remaining republics under his leadership, similar to the way the aborted New Union Treaty was intended to function. The tide had already turned, however, and more and more republics seceded, beginning with the largest of them, Ukraine, a few days later. In the months that followed, more dominoes fell, and on Christmas night, December 25, 1991, the Soviet Union was formally dissolved forever, and Mikhail Gorbachev left power for good.

Perhaps the biggest real-life mystery contained in this story, according to Russian defector Sergei Tretyakov in a series of interviews he gave in 2008, is that Vladimir Kryuchkov did indeed secretly send $50 billion US dollars' worth of funds belonging to the Communist Party to an unknown location out of the country in the months leading up to the Soviet Union's collapse.

Sometimes truth may indeed be stranger than fiction.

Acknowledgments

Writing is often seen as a solitary endeavor, however anyone who has put in the time and effort to create something worthy knows this is never the case. Regarding *Red Moscow*, my heartfelt thanks go to many individuals who have walked this journey with me.

First and foremost, the great folks at Jumpmaster Press deserve a round of applause. They've made me a better author and helped elevate this book into something to both entertain and be proud of. My heartfelt thanks to R. Kyle Hannah, E.G. Rowley and the entire crew. They are indeed the best of the best.

On the home front, my wife Susan deserves the lion's share of praise, even after she told me not to read her any more scenes. ("I want to read the final, printed version," she told me.) Our daughter Carolyne has been my writing inspiration as she works on her own projects, and our daughter Emily is my strength and rock. And, of course, there is our son Thomas, whose recent MFA and poetry awards have warmed his father's heart. With all my children it seems, the apples and the trees share a lot in common.

To my circle of friends and supporters, so many of which I am not able to name, I give great thanks. Special mention goes to my great friend and alpha reader Evan who took the time to read it all and give me detailed feedback. The same goes for my wife's Uncle Tim for his invaluable professional advice.

Finally, there are my close, special friends of long acquaintance. I thank Marcus and Andre for their unflagging encouragement, Martin for his superb technical suggestions and of course Robert for his early forensic line edits and honest advice. Your support—and most importantly your friendship—is amazing.

Extra special thanks go to my friend Cajun, who writes under his real name of Tim Bischoff, for his tireless developmental editing discussions and especially for listening to my early concept ideas and telling me this story was too good not to share with the rest of the world. That conversation was, as they say, the "inciting incident" from which everything else flowed.

About the Author

Born and raised in the heart of Kentucky's bourbon country, R. C. Reid is an amateur historian and espionage aficionado who always wanted to write fiction. An uber fan of the works of John D. MacDonald, Edward S. Aarons and Daniel Silva, he always longed to see a well-written female protagonist in the action-espionage genre, and so created the *Mother Russia* thriller series.

Star Trek, Shakespeare and English history are several of his other passions, and with five friends, he is one of the producers and hosts of the *Snakes and Otters* podcast (available on all major platforms) with 10,000+ downloads to date and counting. He is active on both Instagram and Facebook and his website is www.rcreidauthor.com.

He and his wonderful wife Susan have three adult children—daughters Carolyne and Emily and son Thomas—and live in Louisville.

Other exciting titles from

JUMPMASTER PRESS™

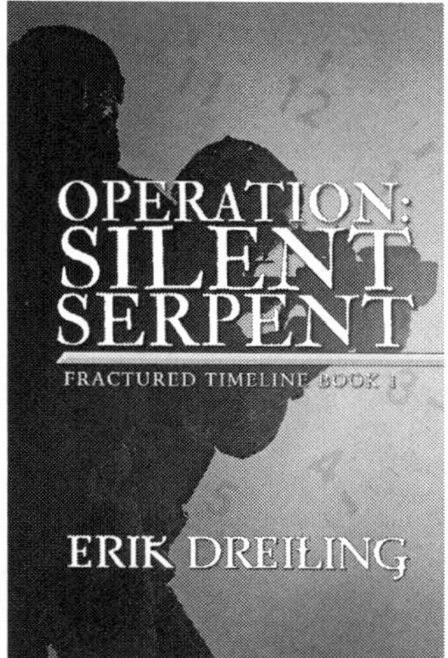